CRITICAL ACCLAIM FOR *SALVADOR*

Margaret Young's *SALVADOR* is the finest Mormon novel in today's market. The kaleidoscope of rich images and striking characters converge in a story of idealism and initiation. Margaret brings to her considerable gift of imagination the factual description of an exotic place she knows well. The combination is stunning. Setting, characterizations, dialogue—all are interestingly played off against some hard gospel questions. The winners are the readers of this marvelous new book.

—Sally Taylor, Professor of English
Brigham Young University

SALVADOR . . . is written with great energy and sensitivity, is well made, and the voice is at once innocent and aware. Margaret Young's story is set in a beautifully realized landscape; one in which we can feel the heat, see the land, sky and people, suffer the poverty. It is against this brilliance that she has observed her heroine's confrontation with personal and spiritual difficulties. Very much a novel of our time, it also affirms the existence of traditional human values we might think we are in danger of losing. A splendid achievement.

—Leslie Norris, Professor of Creative Writing
Brigham Young University

Aflame with fireflies epiphanal as "Christmas lights" against a backdrop of "El Greco grief," *SALVADOR* illuminates the humor and the terror of our deepest loves and loyalties. "We will eat cake at weddings," celebrates Margaret Young's earthily lyrical novel, "send roses to funerals. We will read great questions and learn the jargon of answer. And in rare moments we will feel close to understanding what is essential about our lives, ourselves, the ties that bind us." *SALVADOR* shares with us those rare essential human moments.

—Steven Walker, Professor of English
Brigham Young University

MORE . . .

I've never met a stronger female narrator's voice in Mormon fiction. Maybe not a stronger voice, period. This one sings: sings in a range from the ragged edge of perdition to the hem of holiness, richest in the middle octaves of mortal passion and travail, doubt and faith, in a fierce dark starlit hunt for glints of grace that may jump you like a jaguar.

—Bruce Jorgensen, Professor of English
Brigham Young University

With this third volume of fiction, Young joins those at the forefront of the growing tide of fiction that is making a rich contribution to Mormon culture. She is unusual in her ability to create a real, complex world of the imagination—where people speak language that is both pungent and exalted and have all the bodily and emotional functions—and to invest that world with troubling and moving moral and spiritual dimensions derived from her devout Mormon concerns and convictions. . . .

The title shows this is a novel about El Salvador (at the height of the recent civil war there) and about saviors; it is also about, as the fascinating narrator reminds us, "gardenias, cows, unborn children, love, manure, memory, sulphur pits, waterfalls, fireflies, blankets, fleas, spinach, murder, orchids, jaguars." Young's mature style is by turns down-to-earth, funny, bravely sentimental, able to rise to an epiphany. She hasn't written the great Mormon novel—yet, but here she shows the way.

—Eugene England, Professor of English
Brigham Young University

SALVADOR, struck me . . . for the author's courage and provocativeness. . . . More than anything, I enjoyed its humorous tone. This author has a strong narrative voice, and beautiful perceptions. Her descriptions and imagery often swept me off my feet.

—Terry McMillan, Judge for Utah Arts Council
Associate Professor of English, University of Arizona

SALVADOR

MARGARET BLAIR YOUNG

 ASPEN BOOKS
Salt Lake City, Utah

Salvador

Copyright © 1992 by Margaret Blair Young

All rights reserved. No part of this book may be reproduced in any form
or by any means without permission in writing from the publisher,
Aspen Books, 6211 South 380 West, Salt Lake City, Utah 84107

ISBN 1-56236-304-2

Library of Congress Card Catalog Number 92-70723

Printed in the United States of America

First Printing, April 1992

Cover art by Simeen
Cover design by Brian Bean

To Bruce Wilson Young
Con mucho cariño

Author's Note

I wish to acknowledge the help of my teachers and advisors, all of whom are totally competent and always supportive. And I wish to acknowledge the constant support of my parents. My mother, Julia Groberg Blair, is a fine writer in her own right and has always encouraged my literary efforts. My father, Robert Blair, is a brilliant linguist who filled my first home with exotic languages and fascinating international guests. My parents never locked their front door—and that symbolic, for they truly have an open-door policy. I would not have had the experiences which lie behind this book's setting without their adventurous, hospitable, ever-evolving approach to the world and its people.

The title of this book, *Salvador*, means savior in Spanish.

Salvador

One

My mother was a scream when I was growing up. She said things like "Let's giggle-dee-go" and "We wiggledy-went." Each of us kids had a nickname. Mine was "Julie Doolie Diggle-dee Doos." "Digs" for short. Even after I was married, she addressed my letters "Digs."

She hated housework, so she invented songs while she scrubbed the floor or windexed the refrigerator. Songs like "Oh beautiful, a nice clean fridge," sung in her quivery, breathy soprano to the tune of "America":

> Oh beautiful, a nice clean fridge,
> How clean it's gonna smell!
> We'll use the Ajax on each ridge.
> We'll wipe it clear to Hell!
> We'll clean the fridge!
> We'll clean the fridge!
> The refrigerator!
> And then we'll take

A well-earned break
And eat a chocolate torte.

Saturday mornings, we kids would yell "Oh shut up, Mother!"

Dad was usually at National Guard on Saturdays, or on some military assignment, so it was between us kids and Mom. Despite all her songs, the house stayed pretty messy.

I have good memories of those days. I hated the ditties, but I liked my mother. I wanted to have lots of kids and raise them Mormon, in Utah, the way Mom had raised us. I wanted to make my home a haven of silliness. I wanted to be everything Mom wanted me to be—and she came from the best dreamers and idealists and religious fanatics this side of California.

Her parents had been mission presidents twice. Her brother, Uncle Johnny, lived in El Salvador, where he had served his mission. He had married one of his converts and was still saving the Salvadorans. I wanted to be like Mom's side.

Dad's side used to be Mormon. Dad even went on a mission—he was Uncle Johnny's companion in El Salvador, which is how he met my mother—but then he went to Viet Nam, served his time, came home, and requested excommunication; I still don't know why. Sometimes I wonder if he messed around with bad girls in Viet Nam. Not that it's my business. And not that I know. I only know he was exed, and that since then, Mom has been after him: praying, nagging, making up ditties about families being together forever. Nothing worked, but something kept Mom and Dad together anyway, though whatever it was, I didn't inherit it. My marriage gave me colitis. I decided guilt over divorce would be better than perpetual diarrhea.

When I told Mom I had filed, she said she had felt it coming. She added, "You know, now he's retired, your old man is edgy as hay-ell." (I write the word thus because when Mom used it, it was more her Sigurd culture—and her "just folks" self—than invective. Mom's "hay-ell" had nothing to do with fire and brimstone.) She went on: "He's restless for something important to do. So guess what? We're going to visit your Uncle Johnny. Why don't you come with?"

I said there was nowhere I'd rather finalize my divorce than in a war zone.

There wasn't much fighting down there anymore, she told me. The stories about the *Guardia Nacional* were red and exaggerated. Otherwise, I wouldn't have been invited.

So I went with my parents in the Greenbriar van—a white monstrosity with a big red stripe around its middle, navy blue hubcaps, and no air conditioning. It looked like a motorized flag, so Mom christened it Yankee Doodle Dan Van. "Doodle Dan" for short. We left, poetically, on April Fools' Day, moving within hours from almost spring to hard-core heat, from the snow-tipped mountains of Orem to the carotene cliffs and jaundiced rocks of St. George, and then to Texas, where we started sweating. We sweated all the way to El Salvador.

After El Paso, only soda pop was safe to drink. Since Mom and I claim a selectively orthodox brand of Mormonism (her family's brand) which permits the use of all swearwords not referring to God or sex, limited divorce, some gluttony, but no caffeine unless it's hidden in chocolate, our pop could be only grape or orange. No caffeine, but sugar crystals so big they scratched like sand down our throats.

Dad guzzled Coke and thanked God for liquid sin. I laughed at his heresy of grace. Mom ignored him. She kept her eyes to the windows and gave us a running report of the scenery, as if we couldn't see it ourselves. She pointed out acres of moss-draped pines and waxy leaves the size of footballs, like she was announcing the Greening of America for a radio audience.

"The greenness is stunning," she said. "Even the insects have absorbed it. My hay-ell, look at the butterflies."

Twice we had to go through blizzards of pale green butterflies. You had to cross these barriers, these natural borders, to get past Mexico, and then it took a half hour to unclog Doodle Dan's grille and clean the windshield wipers. Along with the dead butterflies in every crevice of our van were maybe fifty beetles—inch long things with backs like emerald dust.

Mom offered a continuous commentary on the heat too. "Hotter'n H.E. double toothpick," she said. "Like leather. Too hot for make-up." Indeed, she wore only her orange lipstick and matching nail polish, and pulled her hair back in an orange bandanna. (Someone had once told her she was an "Autumn" person, and orange was "her" color. She wore orange to death.)

Dad invoked the name of deity as soon as we crossed into El Salvador, and said, "I remember this place, all right."

Mom gave him an exasperated sigh for taking the Lord's name in vain.

"Twenty-three years and no change," Dad said.

Mom said, "What?"

"I mean since I was here, Emmie. Since Johnny and I were here."

Mom turned to me. "What about you, Digs? Do you remember this from the last time? What has it been for you—ten years? Is this familiar to you?"

"Some," I said. Mom and I and my two younger brothers had visited Johnny shortly before the civil wars began in El Salvador. We had come during one of Dad's tours of duty. We always did exotic things during Dad's absences.

"What do you remember?" she asked.

I shrugged.

"Come on, Digs," she prodded, "what do you remember? Cat got your brain?"

"I don't know what I remember," I said. "Fireflies. And gardenias."

"Oh yes, yes," she said. "Luisa's gardenias. Luisa's glorious gardenias. I can almost smell them. Gardenias!"

"And fireflies," I said.

"Uh huh, the bugs are something too, aren't they. The lightning ones and the bitening ones. Now Digs, are you doing all right?" No break between the sentences. No transition. She tucked that intimate little inquiry into the nearest available space in the pseudo-conversation.

I answered, "Yes. Fine."

This was the closest Mom had gotten to asking me about my divorce. She wasn't accustomed to openly addressing such serious topics. She used to giggle when she started talking serious—except when she was arguing with Dad. Besides, that word—"divorce"— had only recently secured itself in her common vocabulary.

"Fine?" she repeated, then gave me an orange smile and let me be mute.

It was night when we arrived at Zarahemla, Johnny's plantation. The name is taken from the Book of Mormon. It's a center of peace in our scriptures, a sort of Zion.

Johnny lived in a pine cabin in the middle of the place. It was easy to find, though it had shrunk from the way I remembered it. It bordered an Olympic-sized pond we called a lake. Beyond the lake were farm makings, invisible in the dark; on the other side of the cabin sprawled jungle.

Mom and I stayed inside Doodle Dan while Dad knocked on the cabin door and yelled, "It's Chuck and Emmie! And Julie!"

The door swung open. Uncle Johnny stood before us wearing a salt-and-pepper beard. He had been smooth-faced and dark-haired ten years ago. He was still a tall, handsome stereotype. In the dark, he could have passed for a native Salvadoran. In the light, his eyes were utterly azure.

Mom climbed over me to get at the door handle. She leapt from Doodle Dan right into Johnny's arms. He hugged her tight, and they said each others' names like they were lovers. "Emmie," he said. "Skinny as ever. Hot damn, will you look at you. Gosh, it's good to have you here."

Mom turned to me as I stepped out. She said, "Look who's even thinner."

Johnny took me in his arms and whispered low and sweet, "I've heard all about your troubles, kiddo. I'm real sorry."

To me, Johnny had always been a sort of middle-deity—a few notches below the Holy Ghost. I figured he had seen visions and been lit up with God-fire and had to keep his vocabulary spicy so heaven wouldn't find him irresistible. I felt I was enfolded in angel wings, and cried a little, till Mom started hovering around me like a moth. She didn't say anything, but kept trying to find my eyes. Finally she gushed, "Oh my hay-ell. No wonder you remember the fireflies, Digs. They're gorgeous. Like Christmas lights! Oh honey, look, would you?"

Johnny squeezed me to him one last time and I pulled away. The first thing I saw was not the fireflies; it was Aunt Luisa. She was diaphanous, standing in the doorway, wearing a white nightgown. Her hair was regally sleeked back from her face, and the moonlight made her cheekbones and forehead white. When she held out her arms to me and said, "Welcome Julie," she seemed to be calling from the stars. Her arms were limp and flat around my shoulders. And in that loose embrace, I smelled the gardenias and saw the fireflies.

Johnny said, "Well, you must be hot after that trip." He pointed to the lake. "Nothing like a little early morning swim." I followed his finger to the reflections of stars glittering on midnight water.

We changed and dived in. The carp darted from us everywhere, tickling our feet in their frenzy.

Mom had teased me the last time we were here. She had told me the piranhas would eat my toes. I had leapt out of the water and stayed on land for a week. "Piranha Lake" she had called it, mocking me. Ten years ago I was gullible. Now I wasn't fooled by carp.

It was 2:00 in the morning when I left the lake. The others were sitting around the shore joking and remembering their silly pasts. By the time I joined the conversation, Dad and Johnny were talking about their hair. Dad's was receding; Johnny's was growing. The beard, Johnny said, stroking it, was "a sign of apostasy" to a guy named Piggott.

"Piggott's here?" Dad said.

"Oh yeah. We call him 'The Pig' when we're being rowdy. He's with Westinghouse, I think. He's the District President for the Church. Lives in a mansion, Chuck. You ought to see it. Blue carpets, chandeliers, Indian maids from Izalco. He dresses his maids up in blue too. So they match his rugs, I guess. Wouldn't want the natives clashing with the carpets, right?" Another laugh.

Mom gasped.

"Well it's true," Johnny said. "The Indians match the damned floors. Seriously." With that word he turned sober, even mournful. "You know as well as I do, Em, the Indian's costume is her culture. Once the Indian woman wears a dress, she can't return to her *huipil.* She loses her way back forever. So basically the Pig," he said, "is butchering Indians. Slaughtering them right and left. In his own front room. And he hates me, you know. Hates me like the devil. Blames me for his wife's leaving. That's a long story. Anyways, him and me, we're opposites. Night and day, and I won't presume to say which one's which. It's just I could never live in a mansion."

"Well Good Gosh, Johnny," Mom said, "neither could Jesus Christ!"

Dad sat in a tattered wicker armchair and began at once to snore.

Two

In the morning I met Alberto again. Ten years had passed since we had been together. Though he was a year younger than I, I had had an excruciating crush on him when I was twelve. We had played tag around the lake and flirted desperately. He was much taller now. His eyes were still large and dark and intriguing. His skin was lighter than what you might expect, and, since Johnny had raised him, he was fluent in English. His father, from what I understood, had been executed by communists. His mother had come to Zarahemla shortly afterwards and died in childbirth. Or so we had been told.

Alberto and I were the first ones to the breakfast table. Aunt Luisa told us to sit; she didn't need help with the preparations.

Alberto said, "Good morning," that he had heard all about my difficulties, and that I looked good despite them. "Still the cornflower angel, Julita," he said.

I smiled, pleased that he remembered what he had called me back then, when I was barely budding. He had stroked my hair—even kissed it, I think—and called it the color of the best *maiz*, brilliant as spun gold. My skin (ignoring the twenty-eight freckles across my nose and cheeks) was like a gull's breast, my cheeks the pink of an apple blossom's heart. He had invented all sorts of poetic metaphors that made me feel like an angel or a goddess or at the very least a beauty queen. I know now that he was merely practicing for his future as a Latin Lover. He was mastering the darts of flattery, and I was a willing target. I learned when I returned to Orem Junior High, that I was still "Freckle Face" and "Feather Butt" and—always—"Digs." Still, I had been almost beautiful then. My hair had been long, nearly to my waist, and it had shone in the sunlight because in those days, I brushed it one hundred strokes every morning. Now it was barely to my shoulders, limp from a half-dead perm, dull from my colitis. I was nothing like an angel, and I knew it, but Alberto's expert poetry was more welcome and more comforting—even in its deceptions—than it had ever been when I was twelve.

I said I appreciated his compliment, but, as was no doubt obvious, I didn't care so much about looks anymore. I wanted to work, I told him. Work, I had heard, was the best therapy for people in transition.

"Yes," he said. "Yes, you are in transition."

Mom bounded into the kitchen then, with a big, neon smile. She said, "Good morning, good morning. Isn't it wonderful to not have a stubbed toe!"

Mom always made a grand entrance. I asked her if she had stubbed her toe, though I knew better.

"No," she said. "But think of the times you have stubbed your toe on the bedpost or something, and how much it hurts and how you think that you always take your unstubbed toes for granted. So this morning, be grateful for unstubbed toes, Digs. Hi Alberto."

He lifted a bare foot and waved with it.

"Attaboy," she said.

Always an entrance. Always a flamboyant line.

"So," she said to Alberto, "are you going to show my daughter the ins and outs of cow milking this morning?"

He said he was.

Mom talked exuberantly about her farm-girl days in Sigurd, about the joys of raising corn and cane and milking cows. Then she stopped reminiscing and instructed us to smell. She inhaled deep, as an example. "Do you smell it?" she said.

I did. Smoked black beans cooked with onion and garlic. Hot, thick tortillas. Fried platinos with cinnamon sauce. "Ooooh, I have been craving this food," Mom said, just as Luisa appeared at the cabin door with the food she had cooked over a fire outside. "I have been craving this food for years."

I hadn't realized it until that moment, but I had been craving it too. When Mom asked me to pray—ignoring the fact that Dad and Johnny were still outside doing miscellaneous farm chores—I made my quickest grace and dug in. So did Alberto. He downed a beaned-tortilla in three gulps, put on his shoes, and excused himself. I dropped my half-eaten tortilla to my plate and followed him out the door.

"Hey," I said. "Weren't you going to show me how to milk?"

"You really want to learn?"

I rolled my eyes in answer and looked up the hill where he was headed. This was my first view in ten years of day-lit Zarahemla. I hardly recognized it. The cabin had shrunk, yes—but everything else had expanded. There were barns on the hill, chicken coops, feeding troughs, cornfields, trees, shrubs, gardenias. The place had bloomed.

There were seven heifers in the barn. Auburn, tender-eyed creatures with brushed, shiny flanks. Alberto taught me to stroke the hide, to coax the milk in soothing tones, to grasp the teat firmly, still whispering comfort, and squeeze and squeeze and squeeze in four-four rhythm.

"The milk will only come," he said, "if you are gentle. It is important to be gentle." The milk squirted blue-white into the bucket. He called the cow by Spanish endearments. "*Mi virgen*," "*Mi amor*," "*Querida*." The cows moved their necks like they were nuzzling Alberto's words in the air. The cows were in love with him.

When two buckets were full, he stood. He said, "Do you read Shakespeare?"

I told him Mom loved Shakespeare. Sometimes her entrance line at breakfast came from *Hamlet* or *Macbeth*. Once when I was stirring cereal at the stove, she shouted from her bedroom, "Double, double, toilet trouble; wheat toast burn and oatmeal bubble!" I had also studied the Old Bard in high school, though I had hated it. Seven days talking about why Hamlet hesitated. As though we should do likewise.

Alberto said, "Shakespeare was a miracle. You must read Shakespeare. Often I quote him to the cows. They love the Queen Mab speech, and Hath Not a Jew Eyes. Shakespeare was the greatest writer of all time, and you speak his language, Julita. You and I speak it. That is a blessing from Almighty God. I think, for myself, I was given to Johnny so I could know Shakespeare. I think that was God's purpose. If there was a purpose." He smiled and brought both his hands around my hair. "Cornsilk hair. But you should bind it, Julita. It will interfere with your work if it should fall in your eyes. Take a bucket, please. We're through here. Tomorrow I'll let you do more. Come. Your hands are very strong. *Que mujer!*"

I took a bucket and followed him.

Within a week, I could milk a cow as gently as Alberto, and I could shovel manure as fast. My days were smelly, chock full of cow dung. I collected it, spread it, hoed it into the cornfields. Dad and Alberto did the same. Mom didn't. She sewed clothes for the orphans who lived on Zarahemla's second biggest hill in a sort of dormitory—really a big adobe box with little adobe rooms. A couple of the younger orphans visited Uncle Johnny daily. There were two that Mom had fallen in love with. She dreamed about taking them home with us, even gave them nicknames. The three-year-old boy was "Benjer Bom Boop-ups"; the four-year-old girl "Munchy Crunchy Cha Cha Cha."

After manuring was done, I usually picked spinach, which Johnny had planted everywhere. Mom accused him once of having a Popeye complex, and he took that as a compliment. We always had some kind of spinach for lunch: spinach soup, spinach souffle, spinach salad. Aunt Luisa liked to grind the spinach into her corn meal, too, and serve green tortillas.

Living in Zarahemla was going back to agrarian times, and back to the kind of charity Wall Street doesn't understand. Johnny took his milk to people in need, offered his spinach to anyone hungry. People came from all over to live by Johnny, to learn how to read, to have a piece of untaxed land, to feed their babies, to get some nourishment from Johnny's spinach and love.

And though he was their savior, Uncle Johnny didn't want to appear rich. The only signs of wealth were those Luisa had provided: she had turned her satin wedding dress into oversized drapes for the front room window; a lacy yellow formal she had worn as "Miss San Cristobal" had been transformed into curtains and pillow shams in the bedroom. These isolated details from another world she called "The Feminine Touch." Otherwise, the house was impoverished. We had outhouses instead of bathrooms and old newspapers instead of T.P. We kept clean by swimming in the lake, and we did our wash (clothing and hair) in a stream a couple of miles down the road, where women from three nearby plantations washed and gossiped.

It was a rocky stream; you wouldn't want to wade in without shoes. Even women who went in naked wore rubber sandals. Water foamed around the rocks, and topless women chattered and waved to each other, undid their long, black braids and scrubbed their laundry with lye soap against flat limestone.

Alberto taught me a few Spanish words to say to the women, but Mom just chattered to them in English. She'd step into the water and shout to some laundress, "My Gosh, it's cold, isn't it! Feels great!" Then she'd crinkle her face into an exaggerated, orange smile and the woman would laugh and she'd laugh back and wave. While I was struggling with *buenos dias*, Mom was playing Queen for a Day at the stream.

At night, when the cows were milked and the other chores done, I liked to walk around the plantation. I liked to smell the gardenias and hear the frogs and distant monkeys, and watch the fireflies. And I liked to listen to Alberto, who sat in a little bamboo cove beside the lake singing Spanish songs and playing his guitar.

I never let him know I was listening. But to me, his music was ethereal as an herbal bath. His notes seemed suspended in Zarahemla's night, like tropical moisture, caught there with the scents of gardenia and hibiscus and pine, melting onto the spinach, becoming part of everything. His songs were simple. The one I remember best went like this:

> *Al decir adios, vida mia,*
> *Te digo eso: te quiero*
> *Y te estoy agradecido.*
> *Te veré, amor, en los cielos.*
> *Te miré, amor, en mi jardin.*

The melody was light, the plucking of the guitar delicate and silver. When Alberto was singing, I could relive the ugliest moments of my life without bitterness. I could hear the worst things my soon-to-be-ex-husband had said to me, and remember them as though they were innocuous and lyrical. I could hear his insults like nursery rhymes:

> Your face is hideous,
> don't you know.
> As hideous as Springtime snow.

Alberto was massaging the underside of my life with his songs.

"I wish I could push you out of the car," my husband had once said to me. "Push you out and watch you writhe to death. That would give me great pleasure."

Alberto was singing about sadness to take it away. Alberto was making me cry with his music, night after night. Quiet tears. Peaceful letting go. He was as gentle as the moon. It was no wonder the cows adored him.

Three

We had been in El Salvador for three weeks when Johnny had his first revelation. His first, I should say, regarding us. Revelations were a common thing for Johnny. From what Mom had said, he had them constantly. The heavens just opened up for him, and God made conversation, called him by name like the two of them were pals.

I always figured revelations from God would sound like the Old Testament or Doctrine and Covenants—lots of "Thee's" and "Thou's" and "Thou Shalt Not's." Johnny's revelations, though, were home-style. The way he explained it, God has to work through whatever tools are available. He speaks in ways His audience will understand. "Oh sometimes He gets fancy," Johnny said, "if there's a need to sound real official. But mostly, He just talks. And you know, what is remarkable to me is how He never puts you on hold. Never does that. He never puts on musak while he solves a war or knocks off a sinner. He's an amazing fellow, God is. Just amazing. The things He's told me—well, you'd never imagine."

Johnny got the revelation about us—or about Mom and Dad, I should say—while he was riding his appaloosa, Yermo, around the plantation. He was jumping the horse over a stream and God called to him to slow down and take a listen.

Johnny, having gotten accustomed to the still small voice of deity, let the horse drink while he got on his knees and asked what was wanted.

"You know, John," said God, "I think we may as well open up a new place. Zarahemla is going so very well, I think it's time to expand. So, since I've seen fit to bring you your sister and her husband—albeit an apostate—" (Johnny winked at Dad when he said that) "I think they may as well head up the thing. Send them to Belen, by San Salvador. Instruct them to set up a school, to plant a garden, to teach my word to the people up there, worlds without end." He went on to describe how they would wipe babies' runny noses and teach old people to read and start cooperative farm projects and mostly be good examples of Mormonism in action.

Mom dabbed at her eyes. She said she could feel the Spirit confirming this move.

Dad wasn't so easy. He said, "Now hold on, John. I hate to mention it, but God hasn't spoken to me."

Johnny lifted his eyebrows sardonically. "Did you try tuning the radio, Chuck?"

"Oh John, get off your high horse."

"Funny, that's just what God said. And I listened, Chuck. Just like I'm listening to you now. God is very real, my brother-in-law. I might venture to say that God is realer than you are."

"Right," said Dad. "Now am I mistaken, or didn't we missionaries used to say God revealed his will to all the parties involved? Emmie, remember that guy who said he had had a revelation about you? That fat guy—what was his name?"

"I forget," Mom murmured.

"He was a forgettable character. Our most forgettable character. Harold or something. Harold or something told Emmie he had had this revelation: if he married her, he'd become president of the

Church. Well, for some reason, God didn't reveal that information to Emmie. Get what I'm saying? You put your will in God's mouth and you're headed for some major disappointment."

"The voice of experience, huh." Johnny grinned and winked at Mom.

"Voice of caution," Dad answered. "Cause you know, John, God hasn't told me to go to this little *aldea* you're talking about. To be blunt: I don't much like the idea. I don't relish—God forgive me—going where I don't know anyone. You may not realize it, John, but El Salvador is a bit tumultous right now. I took my chances in Viet Nam. I'd rather not take any more here—especially not with Emmie and Julie."

"Just Emmie," Johnny said. "Julie's staying here."

"God told you that too, did he?"

"Words to that effect. I don't know why, but he seems to have some purpose in mind for her and she needs to be here."

"Fine, John, fine. You seem to have things all neatly planned. I'm sorry to turn you down. Real sorry. I feel like a jerk turning you down, but, well, God didn't tell me to change tents."

Johnny turned to my mother. He asked her if she had felt the Spirit. She repeated that she had. He shrugged at Dad and proceeded to tell them about Belen and God's plans for it.

Eventually, there was a full-fledged fight between Mom and Dad. Mom called Dad a war-mongering heretic; Dad called Mom a hippie sheep. They both dished each other very poetic, totally stupid insults.

It sounded so familiar and so stupid I nearly laughed. I ended up with empathetic diarrhea—as though it had been me fighting. Dad ended up in unilateral surrender, loading Doodle Dan Van and packing it and Mom for Belen. We would be out of communication for a few weeks. Eventually, mail would work between us, but it would take time.

"It's not the end of the world," Johnny told Dad as the last medicine boxes were loaded.

"Of course not," Mom said, kissing Dad's cheek, assuring us, "It's just his macho identity makes him resist these things. That and his apostasy." She jabbed his shoulder, teasing. "He feels simply great about the trip now, don't you, Pop."

"Simply great about it," he said, finally smiling when Mom kissed his chin.

Johnny gave final instructions as to who to see, where to go, what to say, etc. Luisa came from the cabin and held my hand as Dad started the van.

I assured her I was all right. I had been away from my folks before; this was no big thing.

"You mistake," she said quietly. "I wanted *you* to comfort *me*."

I put my arm around her. She was trembling.

Mom waved her orange scarf as they drove off, making a grand exit like Gypsy Rose Lee.

Bye bye. Tah tah. Toodle-ooh.

Five days later, I found Manuelito.

I had met him once already, two weeks before I found his body hanging from a mango tree. I remember the meeting vividly, probably with exaggerated detail, since the sight of his suspended corpse made him so important to me. He was gutting chickens just outside the cabin when I met him. His hands were covered with grainy, white paste and he was smiling at me. He said, "*Hola, me llamo Manuel.*" I managed to answer back, "*Hola,*" then went to milk the cows.

I was on my way to milk again when I saw him hanging. I thought at first it was someone's laundry. When I got closer I smelled his last act. Then I saw the bulging eyes and the black tongue. The arms were held at an angle from the torso; the legs and fingers were spread. The body seemed to be floating in the tree. I heard the buzzing of flies, the metallic rattle of cicadas, and saw three drops of honey moving down the swollen hands. It took a few seconds before I realized the honey drops were cockroaches, crawling on the wrists and fingers with dozens of red ants.

I stood there staring, as though I did not understand what this was hanging from the mango tree. I stood there wondering, what do I do now?

I turned and slowly went down to Johnny's cabin. Luisa's face, when I told her what I had seen, stretched into El Greco grief. She ran towards the tree. I did not see her again until supper. She had been crying.

Uncle Johnny said the dead man was Manuelito. I remembered I had met him gutting chickens.

"I warned him," Uncle Johnny said. "I told him he was playing with *fuego*. How many times did I tell him that? How many? Kid was a convert to danger. Always flexing at the borders. That kid! Mani!"

Luisa nodded, then sprawled her hand over her face and ran to her room.

Johnny told me Manuelito had been involved with an organization called "Guerrilla Army of the Poor." The kid's life had been threatened before, but he wouldn't stop. It was probably *Orden* that did it. God only knew.

"This is rare," Johnny said. "Very rare. Manuelito was a case. First time I saw him I smelled defiance and greed. Damn. He would have been a missionary next year."

Johnny stabbed his spinach with his fork. Alberto picked up a tortilla and sat looking at it for a full minute before biting. We could hear Luisa sobbing in her bedroom, weeping Spanish.

Would she be all right? I wanted to know.

Alberto and Johnny commented to each other in Spanish. Johnny said, "It's just that life gets awfully serious for her sometimes, kiddo. She's a gentle sort, Luisa is."

"*No lo creo,*" she was weeping. "*No lo puedo creer.*"

I asked Johnny who he thought had murdered the boy. It was *Orden*, he repeated.

So just outside the cabin, while we all had slept last night, some local politicals had been hoisting Manuel up a tree.

Alberto ate intently. He seemed unaware of anything but his food. When his plate was clean, he glanced at Johnny, then turned to me, stroked my cheek with his finger, said, "Don't worry, Julita. Let this horror pass." His eyes returned to Johnny as though for his approval. Johnny nodded.

"Can I get you anything, kiddo?" my uncle said.

"Can I get you anything?" Alberto repeated, almost at the same time, as if Johnny had cued him.

I said no, and thanked them both for their concern. Alberto moved his palm down my hair. "*Tranquilo*," he whispered. "*Mi angel. Tranquilo.*"

I wanted him to sing. I wanted his songs—wanted them; I *needed* his songs. But I knew there would be no music that night. Everything had changed.

I walked around the lake after supper and breathed the gardenia perfume, waiting for the music that wouldn't happen. There was a shadow behind me, not mine. I watched it approach, my gut twisting. I imagined myself strung up in the mango tree.

The shadow said, "Hi, kiddo." Johnny's voice.

I turned to him, my insides knotted. I answered "Hello" like I hadn't been ready to wet my pants.

"You doing okay?" he said.

I said I was.

"I know what you saw was—well, it was pretty awful, wasn't it?"

"Pretty awful. I'd say that, yes."

"Not a sight you should be seeing. Nobody should see things like that."

I told him that with today's movies, everybody sees everything. I said, "I'm not going to have a breakdown, Johnny."

"Well I know," he said. "You're a strong girl."

"No, it's not that. I'm a wimp, really."

"Naw," he said. "You're strong. A survivor." He sat on the stone bench where I always listened to Alberto. He stroked his beard. "If you want to know the truth, I think God knew what would happen when he told me to keep you here. Sounds strange, doesn't it."

I nodded.

"I think God wanted to put you to the test. I think he wanted to see if you're ready for whatever you may have to see in the next few years. See if you're ready for whatever happens. Of course, He tested Alberto and me even more, you know. We were the ones had to cut Mani down and clean him up and dress him for burial. That's a bad enough job when you don't know the body you're washing. But when you know him, when you love him—oh kiddo, I can't tell you how that pains. It was especially hard on Alberto. Those two were like brothers. Well, it was hard on me too, even though I knew it was coming."

"You knew?"

"Figured as much, I should say. Around here, you keep quiet about politics. Trees have ears. Mani, he took too many chances. Yeah, I knew it was coming. Didn't make it any easier to take." He took hold of my elbow—a characteristic gesture of his. He said, "I'll tell you something, kiddo, though I don't know as you'll fully understand yet. But I'll tell you this much: God wanted me to know how it feels to love someone like a son and then to give him up for sacrifice. Wanted me to know that. It was like His ultimate test, see? Oh kiddo, I knew, cutting down that stiff body, that body I had raised as my own boy, I knew how Abraham felt staring down at his son on the altar. I knew how God felt watching the Romans pound their nails. I knew those things. Praise God, I knew." He wiped his eyes with both hands and looked at the lake, breathing deeply, controlling his emotions. When he said, "The moon's pretty," his voice was weak and quavery.

I linked arms with him. I said yes, the moon was pretty.

It was not the real moon we were talking about, but its reflection in the lake. A brilliant, perfect globe, dilating and contracting in the ripples of water, translating itself into all sorts of lights as though the lake were a black and white prism.

"Romantic moon," Johnny said. "You don't see it like this stateside. Too much competition from the 7-11s, right? I love this moon. In a way, it brought me here. I remembered it that well."

"Hard to forget."

"Oh yes. Yes it is. There are a lot of things hard to forget." He stood and skipped a stone. It caught the moonlight; looked like a dying star hobbling across the water, becoming a reflection.

"Isn't that pretty," he said.

"Gorgeous."

He skipped two more. You could hear them touch the lake. You could see the water beads spray up.

"Yeah, you're strong," he said. "You'll do what you need to do. Won't you, kiddo."

"You know I will."

He bent down and kissed my cheek. "I do know that," he said. "And God does too. That's why you're here." He turned towards the cabin.

"You going in?" I said.

"I think I will. It's getting chilly." He stayed there for a moment like he was waiting for another conversation to start up or some smashing exit line. "Goodnight," he said.

"Goodnight, Johnny. Thanks."

"Thank *you*, kiddo. You passed this test, I think. That's a lot to say. I'm very proud of you."

The light from the house made everything a little hazy when Johnny opened the door. Then things got blacker.

I stayed by the lake for another hour before going to bed. I had nightmares all night and was desperately sick the next day. The *dengue* had seized me. My joints felt soldered, my organs on fire. I was delirious, dreaming terrible things, having visions of hell, though the only nightmare I remember in detail involved Manuelito: I'm walking out to the mango tree, which is filled with red fruit. Each fruit is Manuelito's head, bleeding.

The dream is like an episode in the Indian book *Popol Vuh*, in which Xquic, the princess of the Underworld, goes to the forbidden tree where two decapitated heads have become fruit. Not mangos, as far as I know, but whatever fruit skulls become in hell. One of the fruits speaks to her, tells her to hold out her hand, which she does, and then spits into her palm. This makes her pregnant. She has twins who eventually kill off the Lords of the underworld and become culture heroes.

In my dream there was no spitting, but the Manuelito Mangos screamed like they were pieces of his dismembered body, all in separate agony. I was crying, "It's all wrong!" when Johnny shook me awake. Perhaps I would have forgotten the dream if he hadn't wakened me.

I had nightmares like that for a week. Even after my body had sweated itself back to normal and my joints had loosened, I moaned through my nights. Johnny suggested I leave Zarahemla for a time and go with him and Alberto to the village of Izalco, near the Guatemalan border. Johnny had another salvation project in the works there. He said I would be an inspiration to the natives. And I would forget to dream bad dreams.

Four

It was a four-hour trip by jeep. The three of us sat in the front, Alberto and I crowded into one seat. The back was filled with medical supplies and food for the Izalco Indians.

The last hour of driving was up a winding dirt road. We passed an Indian with a load of wood tumplined to his forehead, and I began to feel the romance of the place. No industry. No technology. Johnny said he had once seen an Indian hauling a haystack on a tumpline. "Nobody's weaklings," Johnny said. As if we needed to be told.

I thought it took strength to climb the road even in a jeep. You had to keep your eyes forward; if you looked into the ravine, you got faint. It was like going up a roller coaster. The one time I did look, I saw a canyon of pine trees with flexed trunks, moss draping the branches, little yellow flowers clustered around the roots, fog hanging everywhere like foamy mousse, moving, changing. I felt dizzy, on the brink of a kaleidoscope. Green arrows, yellow dots. Moving.

I took deep, silent breaths. "So," I said, "what are the yellow flowers called?"

Johnny said, "Coli. Tastes great boiled with spinach and salt. Gorgeous down there isn't it."

I moaned.

"Yessir," Johnny said. "Izalco is a great place. Sacred place. It's where Alberto is from, you know. Anyways, his parents were from there. So you're going to be meeting his relations." He pointed straight ahead. I saw a few adobe shacks and a bright, flamingo-pink fountain. This was the place. "And, kiddo," said Johnny, "you're going to meet Primitivo. Distant relative of Alberto's. Great uncle or something."

There were a couple of naked boys just ahead of us, playing with a bicycle tire, squealing words I couldn't understand, waving to us with both hands and jumping up and down, holding their tire up like a wreath of triumph.

Johnny told me about Primitivo Santos, to whom an angel had appeared. The old guy wore his hair long now, because that's how the angel had worn his.

I pictured the kind of long hair Mormon artists portray: gleaming, just-brushed perfection—exactly what you see on Christmas trees—sleeked back from the forehead and ears. Mormon angels are not hippies; in order to get past the Correlation Committee they have to be conservative and well-groomed. Nonetheless, they transcend time and culture and make implicit statements about barber shops in heaven.

Primitivo's angel would not have made it past Correlation. Primitivo was a punker.

He stood before an adobe shack like a monument to Einstein after a tough day and no comb. His arms slowly rose as Johnny parked. Primitivo, it seemed, was conducting the weather. Johnny copied the pose when he got out of the jeep. The two men approached each other and made a great *abrazo*. Primitivo kissed Johnny's cheek and grinned at Alberto and me. His teeth were half rotten. What was left of them was sharp, canine, brown. But his eyes glowed.

Alberto and I got out. This, somehow, was a signal to the rest of the community; we were instantly surrounded by laughing, shrieking, jumping children—most of them dressed, all of them dirty. They were shouting, "Don Juan! Don Juan!" running around the jeep in their bare feet, bringing a fine, amber dust around their legs and the wheels.

Then from a distance, as though emerging from the mists, a woman appeared. She had a sandy-haired baby shawled to her back. She walked towards Johnny and swirled to her knees, drunk or in ecstasy. Johnny helped her up and embraced her. She held her baby to him and he smacked his lips around its little ears until it gurgled and laughed. "This woman is Marta," he said to me. "She's a convert. One of the greatest converts of all time, I should say."

Marta wiped her cheeks. She was gazing at Johnny like he was God. Eventually she came to Alberto and kissed his cheek.

"Over there," Johnny said, "is Cordelia, the old guy's daughter." He was motioning to the open door of the shack. A girl stood in it now, looking at the ground, hiding the beginnings of a smile. "Actually," he said, "her real name is Maria. Alberto renamed her. Alberto and her are relations."

Alberto said something to her in Spanish. She lifted her eyes to him and grinned like the Spirit was beaming from her teeth.

Cordelia looked like a Rembrandt model, shadowed in the door, her hair invisible in the darkness, cheekbones high and bronze, eyes black. She looked like she should be holding a baby and a threaded needle or some other emblem of fertility. She looked like some artist's magnificent, nubile mystery.

"Now kiddo," said Uncle Johnny, "you and Cordelia, you be friends. She's not too much younger than you and she'd love a sister. How does that sound?"

"Great," I said. "Fine."

"While you're at it, teach her to read," he said.

I made a limp salute. I thought of my mother teaching me to read when I was four years old, a dish of cinnamon candies between us. The candies were called Hot Tamales. They looked like suppositories made of cherry jello; they tasted red and spicy. I got a hot tamale for every word I put together. Mom would pop it in my mouth and say, "We're groovin' now, Digs." I'd chew the cinnamon and feel proud.

Dad was in Viet Nam then.

Dinner that night was what you'd expect: thick tortillas and garlicked beans. Indian food.

There was a fire in the middle of the hut, surrounded by large black stones. This was the only light we had.

Primitivo's wife—a silver-haired lady with one eye completely encircled in black warts—turned the tortillas. She jabbered away in her dialect, apparently to the food. When she got very close to the fire, the embroidered flowers of her *huipil* jumped into color—red and blue and purple—and her face shone like it was golden.

The rest of us conversed mostly in Spanish, though sometimes I interposed an English question to Johnny. We had no utensils, but spooned up the beans with tortillas. Afterwards we dipped our fingers in a dish of warm water.

It was dark when dinner was over. Our only light was the fire.

Johnny said it was sleepytime now, and that if I had any biological needs, I should attend to them. There was no bathroom, he said, or even an outhouse, but there was a cornfield. He instructed me to use smooth leaves.

When I returned, Johnny gave me a mat and showed me the hut where we all would rest. Primitivo stood by the door. He shut it as I entered. I could still hear the breeze outside like the rustle of taffeta, playing in the cornfields, sighing unknowables.

Johnny whispered an evening prayer in English and added as an aside to God that tomorrow we would visit the prettiest place on His good earth.

*   *   *

I didn't sleep. Not for a long time. There were fleas nesting in my mat. They bit wherever they found exposed skin. My wrists and ankles and stomach burned. But the fleas weren't all that kept me awake. I was thinking about my husband too, wondering if he was feeling abandoned, wondering who would take care of him now, or if he would kill himself. I thought, too, about the prowling horrors outside: *terroristas,* revolutionaries, executioners, deadly snakes, baritone felines. Nighttime was full of awful stuff. It was hours before I slept, and not long at all before the roosters of Izalco began braying to each other across town.

Primitivo's wife and Cordelia were already turning tortillas on the *comal.* They spoke to me when I joined them, as though I could understand. Their Mayan dialect was guttural and rhythmic.

I helped them wash the dishes after breakfast. We used water stored in an earthen jug and washed the plates with a cornhusk rubbed in lye soap and dirt. The floor we swept with a corn-husk broom. Then we fed the chickens, the rabbits, the hog, and returned to the fire to make lunch.

It was afternoon before we went to what Johnny had called "the prettiest place on earth": *Salto Blanco.*

"Salto Blanco" is a hundred-foot waterfall that cascades into steaming craters. You hike up a mountain, then descend a ravine that rivals the Grand Canyon. Half way down, you hear the crackle of the waterfall and see the craters' steam rising as during creation. Clo0ser, and you see "Blanco" foaming over the cliffs like milk; leaves and moss glistening under it; steam rising from the craters, mixing with its spray. You are descending into an inferno made lovely. Iridescent blue butterflies the size of a child's hand are hovering everywhere. There are purple-veined green orchids, hibiscus, coconut palms. There are people inside the craters, like something out of Dante. But this is their bath, not their punishment. They know which pits scald, and they add cold well-water to the safest ones. They are washing themselves in perfectly warm sulphur water, jumping around happily like brown frogs.

Rocks jut out everywhere. The ground itself is a huge rock, pocked with these sulphur pits. The place looks like the inside of an ancient volcano. There are stones shaped like camel humps and stones that are tunneled; stones that rise like petrified pines; stones like pleated walls; stones like stalagmites gone wild.

We dressed behind the tallest rocks, Marta and Cordelia and I, and put on muslin tunics called *camisones* to guard our modesty. The men put on their tunics behind another rock. Then we sat in a crater together: Primitivo, Cordelia, Marta, Uncle Johnny, Alberto, and I.

The water was hot enough to steam, but not to burn. Still, my skin pinked where the muslin didn't protect it. Cordelia scrubbed her father's back, then unfastened my tunic and rubbed my shoulders with a pumice stone. I could feel my skin peeling into fibrous strings as she circled my bones with the rock. She massaged my neck with her fingers, then scooped the hot water into her hands and poured it over my back, again and again and again, rhythmically, ritually. She was anointing me with sulphur. After-wards she did the same to Alberto, then offered him the pumice. He untied her tunic and rubbed her back gently, as though her skin were satin. She let the muslin fall below her breasts.

Johnny said, "Now don't get shocked, kiddo. A woman's—you know—her breasts—they aren't the same here as in the States."

"I know," I said. "They're darker."

He translated, and everyone laughed. I was a hit. They loved me here. Like people loved Mom at Zarahemla.

Marta spoke in the dialect to Alberto; he answered in the same. It was strange to hear these foreign sounds coming from a peer. These were the same guttural sounds I had heard from Cordelia and her mother that morning. Clicky sounds: shallow clicks, deep clicks, clicks from the hard palate, clicks from the tonsils. This was an exotic, a romantic language—almost birdlike, with deep-throated caws. It surprised me to hear Alberto speak it, but soon it seemed just the right language to use in a crater.

Marta and Cordelia laughed at Alberto, teased him with their clicking words.

I asked Johnny, "Are you getting any of this?"

"You kidding?" he said. "I'm a farmer, not a linguist. The only thing I can say in dialect is 'I love you.'"

"Say it," I said.

"What?"

The Indians were laughing at their laughter, oblivious to me.

"Say it," I repeated.

"*Ya tinwaho*," he said.

I repeated the words and the laughter stopped. "*Ya tinwaho*," I said to each of my fellow bathers. "*Ya tinwaho*."

Cordelia embraced me and giggled something in her language.

"She says you're one of us," announced Alberto. "Only one of us says those words."

They laughed again. Cordelia kissed my cheek and whispered more dialect sounds to me.

The sulphur got hotter the longer we stayed. Primitivo went to the well three times for cool water. He stood over us after his last trip, pouring the coolant into our bath and making a speech, half in Spanish, half in dialect. Alberto translated:

"The old man believes this place was made when Jesus came to our people. He believes this place was called Desolation, but that after the destructions, Jesus redeemed it. We have all been redeemed, he says. All of us are the fruit of desolation, the flower of the desert. It's Isaiah he's quoting. He says the angel read him Isaiah over and over again, so he would not forget."

Primitivo's hands and arms were signing the meaning of his words. He made circles and prayer poses. He motioned to his long hair as hula dancers motion to their flowers.

"He says Jesus will visit this place again."

The old man pointed with both hands to the waterfall and made a slow circle, as wide as his arms would spread.

"He says Jesus will visit the poor and the humble before he goes to the rich. He says we will be the angels who announce His coming to you. He will know us first."

Primitivo's speech was slow and punctuated. Then, abruptly, he turned to Johnny and scolded him. Alberto translated for Johnny into Spanish—which was still Greek to me. Johnny seemed merely amused. He made some sort of humorous reply, which Primitivo clearly didn't accept.

"What's he mad about?" I asked my uncle.

"Oh, his blankets. He thinks I didn't pay him enough for one of his blankets."

Primitivo pointed to Johnny, then to the sky, and shook his finger. Johnny shrugged. Primitivo watched him, sighed, then climbed back into the sulphur and was silent.

It was dark when we walked home. We used candles to see the path, as did the others around us. All up the ravine were little yellow lights. All through the cornfields that surrounded the cliffs were fireflies, flaring and fading and flaring again. The cornfields and the canyon seemed to undulate with the flashing of the bugs, like Johnny's lake reflecting the stars. And we were there, making some of those stars, holding pieces of light in our hands, blowing them out when the wicks got too low, starting over with new candles. We were fireflies too, with longer lights.

Primitivo's wife gave us tortillas and beans when we returned, and a tart fruit juice that reminded me of what Mom had served at my wedding reception: a blend of cranberry, apple, and raspberry that Mom called "crappleberry."

After dinner, Johnny walked me to the cornfield. He said he wanted to talk to me. I figured he wanted to know how my nightmares were coming, and if I was really going through with the big divorce. This was "The Talk" coming up. I got my answers ready.

He stopped at a rock and lit three more candles. I said we looked like a couple of icons. Johnny chuckled. His hands were curved around the flames, red between the fingers, yellow at the palms. He said, "So, how are you liking things?"

My nightmares had ended, I told him.

He said, "Primitivo's quite a guy, isn't he."

I said he was.

He told me about Primitivo's wife, Josefina. She was born with that black, warty shiner, he said. Johnny had thought it was cancer the first time he saw it, and took her to San Salvador to see a doctor. But when the doctor offered to remove the birthmark and both the old lady's cataracts, she had whimpered that she wanted to go home and live the life God had given her. No big-city charity for her, thank you. So she was basically blind, and the birthmark was still a monstrosity. Johnny said, "What do you think of that?"

I said it was an interesting story. I was still waiting for "The Talk."

"I told your Mom that story. She said the doctor ought to come to Izalco and dope Josefina in her sleep and go on to do the operations. That's your Mom. Oh, that Em! I'm real fond of her, you know. Wasn't always, of course. You might know we hated each other when we were kids. She was a brain and a beauty, and I was a dunce and a klutz, but I was still the family favorite. Has she told you about that?"

"Some."

"It was hard on her. But when I came off my mission she softened up. Half my ex-comps wanted to date her. I suppose you know all about that too."

I shrugged.

"Actually," he said, "the first guy she fell for, it wasn't your old man. It was Daniel Castillo. He's from here too." He blew out a flickering candle and took another one from his trouser pocket. He lit it while he explained how Mom had written Daniel for nearly a year, and fallen in love with him by mail. Their family had sponsored him to come to the States. He had been like another son for their parents. "If things had worked out," he said, "you would have known him well. Maybe he wouldn't have married your mother; that never did seem right to me—they were so different. But he would have been like an uncle to you. We loved that boy. Isn't that something how things work out? I never guessed we'd have a parting of ways like we did. His doing, mostly. You see, kiddo, he did learn his English," Johnny said. "But he won't use it now. Hated it over there. Used to watch 'Let's Make A Deal' on the boob tube. And one morning during a commercial break he says, and I quote, 'North Americans are plastic idiots,' and he wants to go home. I remember his speech because Luisa and I were there together. We had announced our engagement the night before. So when Daniel says all of this, Luisa starts to crying like her heart will burst into smithereens. 'Americans' he says—I remember the words exactly—'Americans worship Gucci cufflinks and ceramic dogs.' That's what he said. And he had had enough of it. So he left, just after Luisa and I married. Lives in San Salvador now. Big-shot doctor. Never did marry. Him and Piggott are buds. And if that's not some huge irony, I don't know what is."

"So he and Mom broke up?" I said.

He grinned. "What do you think, kiddo? Think your Mom's doing something clandestine?" He drew the word out long, made it rhyme with brine. "They wrote for a while. When Daniel got polio your Mom and me and Luisa fasted for him to survive, which he did. Then he wrote your Mom to say he knew he wasn't supposed to marry her. So meanwhile there were about five other friends of mine or ex-comps waiting. Your Dad was the first in line, and you know the rest. I'm surprised your Mom hasn't told you that story. It's a fine story. She probably doesn't talk much about the men in her past. I guess that's a good idea. I don't talk about the other women in my life either." He rustled his hair and scratched his beard.

"So what did you want to say to me?" I asked.

"Aw, nothing in particular. I just wanted to jabber is all. It's been ten years. I wanted to see how you're doing, chew the fat, pass the time, shoot the breeze." He grinned. "I tell you, your old man and me used to talk on our missions, when we were comps. Oh, we were close. You gotta know about that, don't you?"

"A little."

"Oh I loved your Papa. Him and me and old Mr. Piggy were all three of us musketeers. We were going to find us some good women and come back here to El Salvador and build Zion. I was going to be the farmer, your Pop was going to be the lawyer, and old Piggott, he was going to be the engineer and architect. Can you believe it? Makes me want to kick dust. My, oh my. Things change." He lit another candle. "You know, when your Mom wrote me about the excommunication—do you mind if I mention it?"

"No."

"When I got that letter, oh kiddo, I cried. You may find this hard to believe, but your Dad was the most idealistic of the three of us. Back then he was a visionary. He believed in things better than I did."

"I can't picture Dad like that."

"Oh let me tell you. Cheeks like polished apples and eyes bright as the stars overhead. Oh yeah. Couldn't bear his testimony without bawling. Couldn't see a kid without hugging it. Your Papa to me was just about how I'd picture Jesus. When your Mom and Dad got married, well I figured our family had just been guaranteed a condo in the Celestial City. Your Dad had this sanctifying effect on everything. He still would if he'd just let go some. Let it out. It's still there inside him, just covered up like a candle in a bushel." He covered one of the candles with his hands, for emphasis. "What he reminds me of is a soft vanilla ice cream cone with a chocolate shell. They used to call them Brown Toppers. Ever had one of those?"

"Sure."

"Hard on the outside, soft inside. That's how your old man is. Oh he's a good one. I'm sure you know that."

I nodded, still waiting.

"We were going to be somewheres around here, the three of us, and have us a little school and a church and live the Law of Consecration. All things in common. No rich nor poor. Everything the way it should be. Call our place *Justicia.* I wouldn't have guessed things would turn out like they did, not in a thousand years."

"What about Piggott? He's here."

"Yup. Yup, he is. But him and me, we don't have right feelings between us. You may have picked up on that."

"Not hard to pick up on."

"It's a long story, and this probably isn't the place for it." He looked around, up at the Milky Way, around us at all the foliage, down at the rock where our candles were leaving green spots of wax. "It's not hard to believe that Jesus came here, is it. There couldn't be a prettier land, I don't think. I imagine every place Jesus stepped just bloomed up a storm afterwards. Touch of the Master's foot. This place has God's mark on it everywhere. You may find out more about that later. Some things I can't tell you just yet. But I'll tell you this much: the land you see around you, it's tattooed with grace." He sat there, breathing in the smells of chlorophyll and pine, looking up at the spiralled stars.

I could feel everything he hadn't said hanging around us. I volunteered the beginning. "Did you want me to tell you about my divorce?"

He put his arm around me. "Aw kid," he said, "that's your affair. Things'll work out for you. We all have to make our own decisions. We have to do what we think is right. Not everybody will understand your decision, just like not everybody understands mine. But you're the one in your mirror. I'll stand by you if you stand by me, kiddo."

I leaned my head to his shoulder. We talked about the economics of El Salvador, the future and the past of Zarahemla, how beautiful the world is by candlelight. I felt closer to him in those moments than I did to anyone. He was the man my father would have been if Viet Nam had never happened.

*   *   *

When we got back, Primitivo was waiting for us by the door, but the only person inside was the old blind woman, who lifted her head off her mat when we entered, and gave us a tired smile. Cordelia's mat and Alberto's were empty.

I awakened burning sometime in the middle of the night. I could feel the fleas crawling on my stomach and legs, biting my skin, crawling, biting. When the roosters crowed I sat up, drugged with sleeplessness. Cordelia was kneeling by my mat, looking at me. She motioned me to get up, and swung open the bamboo door. There was a ring of turquoise around the sky. Cordelia raised her arms high like she was worshipping this light, then dropped and swung her hands by her toes. She moved her shoulders in long circles and spat on the ground. "*Buenos dias,*" she said.

I said, "*Buenos dias.*"

She was shaking her hands like a flapper girl and making circles with her shoulders and her head. And spitting.

I tried the spitting too, just to see how it felt. Actually, there was something nice, something earthy about it. You gather up the sleep in your stomach, move it to your throat and spit it straight into the dirt.

Cordelia took a bright green jug which was next to the "kitchen" hut. She indicated I should take the blue one.

The morning skyline was getting thicker; the stars were fading as we started up the cobblestone. I wore wood-heeled sandals that clicked like horseshoes. Cordelia was barefoot. She seemed to glide to the center of town, to the *pila* where the Indians got their water.

The *pila* was a natural spring, a rivulet cascading over copper stones. There were twelve other women there, extending bamboo poles from their jugs to the spring, waiting, gossiping until the water bubbled around their bamboo. Then they put their jugs on their heads and walked away, straight and graceful, and other women replaced them. (When I was in fourth grade, I was voted

"Miss Posture"—my one success in Granite Elementary School. But my back was nothing to these Indians'. My perfect posture was upstaged by every one of their gazelle steps.)

Cordelia put her pole to the well. She glanced at me and radiated a holy smile every few seconds, trying to make friends through her teeth. I went along with her, smiled and smiled and smiled back. When her water bubbled, she removed the pole and filled my jug. She gave it to me and hoisted hers to her head as though it were a bonnet. I found mine leaden. I hugged it home, clicking, bent-backed, horse-heavy all the way down the cobblestone, with Cordelia grinning beside me, floating.

Primitivo's wife was already making tortillas at the *comal.* Cordelia and I emptied our water into the clay vessel in the corner of the hut.

After breakfast, I gave my new "sister" her first reading lesson. I showed her the vowels and pronounced them Spanishly. She mimicked and clapped for herself whenever I indicated she had read a sound right. She clapped for herself when she missed too; the only difference was that she clapped less vigorously and laughed when she gave the wrong answer; she beamed at her right ones.

There was an intentness, an urgency in her studying which I had never seen before. For three hours we worked, until I was bored frantic, and still she wanted to continue. Only the call to lunch saved me. But immediately afterwards she took my hand and pulled me away from my last, half-eaten tortilla. She said something in Spanish. I was sure I was in for three more hours of vowels.

I was wrong. She led me to the cobblestone road again—still holding my hand as though I were a lover or a child—and took me to the pharmacy, where other Indians and a few Latins were also entering.

Inside, between rows of toothpaste and deodorant, was an archaic-looking television set, black and white. Linda Evans in a white silk gown and a heart-shaped diamond pendant was coming down marble stairs. She looked like a ghost behind static snow. The Indian girls were gasping and whispering to each other.

It was *Dynasty*. A Soap in Izalco.

Cordelia asked me questions which I could not understand, and chattered to me in Spanish and in her dialect as though comprehension were irrelevant to such an important conversation as we were having. I nodded and shrugged and said *si* and *bueno*. Cordelia leaned her head against mine and blessed me again and again with her smile.

I laughed at the dubbed voices, though I could not understand a word they said. My laughter cued everyone else's. They all seemed to be watching me, assuming, I suppose, that since this was an American program and I was an American lady, I would know things about it which they could not. I would get all the jokes, laugh at all the right places. They wanted to understand the world that had charmed them.

And they were charmed. Entranced by Joan Collins and her clothes and malevolent looks, mesmerized by Linda Evans and John Forsythe. They loved—they worshipped this stuff.

Cordelia was subdued and dreamy afterwards. She held my hand as we went home, giving me satiated smiles, asking me incomprehensible questions, which I always answered, "*Si, si.*"

This was my pattern for two weeks: in the early morning Cordelia and I either fetched water or washed clothes in the river. Then we worked on reading. After lunch we watched *Dynasty* and took long routes home, during which we had bilingual conversations that neither of us understood. Occasionally in the evenings we went to Salto Blanco and bathed. Sometimes we helped Primitivo with his weaving. (He made blankets and coats and required wool to be spun into thread on his ancient spinning wheel, then dyed green or blue or red by the ink of various and pungent boiled herbs. When the weaving was done, the product needed to be combed with huge burrs that grew outside Izalco.) At night Johnny took me "exploring" or to the rock, where he talked to me about strange and superficial things, asked how Cordelia's reading was coming and if we were getting to be friends, told me about Primitivo, or (twice) recited a Grimm Brothers' fairy tale. It was like he was protecting me or diverting me from nighttime secrets, or maybe filling my mind with fluff so I could sleep without bloody dreams. Every night he talked to me. Talked and talked.

Not so with Alberto, who talked to me rarely, though he did help Primitivo with the weaving and thanked me for the wool I spun and dyed. He had not brought his guitar. But one night after supper, while we were all gathered around the fire, he began singing hymns. Spontaneously, I harmonized. He was singing Spanish and I English, but the blend of our voices absorbed difference.

Singing was one thing I could do. Mom had made me take lessons when it became apparent I wasn't going to be a beauty. Sometimes she told me a joke about an opera singer who takes off her false eyelashes, her dentures, and her wig on her wedding night while her new husband watches in horror and begs her to "sing, sing, for the sake of heaven—sing!" I always figured that joke was the real inspiration to Mom's insistence that I practice an hour a day.

My husband loved my singing before we were married. I used to put him to sleep on his front room couch with songs like "Amazing Grace" and "Chattanooga Choochoo." He said, "Will you always sing when I'm lonely?" and I said, "Why, you'll never be lonely again."

Famous last words.

Anyway, Alberto was impressed. He said, "Nice voice. We're a team."

Cordelia hugged me after each rendition, clapped like her hands were possessed, made smiles of awe. Primitivo sat with his arms folded around his legs, his long, tangled, white hair shining in the firelight. He nodded like this music was no surprise but something he had been expecting for years. His wife knelt beside him. She said, "Aaaah," after each of our songs as though the hymns conveyed some essential bit of information to her—something she had been trying to understand forever and finally had. "Aaaah." The problems of the universe unravelled with "A Poor Wayfaring Man of Grief." She clapped three times, gave a comprehending nod. The firelight showed the warts around her eye, all her black bumps. Her eye looked like it had been singed by lava.

"Aaaah."

Johnny said, "What did I tell you, Alberto? Great things in store."

We sang and sang and sang. "Come Come Ye Saints," "The Spirit of God like a Fire," "In our Lovely Deseret," "Praise to the Man." We harmonized. We filled the adobe with Mormon music. Till deep into the night we sang, and the next morning we slept beyond the noise of the roosters. Indeed, there was no cause to arise early; we were not going to get water or to wash clothing. There was only one thing on our agenda: Johnny and Alberto and I were going back to Zarahemla.

Cordelia could now read the words "*gato*," "*perro*," and "Mormon." Johnny felt our trip had been a monumental success. I had had no nightmares at all in Izalco.

Five

When we got to Zarahemla, Luisa was in the kitchen, chopping carrots. She looked yellow, tired, and pregnant. Yes, there was a little ball, the size of a small cantaloupe, under her ribs. I knew that she had had seven miscarriages and two stillbirths. I didn't say anything about the obvious, but the cantaloupe made me nervous. Death in embryo.

The spinach tasted wonderful that evening—maybe because in Izalco we had eaten in the dark and used prayer more than light to counter maggots. In Johnny's cabin, we could actually see what we were eating. There were electric lights strung everywhere—naked bulbs and exposed wires hanging from the ceiling, but light!

Luisa served the dinner. When I asked if I could help she gave a weak smile and said everything was fine. She had grey lips and purple crescents under her eyes. I watched her moving around the table. I thought, now there's someone you could stick a halo on and pray to. There's the real thing: Madonna in the flesh.

We made small talk as we ate, and then did the dishes together: Luisa and Johnny washing, Alberto and I rinsing. What I noticed was that the sink was chromium and the dish soap Palmolive. These, I thought, were luxuries.

I fit back into my Zarahemla patterns easily. I found myself walking by the lake after the dishes were done and hearing—oh yes—the guitar music. As though there had been no interlude for Manuelito.

> *Al decir adios, vida mia,*
> *Te digo eso: te quiero.*

Soft, siren song. I had forgotten how I loved it.

Again I saw my husband's face while I listened. Saw his face and heard his insults. And then I saw Mom at her most ethereal, saying, "But Digs, women can work miracles."

The words that persuaded me to hitch up.

What I hadn't realized was that it's not easy being married to an angry young man. Not something you want to dress up for.

My husband had one glass eye, his right one, having lost the real thing in a freak accident when he was seven years old. (He had been jumping around in an abandoned house and had fallen on a stick of lumber with jutting nails. Two pierced his hands; one, his right eye.) The glass eye, he felt, changed his life, made him a freak, doomed him to the anger which found its ultimate consummation thirteen years later, while he was a Mormon missionary in Taiwan. It was then his father died in a private plane crash. My husband left the Church within a week of receiving the telegram, and started translating anti-Mormon tracts into Chinese. When he met me, he tried to get me to join him in the ranks of the exed. I stood my ground. Within a month, he decided he wanted to come back to the Church and get married.

Me, I loved his square jaw and didn't mind his glass eye, which never dilated in the dark. I felt sorry for him because he was so helpless and pathetic and out of control. I talked to Mom about it—one of the few real talks of our life. She said a woman could work miracles. No telling what a woman could do, she said. No limits. Women were God's gift to men. Wearing this gorgeous, serene, orange smile, she lulled me to hell with the promise that I could make a metamorphosis. I could consecrate hellfire and turn brimstone to lilies. And I bought it, because I loved her and I wanted to be her and I trusted every word she said. I was wrapped up in her goop like a one-winged fly.

Truth was, I had bought the sugar-coated marriage bar a long time before I actually made my choice of a partner. The whole yummy looking thing. My diary was full of bride pictures and promises that my colors would be purple and lavender.

We got married in lilac season. I had seven bridesmaids and two flower girls all in purple and lavender lace. I carried lilies and lilacs. And two weeks after the ceremony, I had indeed worked a miracle, just as Mom had prophesied. All my husband's anger diverted from the Church—and centered on me.

I said to him one night, "Do you love me?" He answered with this helpless, this apologetic shrug, "I don't think there's a man alive could love you. Not without makeup, anyway."

Sometimes he would dig his glass eye out of its pink socket, lick it, hold it between his teeth, grin at me. "You repulse me," he would say.

My diarrhea didn't let up in four years. It was, the doctor told me, pre-cancerous colitis.

Para decir adios, Alberto was singing. I was humming along with him—I knew his song by now—and thinking it would have been nice to have been warned. Would have been nice if Mom had said after her miracle speech, "Of course, you realize miracle workers do get wasted every now and again. You could die or go loony or come home humiliated. You might have to give up a lot: your heart, your soul, your intestines—who knows?"

Alberto finished the song and plucked the guitar strings.

The lake was glittering with stars. The smell of gardenia was thick. This could not be a place, I thought, where people are cruel to each other. This could not be the place where they don't love a face with no makeup. Not the place where kids get strung up on mango trees like laundry.

Alberto made the guitar strings quiver like something magical. I watched the stars' reflections, and felt that someone—God, Jesus, or Johnny—was watching me too. Loving me, protecting me, preparing my path to heaven.

But the next day, like an answer to my hope, the weather changed. Rainy season came, and with it lightning. As abrupt and violent as a Shakespearean storm.

Alberto and I were walking back to the cabin after milking cows when the clouds converged. Slate clouds, weighted with rain, ready to explode. There was sudden war in the sky. Brilliant spears slashed and were answered by claps and rumbling pulses of light. Sometimes the whole sky raged at once. We stopped walking and watched.

The lightning and thunder were almost simultaneous. The cornstalks around us turned silver-blue in sheets of electricity. Alberto started telling me about one of his friends who had been struck by lightning: how the bolt had entered the guy's head, exited his toes, burned all his internal organs and scalded his blood, but left him looking unscathed.

"I don't want to hear this," I said. "Not now."

The sky was teasing us with electric darts, like God's avengers.

A sheet of lightning illumined Alberto's face. He was looking at me hard. Then it was dark and the thunder was swelling around us and Alberto was kissing my neck and my hair and my mouth. I was thinking, if we do get electrocuted, this is a helluva way to go. I was loving his arms around me, his mouth, the smell of his hair. I had had a crush on him ten years ago. It was coming back full force.

We lay down. We were flying. Floating through blue clouds.

"Do you want to?" he whispered.

"To what?"

"Make love with me."

"What?"

"Make love." He said the words softly, and let them sit in the air for lightning to strike.

What he was suggesting was that I commit adultery. A pretty grievous sin in Mormondom. You get excommunicated for adultery if you were married in the temple. You make covenants of fidelity and chastity in the temple. You can't break them without getting exed.

I said, "I'm married."

"Let me," he said.

"No." I pushed him gently away. "Are you serious?"

His eyes turned suddenly playful. He laughed and held me close. "A joke," he said. "A test. Congratulations, you passed."

"Oh thanks," I said.

"But you did. We knew you would. I knew you would." He was serious now. He brushed my lips with his, softly, softly (oh, the boy was gentle!). "Someday, there will be more," he said, "and the time will be right."

The storm subsided, just as his passion had. The clouds broke up and let the stars come back. Things were like that in El Salvador: abrupt and unpredictable.

He kept his arm around me as we walked home. He told me the story of *Hamlet*, with which I was already familiar. But he told it as though it were his own story, something intimate and essential.

"*Hamlet* is the greatest play ever written," he said. "You must learn to love it. This must be part of your destiny."

Six

The rains would keep up for about three months. Mornings would be misty and warm; evenings would get soaked.

So the rain was added to the nighttime sounds of the wind and the frogs and the monkeys. Just taps at first, like clicking fingers, but swooshing suddenly to violent storms. Sloshing, pelting, slapping rain. In this weather, you could imagine a Death Squad gathered around a sharp-toothed idol, making lists.

And the weather was not the only sympathetic vibration of restlessness in El Salvador. The earth also became uneasy, started quaking. Alberto told me that this was simply part of rainy season, and that I would get used to it.

He was wrong.

I got so I could tell when one was coming—a stillness would settle around us and even flower petals and leaves would seem to be braced on their stems, waiting—but I never got used to that underground thunder rattling tables and chairs, making pictures sway on the walls. This, to me, was not ordinary. It seemed in these moments that something or someone was trying to crash out of the underworld.

No one else appeared concerned. The cows still gave milk; Alberto and I still talked between their udders—usually about Shakespeare.

But there was no more guitar music by the lake, and I lay awake at nights listening to the rain in its various stages and thinking mostly about divorce. Sometimes I pitied myself; more often I pitied my husband and regretted my failure to save him, my lack of love. Though I understood the psychology, the rationality of my situation, I still had to face my Mormon guts. Which was enough to give me diarrhea.

I got it a lot during those rainy nights. During midnight hours I went to the outhouse and watched the rain making blue streaks in the mother-of-pearl sky. I was coming apart, and there was only wet newspaper to wipe me up with.

Once, when I was making one of those trips, I saw Aunt Luisa crying by the gardenias. Her hair was down, hiplength, blowing around her face, lifting in the wind. The moon behind the sky made everything glow. The clouds, the gardenias, Luisa's nightgown were light silver; the leaves and her hair and hands and eyes were black. It was a ghostly vision. I stopped, very near to her, but she made no sign of seeing me. She raised her arms like she would embrace some angel or catch a slow comet. Over and over she said, "*Dios, Dios, Dios, Dios.*" I wondered if she had lost her baby. I wondered if it was the baby's spirit she was reaching for, trying to hold.

I didn't mention anything to her at breakfast. I pretended all I had seen in the middle of the night was the relief of the john. Nor did Aunt Luisa volunteer an explanation. She looked weary, but she always looked weary. The little cantaloupe of a baby was still visible under her sternum.

I wanted to understand her, to talk to her, to be her friend. She was timid, though, almost frightened at times, and rarely said anything directly to me. I had heard her laugh only once, when

Mom was teasing her—telling her to be alert because the world needed more lerts. I tried daily to get some kind of conversation moving; Luisa always had some task that took her away from my efforts. But one afternoon, when Johnny delivered a letter from Mom and Dad, Luisa started talking. The letter said very little. It described the work Mom and Dad were doing, the literacy program Dad had begun, the children Mom had fallen in love with. Mom spent two paragraphs asking about Boops and Munch (her Zarahemla orphans) but made no mention of the letters I had written her and Dad, or of Manuelito. Out loud I supposed that the whole awful event was just too much for Mom to handle. She couldn't take much reality.

Luisa came to her defense, told me I underestimated my mother; more likely my letter had never reached Belen.

"You mailed it?" I asked John, and he said he had, but that mails were unpredictable in Salvador. Mails had always been unpredictable.

"Your mother," said Luisa, "she sees more than you think. She doesn't always know how to answer." Johnny started to speak, but something in Luisa's eyes stopped him. He excused himself and went out to ride Yermo. It was then that Luisa and I talked.

At first, we reminisced. I told her my first memory of her: when she and Johnny were taking off for El Salvador. I remembered Johnny giving everyone goodbye hugs and kisses, and Luisa doing the same, and people saying things like "God bless you" and "Drive safely." Grandma had cried. She had kept hitting her cheeks and saying, "Oh for heaven's sake, I wish I'd stop doing this." She was talking about her crying, of course, but I thought she was wishing she'd quit hitting herself.

Luisa smiled. She told me her own memories: first about the trip she and Johnny had taken after our send-off—about how funny it had seemed to her to be travelling back to El Salvador with her Gringo husband, when she had always dreamed of living in the States. Then she told me about her youth. "I was a superficial girl," she said. "Very rich compared to now. Sadly rich." When she was made Miss San Cristobal, she had felt like a little goddess. Her picture was in the paper; she rode a butterfly float in the Independence Day parade; some half-famous local artist did her portrait.

"I'll bet people fell in love with you," I said. "Right?"

She waved the thought away, then admitted, "There was one, yes. I broke his heart." Her eyes teared. It surprised me that she could still feel pity for this guy, this thwarted teenaged lover. "But John is my husband," she said, as though to this old boyfriend, not to me. "I have covenanted with God for that."

Those words hit hard. They came at me like an angelic accusation, reminding me of my fantasies of marriage, my illusions, my diary brides, the cliches that had justified my innocent, naive committments. The great "Covenant with God." Marriage. The tie that binds, that bound, that strangled. Sometimes at night I had been startled from sleep with echoes of Mormon cliches humming in my head like muted alarm clocks. I would shout at my past self, at all my elementary school pictures, at my trashed bridal album, "I'm sorry, okay? I'm Sorry!"

My eyes teared now. Luisa took my face in her hands, and kissed both my cheeks. I sobbed, and she held me like she was my mother. I found myself telling her things I had told nobody.

It wasn't that I hadn't loved him. That wasn't why I left. I had loved him too much, with my heart and soul and my aching, bloody guts. The day I went, I froze two tunafish casseroles so he wouldn't go hungry. I wept for him, as I was weeping now. "But he tied me in knots," I told her. "I'm blistered inside. Still blistered inside."

"If you loved him," she soothed me, "then you were loyal. You need not torment yourself if you were loyal."

"I wasn't," I said. "I flirted." This was the first I had confessed my sin. "There was a bus driver," I told her, and unloaded the image.

The Woodward Avenue bus driver. I hadn't ever known his name, but I could still smell his cigarettes. Once when we were alone on the bus, he said he wanted to kiss me. He pulled over, stood, walked to my seat. He was a huge black man with tender, fiery eyes. He said, "Stand up." I did, and looked into his eyes, saw the sweat above his lips, the little whiskers like sandpaper on his chin. He put his hand on my waist and moved his face close to mine. I pulled back, told him I was married. He cursed and came for me again. I said I was a Mormon—a member of Christ's true church and I couldn't commit adultery or do anything like it or I'd go stark crazy. He moved his other hand to my waist so he was holding me like a big vase of flowers. He said, "I want you. And I could."

I told him I knew that.

"Can't you," he said, "quit Mormon?"

I said no.

"You want to kiss me?" he said.

I did. I told him I did.

"But you won't?"

"No."

He pinched my waist hard, then dropped his hands and returned to his place. I kept standing there. When he pulled back onto the road, I fell to my seat. We watched each other in his mirror, glaring, the angry lust almost palpable between us. It felt like adultery to me.

"But it wasn't," said Luisa. "You kept your head. You were tempted. You did not yield."

"I wanted it," I cried. "It felt like a sin to want it so much."

"Oh *hija*," she said, "you are so young, so pure. God forgives you, *hija*. Let it go." She massaged my temples as though preparing a place for the memory to leave my mind. She kissed my forehead. "We all have tests. We all are tempted. This is life."

Another Mormon cliche, but coming from her it consoled. I felt forgiven, unburdened. I felt like a baby in its mother's arms, certain of love, protection, comfort.

It was dusk outside. We could see Johnny, shadowlike on his horse, galloping over the hills like an apparition from the Spanish conquest.

The sky was clouding as the stars turned on. Luisa named constellations even as nimbus hands were covering them.

"Too bad," she said.

I asked what was "too bad."

"You didn't get to see it. The clouds were in a hurry tonight."

The "it" I wouldn't see was the Southern Cross. I would never see it from Orem, Utah. She informed me the crux would travel the sky until an hour before first light, and then sink from view. "If the clouds part before it leaves," she said, "I can wake you. If you'd like."

I said yes. Absolutely. I wanted to see this new detail of the cosmos.

It happened that I was awake when the clouds retreated. I had been awakened by my blanket—a beautiful but scratchy thing, all undyed wool save the center where two green quetzal birds faced each other. No doubt, Primitivo had woven the thing himself. It felt raw, unrefined, ancient—just like its artisan. Apparently I was allergic to it, and had been since it first touched me. Most nights I cast it aside, but I never requested a softer one. I did not want to confess how the wool hurt; that would be such a *gringa* thing to do—as if I were suggesting there was something wrong with Indian ways, Indian culture, Indian art, Indian lambs. It would be like wanting to make over Primitivo, cut and comb his hair, give him a three-piece suit and dress shoes. I was too converted to Johnny to make such insults. I had used the blanket that night because it was cool outside. I had hoped I might be accustomed to the wool by now, that I might use it without burning.

I was still allergic. I could feel welts and pimples grow where wool met skin. I was about to sit up and throw the blanket off when my door opened and Luisa approached me. She was holding a kerosene lantern. A dimly glowing, orange ball at its base illuminated her chin and nose. When she stroked the blanket to nudge me from sleep, my itching stopped. I looked at her. "It's here," she whispered when I sat up. "Julie, it's here."

I thought "The second coming?" then remembered I had asked her to show me the Southern Cross. I followed her in that circle of lantern light, both of us silent, reverent.

The stars were out in glory. The Big Dipper, directly overhead, was pouring Tinkerbell dust into the night.

Luisa directed my eyes to the horizon. She pointed to four stars arranged in a diamond. "There," she said. "The Cross." Four lonely stars. "There are people," Luisa said, "who worship it. And that river of stars, that is the Milky Way. You knew that, yes?"

"Yes." It was like milk—dense with nearly indistinguishable specks of light.

"Glorious," I whispered.

"Glorious," she repeated. "On a night like this, you can imagine Moses, yes? Falling to the earth, sure that man is nothing." I looked up, turning my head to the eternal north, the eternal south, the eternal east, the eternal west. There was more glitter than sky. I imagined music—a cosmic orchestra of harps and bells and windchimes. "The sun will come soon," Luisa said. "Almost a pity, no? The stars will fade." There was a heavy, moist fragrance around us, a cool breeze. Both of us were wearing only our nightgowns, but we were not cold.

"My mother showed me the stars many times," Luisa said. "She told me stories about them."

I had never heard her speak of her mother. I wanted her to, and asked her to tell me. She sighed.

Last night, I had felt that I was the baby and she the grown-up. Now we were peers, both of us young, easily amazed. If anything, Luisa with her hair down looked younger than I did.

"My mother," she said. "She is no longer living. Some years ago, my brother was killed by *guerrilleros*. He was too rich, you see. It was dangerous to be rich in those days. Perhaps it still is. Dangerous. Jorge, my brother, he was not yet twenty. Younger than you. They took him off a bus and they shot him many times. Even after he was dead they shot him. As though they were shooting all of us through him. Perhaps they killed us, too. My mother began to die, a little every day until only her heart was beating—whipping her blood. Then it stopped too. Others of my family disappeared, or lost hope. It was a terrible time." She stopped. "Look there, Julie—did you see it? A falling star."

I looked where she was pointing. I saw only stationary stars. Some of them seemed to be beating, as though there were a pulse of the universe.

"I missed it," I said, then admitted that falling stars were stubborn superstitions for me. Mom always said that a falling star meant someone had died. Once or twice, when Dad was in Viet Nam and we kids were driving Mom crazy, she had taken us up the Utah Valley mountains to a viewpoint on Squaw Peak and had us count falling stars. The next day, we'd compare the numbers with the obituaries. Sometimes, we were right on. Once in mid-August, there was a meteorite shower. We counted fifty-seven shooters in thirty minutes. Mom said, "Catastrophe around the corner, watch out." The next day, sure enough, there were reports of a hurricane in Florida. Thirty-six dead. "They just haven't found the rest," Mom said, and I believed her. Falling stars have spooked me since. I have seen them losing their places, becoming disattached, and I have imagined cliffs and graveyards. "Pretty silly," I said to Luisa, "isn't it."

She took my hand. "I suppose," she said, "it is silly to count stars that fall. Silly perhaps. Now maybe I will get frightened. Maybe what you told me will haunt me, yes? I will think what I saw was my own star. It will give me bad dreams."

"Pretty silly," I repeated.

"If it were true, there would have been comets and meteors all over the sky during the last years. Hundreds of them. Like old coins with no more value. Thrown away."

"Do you look like your mother?" I asked after a moment.

She nodded, and said her mother was much more beautiful than she, but that there were similarities.

"I think you're beautiful," I said.

"My mother," said Luisa, "was once the most lovely in all of San Cristobal. Queen of everything, yes? She had many suitors before her marriage. I think sometimes that my father was not as kind to her as she deserved. It's the *machista*, you see. The great temptation for the men of my country. I wanted to marry a Gringo to get away from *machista*. My father loved too many women; Mother was only one of them. But she was loyal to him, Julie. She was great in that way. No matter what he did, she was loyal and she was silent. She told her sorrows to The Virgin, to no one else."

"You were Catholic before Johnny converted you?"

"Of course," she said. "El Salvador is Catholic. My mother cried for two days when I joined the Mormons. It hurt her more than my father's adulteries. It was her greatest pain until my brother. There, Julie, look again at the Cross. It's leaving us."

The bottom star of the diamond had already sunk below the horizon. Within a half hour, the rest of it was gone as well. Then came the first hints of sun. Orange light moved up around the cornfields. "Mom's color," I said.

"Another remarkable woman," Luisa said. "Your mother."

"Right."

"A good mother too."

I didn't answer.

"A good mother," Luisa repeated.

"We came out okay," I shrugged. "Only one divorce in the family."

She reached over and hugged me. "You must not be bitter," she whispered.

"I'm not bitter."

"You love your mother, yes?"

"Sure."

"And you forgive her?"

"Forgive her?" How could she know, I wondered, about how I had been betrayed by Mom's "women can work miracles" speech? How could Luisa know how much there was to forgive? Not just that lying speech, but Mom's whole lovable self that she hadn't passed on to me. The ease with which she slid through things, the blindness she boasted, her simplicity, her joy. I had gotten her skinny bones but not her carefree laughter. My outside was all her, but Dad's genes made up my personality. I got Dad's somber, pensive, cryptic ways, his cloudy perceptions, his negative heart. I was both Mom and Dad, thesis and antithesis, but the synthesis was incomplete and, so far, unsuccessful. I still had not become distinctly separate and lovable. I vacillated between faith and despair, good and evil, love and hate, joy and bitterness. I adored my mother and I wanted to smash her orange mouth.

"You should forgive her," Luisa said. "We need to forgive. Everyone tries his hardest, does his best. We must accept this and forgive. Even if we die through their errors, Julie."

"Right," I said, feeling the gnaw of my pre-cancerous colitis.

"Venus is disappearing," she said. "The Mayan star. You know more about Venus than I do."

I did. I had a B.S. degree—which is just what it sounds like—in anthropology, an emphasis (inspired by Uncle Johnny) in Mayan history and ritual. (Alberto and I were going to visit the ruins of Tazumal soon, and I was going to play scholar.)

Luisa's arms were still around me, loose now. A few roosters crowed.

"Did you ever see the sun come up?" she asked me.

"Yes."

"Aurora's pink fingers. I remember that from *The Iliad*. I have loved literature, you see. Aurora's pink fingers. Are you tired?"

"I'm fine," I said.

"You can take a nap this afternoon."

"No need."

"No? Very well. Thank you, Julie, for sharing the stars with me."

"You're welcome," I said.

The roosters were really crowing now, and the morning mists were settling on the trees and the cornfields. The kitchen light came on.

Seven

Johnny and Alberto and I went to the ruins of Tazumal a week later, on one of those humid, rainy-season sunny days.

I had seen Mayan ruins before. I went on a couple of digs when I was in college. The ruins of Tazumal weren't as impressive as others, but not as crowded either. We were the only people there, although there were a lot of emerald-backed beetles and oversized field mice.

Tazumal's biggest building is a pyramid with about a hundred stone stairs. From a distance it looks like a huge lump of tar. Up close it is eroded stone. The front has been cleared, so the stairs, though cracked, are accessible. The sides are overgrown with weeds.

What you have to wonder about the Mayan temples is if they were used once for human sacrifice. There were no guides at Tazumal to tell us its history, but I knew about other sites: Mayan gods were hungry SOBs. They demanded blood. Their victims— often willing, since a human sacrifice went to the highest heaven— were usually drugged with simple herbs before having their hearts cut out by a well-trained priest. The heart was divided; the priest and his helpers partook of it sacramentally. The body of the offering was rolled down the steps. Sometimes hundreds of sacrifices were made. After a war, all the captured soldiers were sacrificed. A ritual offering could go on for weeks. The most I ever heard of being offered at one time was seventy thousand.

You look at the stairs, with innocent dandelions growing in their cracks. You have to wonder how much blood the centuries have washed away.

Both Johnny and Alberto asked me a lot of questions about the Maya. I gave them undergraduate answers. Johnny observed after I described some of their practices that "people can be pretty brutal." Well yes, they can. But the Maya weren't total barbarians; they just didn't have the technology to be pristine. There are ugly aspects of Maya culture (there are ugly aspects of all cultures), but the fact that they knew the stars well enough to chart them, that they farmed the land, that they built beautiful buildings and made beautiful art, says at least as much about them as the fact that they dug out human hearts.

Today, of course, the Mayans have been assimilated into Spanish blood. I have heard that there are still idol worshippers among the Indians, and that there were secret heart sacrifices as late as 1940, but the Indians are fundamentally conquered. Their conquerors have now been weakened by other forces: wicked men, rotten leaders, materialism, communism, fascism. El Salvador is disintegrating under the pressure and expense of all sorts of isms. Truth is, no one here could make war without a lot of help. The little soldiers of the current conflict are pawns of the bigger powers, supplied with guns and instructions, depended upon to find their political passion and use it, while the rest of us make rhetoric. El Salvador is a nice place to put on a battle. A good arena for judging Karl Marx. I said this to Johnny.

"I reckon," he answered, "that's why your old man came here, right? God knows it wasn't to help spread the gospel of peace—no offence. I suppose he's killed people, hasn't he—your Dad. I suppose he's committed murder."

"Yes," I said, "I suppose he has." I didn't know this for sure, but it wasn't hard to guess. I knew what he did at his summer retreats with the National Guard: he taught fellow warriors how to make sure a guy is dead. They used dummies, and Dad showed recruits just where to aim a bayonet, just where to stab, just where to shoot. I don't suppose he took that knowledge to Viet Nam for nothing, but until now, I had avoided thinking about what he might have done. That image—my father with his fist around a knife, pounding some oriental guy's chest—that image was too terrible to keep.

"Murder. Well, that must be why he asked to be exed," Johnny said. "That sin would plain be too much to bear, unless you knew in your very soul that it was the right thing to do. Like Nephi, when the angel commanded him—commanded, you remember—to kill Laban. See, kid, it's not that your dad doesn't believe the Church. He believes the Church. I know him too well. He believes, just doesn't think he's good enough for it anymore." We were sitting on the steps of the past. Johnny took our lunch from a paper bag: chicken sandwiches, with tortillas in place of bread. He took a bite, and talked between swallows. "What your father has to understand, though, is that sometimes people have to die. Sometimes it's God's will, understand what I'm saying?" He took a swig of water from his canteen and offered it to me. "It happens that I don't agree with what America did in Viet Nam—your mom and I are real pacifists, if you want to know the truth. Hippies from the word go. But if you're fighting for a good cause, and you feel like there's reason for what you're doing, God's not going to hold you back from the C.K."

"C.K.?" I asked.

"Sorry," he said. "My own lingo. Celestial Kingdom. Sometimes God himself calls it C.K.—to save time, I suppose, and I guess I've just picked up on it. C.K.—Celestial; T.K.—terrestrial; turkey—telestial. And you know what the Big H is." We laughed and ate. Alberto put his arm around me.

"So," said Johnny, "maybe that's why your dad's here. Maybe God's sent your father here so he can remember important things, and forgive himself some. I think the work he's doing in Belen will bring him part way back to God. And there are other things too. Other ways he'll be redeemed. Maybe even through you, some. What do you think of that?"

I shrugged.

"He may think he's here to check out politics," Johnny said. "God sees a bigger picture, though." He passed me the canteen again. "How about you, Julie? Where do you stand? Politically."

"I don't believe in politics," I said. "Politics are an excuse to be rude and brutal. Rude in election campaigns, brutal in battles. That's where I stand. Call me a wimp, Johnny—I won't deny it."

"Naw, kiddo, you're no wimp. Just not converted to a cause yet. We'll see how you feel later, though. Maybe you'll see some things—well, let's not rush." He grinned, then said he guessed he was ready for a nap in the jeep. Alberto and I, he instructed, should "get to know each other better."

The sun gleamed on the jeep's headlight rims and hood. It was too bright to see Johnny climb inside and lie down. It was like he was mounting a chariot of fire.

The heat was also baking our bodies. I knew my nose would be sun-bubbled when we got back to Zarahemla. Alberto suggested we find shade and pointed to a giant olive tree, its trunk gnarled and knotted, its branches twisted, untamed. We lay under it and looked up to the silver side of its leaves.

"What are you feeling?" said Alberto.

"Hot."

He leaned over so his face was directly above mine. He looked young, almost androgynous with his long lashes and smooth, nearly fair skin. "Hot?" he said. He came very near my mouth; my lips parted for his kiss. He only brushed them with his lips, and then smoothed my forehead, my nose, my cheeks, my neck with with his soft mouth. He kissed both my eyes. He was God, and I was Eve. Little by little he was breathing life into me, creating me anew, consecrating me bit by bit for his use. We would sleep, and when we awoke the world would be changed. He moved his head to my breasts and laid it there. I could feel his heart beating over my right hipbone; his head moved with my breaths. For a long time we lay like that. He slept; I did not, though I tried. I found myself checking out the world from this half-conquered, half-loved vantage point. I saw a family of seven ruby-throated hummingbirds moving their needley beaks into yellow flowers—weeds of some sort, like overgrown hollyhocks—whose like I have never seen since. This, I thought, is the hummingbirds' job: to keep those flowers pollinated in memory of what used to be here. Or to keep the place pretty for tourists like us. I saw the towers, too, as though they still functioned, saw them as a ready-to-die-virgin might. If you didn't look closely, you could pretend that this was the hub of civilization. The biggest tower seemed to touch the clouds. You could maybe jump into heaven from its top step.

When Alberto awoke, he kissed my mouth briefly, then knelt beside me. When I tried to get up he stopped me by putting his hands on my head, as though he would bless me. He pushed me gently back to the ground, then traced my face, his thumbs molding my cheekbones, my nose, my jaw. He kissed me again, long now, but not passionately. It was something almost religious.

Johnny appeared, standing over us, the sun lighting him from behind. He looked like the center of his own eclipse. He scratched his butt and yawned.

"So," he said. "You kids ready to go?"

Alberto helped me up, and kissed my cheek once more, not even ashamed before my uncle.

We stopped for gas on our way home, and bought a newspaper. The headline article was about some local genocide. There were photographs of men—former men—with bloody holes for eyes and jagged purple lines across their necks. The victims of the politics.

Of course you can't take newspaper articles seriously in El Salvador (though a lot of Salvadorans do, figuring, I presume, that you have to make headlines to be relevant). Journalism here is yellow as a field of dandelions—and as hard to control. Every paper is a little *National Enquirer.* And the Salvadorans publish pictures even U.S. papers wouldn't touch. Blood and guts and children decapitated in car crashes. You see a newspaper and you think all of El Salvador is being massacred—which is crappola. The murders were as much a surprise at the gas station as a report from Siberia would be at a Safeway's checkstand. As much a surprise as Manuelito had been to me.

I stared at the photos. Johnny put his arm around me. He said we shouldn't have bought the paper, then suggested we get our minds off it and go to *Puerto del Diablo,* a viewpoint just outside San Salvador.

Puerto del Diablo is like one of the rock formations at the Izalco steam baths—an overgrown, mountainish stalagmite draped with moss and leaves. You can see the Pacific Ocean from the *Puerto* on a clear day, Johnny told us. We couldn't since it was getting dark, and darkness in El Salvador is not a gradual process. There's a quick interlude of turquoise and then the stars turn on. The night breezes start. The planets and stars seem to be ventilating the sky.

"I love the nights," I said, trying to push those newspaper pictures away by happy thoughts, a positive mental attitude, etc. "Feel that breeze."

"Nothing like it," Johnny said. "Is there, Berto."

"Nothing," Alberto said. "Nothing."

There was a condor circling above, as though waiting for one of us to drop. I had to wonder if *Puerto del Diablo* had been a body dump during the worst of the revolutions. It would have made a good one.

"You know," Johnny said, "newspapers will do anything for a story around here. The newspapers are probably behind the whole war thing. Maybe it's the journalists sending guns. I heard one time a journalist somewhere in Central America didn't have a story so he bought a wax figure. Then whenever things got dull, he'd pour catsup on the figure's face and click his camera. You never can tell."

"I think you made that up," I said.

He laughed. "You're right. I did."

"No flies," I said. "Am I right? They leave with the sun."

Johnny nodded and stuck a toothpick between his front teeth. "No flies at all," he agreed. "Except maybe a few that got caught in some houses. But they're slow, lazy sons-a-maggots. They'll end up squirming on fly paper."

"You want to hear something funny?" I said. "The first time I saw one of those sap-colored strips of fly paper, I was at Zarahemla. I thought you had made yourself a fly trophy. I thought you had taken all the flies you had caught and glued them to that paper and then hung it from the ceiling. Award of excellence for fly catching." I giggled. "Of course, I know now you're not the type to do that, Johnny. I imagine you hate killing anything—even aphids and flies."

"I do hate it, kiddo," he said. "Hate killing anything. But sometimes, you have to. That's what your Papa needs to understand. Sometimes, you plain have to. It's not the killing but loving it that's the sin. The people who did that—" (He gestured vaguely towards the jeep, indicating the newspaper on the front seat) "now those people will go straight into Outer Perdition—O.P.—when they die. Those people gloried in the blood they shed. And that's a sin, kiddo. That's an unforgivable sin. There's not much the Lord won't forgive. He's not the type to hold grudges, and He's not as harsh as some people think. Mostly He's just amused by us and our weaknesses. But blood-love, that's something He'll take mighty seriously. The people who did that have murdered their own spirits."

The stars started showing. First one, then a few. Within fifteen minutes the sky was full of them.

"Wow," I said. "You can almost see Kolob."

"If you use your imagination, I guess you can," Johnny said. "So, what did you think of Tazumal?"

"Great and groovy," I answered. (Mom's phrase. She liked to say that or "groovy grumptious.")

"That's only my second time to see it," Johnny said. "It is something. I'd love to see Tikal someday."

"Tikal is wonderful," I said. "It's overdone—all the civilizations get overdone in their decline—but it's splendid. Pyramids twice the size of what we saw today. George Lucas shot a segment of *Star Wars* there."

"Well, my gosh," he said. "I would never have known that."

"You probably wouldn't remember it. A couple of storm troopers are on the temples and some imperial planes are flying around. It only lasts a couple of seconds."

"The things I learn from you," he said. "Something special, isn't she, Berto."

"Yes," he said. "Something special."

I saw a shooting star, and then another, just to the left of the Little Dipper. I pointed it out to my companions.

"Maybe it's meteorite season," said Johnny.

We watched. Within seven minutes, three stars had streaked out. Alberto timed them. He said there was a shooting star every two minutes.

I said, "Must be an epidemic or an earthquake ready to happen."

Johnny said, "You get that from your mom, doncha. Well, God forbid another catastrophe."

We got in the jeep. The nighttime clouds were starting to converge. The rain began when we were halfway to Johnny's place. It was torrential by the time we arrived.

Eight

I milked the cows with Alberto in the soggy morning. He seemed oblivious to those intimate moments at Tazumal, and only asked me if I had thought anymore about Hamlet.

I said I hadn't.

"Perhaps you can read it today," he said. "Again, but for the first time."

I said I would, and sat on an overturned tin bucket. I pulled the cow teats and unconsciously started humming Alberto's song. I could have sung the words, I had heard them often enough, but I didn't.

He put his hands on my shoulders. "So you have learned it," he said. "You have come into my privacy."

"Sorry," I answered, looking up at him, waiting.

He massaged my shoulder bones, the same way Cordelia had at the sulphur pits. He reminded me of how beautifully we had harmonized at Izalco, the night we had sung hymns.

"Do you like to sing?" he said.

It seemed an obvious question. Mom and Johnny, whose blood I shared, adored song. Alberto knew that. They could take any composition and make it totally, insipidly theirs. Music was part of their style. I knew Alberto had heard at least one Johnny original— a naughty song about President Piggott:

> The Pig, the Pig,
> He did a jig
> And sold his butt for money.
> But just you wait,
> The pig'll be ate
> And glazed with cloves and honey.

Johnny would sing it when he slopped the hog.

I told Alberto, yes, I liked to sing.

"After we finish," he said, still kneading my skin, "after the milking is done, let's sing. We'll take a break. We'll make some music." He kissed both my shoulders. "Since we can't make anything else."

So in the middle of a spinach garden by the lake we sang Beatles songs I didn't even know I remembered, and Simon and Garfunkel, and Peter, Paul, and Mary. We sang "Homeward Bound" and "For Emily Wherever I May Find Her" and "Puff the Magic Dragon" and "Yesterday." For two hours we sang, Alberto looking at me with his soft libido, making me think temptation. We gazed at each other like James Taylor and Carly Simon before their divorce. We were wonderful.

He kissed my fingertips. He said we would do a great work with our music. Then he took my hand and led me to the kitchen, where Luisa had spinach soup and tortillas ready for us. When Johnny came in, Alberto said to him, "It's time for the tape. Julita and I will sing it."

Johnny explained that for about a year, he and Alberto had wanted to do a tape of gospel songs and messages and broadcast it on the El Salvador radio. But they had wanted a female voice that knew how to harmonize and testify. They had prayed for a voice.

We ate. Then Alberto and I sang again, for everybody this time. We sang "Yesterday" with such pathos and fervor that I teared up. When the last guitar chord was still vibrating the air I whispered, "Dang, we're good."

We were. It was fate.

We recorded fifteen songs on a little cassette player Johnny had, and then Alberto recorded a gospel message. Johnny said he would take the tape to a radio station the next time he was in San Salvador.

From then on, Alberto and I sang as we milked, and afterwards kissed a little, and talked about religion or Shakespeare. Sometimes Alberto brought a Book of Mormon with him to the barn.

It was the second and third chapters of Jacob he was most interested in. Over and over he read me the verses about husbands loving their wives and wives their husbands and husbands and wives their children. The Lamanites, said the scriptures, "have not forgotten the commandment of the Lord, which was given unto our father—that they should have save it were one wife, and concubines they should have none."

"Then why," he said, "did the Church practice polygamy?"

The standard seminary answer was that polygamy is permissible if God commands it for a time, to raise up a righteous generation—but this wasn't totally satisfactory. There are a lot of fundamentalist Mormons who are convinced God has commanded them personally to practice "plural marriage." They do, and get themselves exed. The Church is monogamous now.

"Would it ever be right for a man to have two wives—or more—when the Church says the time is wrong?" Alberto said.

"I don't think it would ever be right," I said.

"And what of a woman? Could she ever have two husbands when the Church said no?"

"It would be adultery."

"But if God wanted it—"

"Is God haphazard about his commandments?" I sounded like I knew the answer.

"What if God wanted Gertrude to marry someone other than her husband? What if it was God who told her to marry her brother-in-law?"

"That's not in the play," I said.

"Maybe it would be if it weren't Hamlet's story. If the play were called *Gertrude*, it might be different. What we do know is that Hamlet's father was a disturbed ghost, not an angel. It was Claudius—the brother of the ghost—who prayed. Remember? Hamlet couldn't kill Claudius because Claudius was praying."

"I think I need to read it again."

"But what if it had been an angel who told Gertrude to marry another husband and kill the first? And what if it was God who poisoned the king?"

I said I didn't like "what if" questions.

"Isn't everything permissible when God commands it?"

"If it's really God," I said. "Sometimes, people—men especially—get revelations from an overdose of testosterone, and think it's God calling. A lot of people think they've found God when they've found their own instincts. I thought God wanted me to marry my husband. It wasn't God."

"Are you so sure?"

"Yes. I know who it was. Sometimes we create God."

"Sometimes. Sometimes not. Take the case of Helmuth Huebener. You have heard of him."

I hadn't.

"Seriously? But Julita, Huebener is Johnny's hero. Huebener, the Mormon who went against the Nazis. Still not familiar?"

Still not familiar.

"He circulated flyers about what Hitler was doing. When he was caught, he was sentenced to death. You see his dilemma: the Church tells us to sustain the law of the land. But if the law is wicked, what then? If God tells us the law of our land is wicked, shall we not rebel?"

"What happened to Huebener?"

"He was excommunicated from the Church. His Branch President, you see, was a Nazi. Huebener had used church materials for his flyers."

"Was he executed?"

"Beheaded. You see his dilemma, no? He was inspired to do something that would result in his excommunication. So, what do you think—was he a coward or a hero?"

"A hero."

"I agree. So does the Church now. His membership was restored—after the fact. Perhaps this will be the way with many so-called apostates. I think Huebener was welcomed into heaven with trumpets. But Hamlet, you see, went to hell."

"That's not in the play either."

"But it's true. The ghost ate Hamlet's goodness."

"You take this stuff seriously, don't you."

Alberto's face was intent. It softened now. He said, "Do you enjoy these discussions?"

I said I did.

"Good. I want you to. I enjoy them. Once, I talked like this to Luisa. I don't do that now. For several years, I have talked only to the cows. You are a more lively audience."

I shrugged.

"And you're very beautiful, has anyone told you that?"

Another shrug.

"You are. You had a complexion problem when you were younger, yes?"

"A little one." (A lie. I had been a zit-face. But what he was noticing was not my past zits but a tiny case of hives, which tend to break out on my chin when I'm nervous.)

"Put pure olive oil on your face. Don't worry. They're not so noticeable." He brushed my cheek with his finger. "Julita, will you do me a favor? Read *Hamlet* again."

I told him I had already told him that I would.

Johnny took our music tape to the San Salvador station within a week of our recording. It was to have been played the following day, but we never heard it. Our well-laid plan tripped on the muck of rainy-season reality. I had been right about the portent of the meteorite showers: there was an earthquake.

The quake probably would have been no big deal in L.A. It would have jostled pictures on the walls, broken a few plates and glasses. But where houses are made of adobe, even a half-wrath quake can kill.

The epicenter had been Mount Izalco, the dormant volcano which had once been so fiery and predictable that sailors charted their courses by it. It was 4.2 on the Richter—big enough to thwonk about thirty adobe shacks in Izalco and snuff out fifty-seven lives. Not big enough to make the CBS News, but big enough.

We had no way of knowing if any of our friends had been affected or killed. Telephone lines were down; even if they hadn't been, there was only one phone in Izalco—in the pharmacy—and the connection was always lousy. Our only real choice was to go there ourselves. I wrote Mom and Dad, told them what we were doing, where we would be. Johnny, Alberto, and I took the jeep, and started up the mountain. Only Luisa stayed behind. Her pregnancy was having its effect; she was too sick to travel.

A mile or two from the village, you could see the haze of destruction. A brown dust cloud hung over the place like a plague.

Johnny said, "Look at that. Smoking again." He was pointing to Mount Izalco, which rose like a purple monolith above the dust. It wasn't just smoke coming out of her peak; there was fire too. The mountain god had resurrected.

There were a few felled trees on the road; Johnny and Alberto moved these. Then we passed the flamingo fountain.

The quake had been discriminating. It had left the rich homes untouched and levelled the poor ones. The wealthy had managed to buy off nature.

We drove slowly, windows rolled up. But we had been seen. Indians were springing up everywhere, shouting, "*Don Juan, Don*

Juan!" We went to the center of town, where the Catholic church was pointing triumphantly to heaven, beside piles of rocks and bamboo. These piles had been Indian vendor stands, where Catholic paraphernalia—rosary beads, crosses, candles, statues—had been sold. Their owners were digging in the rubble now. One skinny old man was sitting beside the rocks, holding an image of The Virgin. Half of the statue's face and part of her blue dress were gone, like they had been bombed away. The rest of her was covered with dirt. The old guy was wiping the filth—licking it in places—and embracing the statue like it was his wife or mother. He was making crosses in the air and on his body, hugging this remnant of his Mary, weeping.

Johnny parked. Indians jumped immediately into the jeep, passing out the food we had brought, making foreign execrations as we unloaded our charity.

Across the plaza I saw Marta running towards us. Johnny held up his hand and she stopped and knelt where she was. I waved to her. Her head was bowed; she did not acknowledge me.

The food and medicine we had brought were haphazardly distributed. Johnny assured me that the Indians were unorganized but just. The goods would get where they were most needed, he said.

It took about ten minutes to empty the jeep. Then Johnny gestured to Marta with both his hands, like he was bestowing a benediction from across the court. She raised her hands like she was receiving it.

"You remember Marta," he said. "She's one of us."

We got in the jeep again, waved to the throngs behind our dirty windows, and started up the hill to Primitivo's hut.

I looked through the dust at the destruction and shook my head. The Latin streets were unscathed. The pharmacy was fine. The Post Office was fine. The white, cement, Latin homes were fine. Only the Indian shacks had been demolished.

There were five funerals in the street: Indian men in white pants and shirts and straw hats carrying coffins on their shoulders, weeping women behind them. Most of the coffins were small. Baby boxes.

I tried for a few moments to make sense of the disaster, to assign some divine purpose to it, but I couldn't. It probably would have tested my faith if I had had more faith. What it did prove to me was that I believed more in entropy than I did in God. Despite my attempts to understand the mess, it was only another instance of sound and fury. Another level of initiation for me. There seemed no use questioning it, though I knew religious people would; they would rationalize and justify and tell about the miracles that had saved their lives while those babies smothered under adobe.

Primitivo's shack was gone. There was a memorial pile of rocks and mud in its place. His loom was cracked in two. He was laboring over it, taping, nailing, hammering.

I saw Cordelia by the cornfield. Her hair was unbound and blowing in strings around her face.

We parked where the hut had been. The air was grainy.

Primitivo stood and came unsteadily towards us. He took a post card out of his pocket, and talked tiredly to Johnny, pointing to the picture of the Mesa, Arizona temple. Twice Primitivo stopped talking and pressed his teary eyes. Johnny wept with him.

"His wife was killed," Johnny said. "There's a twenty-four hour burial law in this place." He put his arm around the old guy. "Primitivo and his wife, they saved up for two years to go to the temple and have their marriage sealed. They went five years ago. But he didn't have temple clothes to put on Josefina and he couldn't reach us to find him some. They buried her in Indian clothes." Johnny had tears on his eyelashes.

Primitivo tapped his fingernails on the picture and spoke in his dialect. He held the picture up to us, pointed to its doors, tapped it again, jabbered incomprehensible sounds, cried, shrugged helplessly. We stood there watching. Finally, I stepped forward. I said one of the few words I knew in Spanish: "*Hermano*," and made lines down my dusty cheeks with my fingers, showing where my tears would fall. "*Hermano*," I said. He held the post card up to me.

Cordelia stood a few feet from us. She looked less purposeful and more bereaved than her father. She was pale, her skin almost green. I watched her, aching, surprised to find my feelings so tender. I tried, for her sake, to imagine how I would feel if it had been my mother killed in an earthquake. It seemed so silly, so ridiculous, that I couldn't picture it. But it was not hard to imagine that black-eyed lady, Cordelia's mother, dying that way. It seemed natural—senseless, but natural—because she was a part of what we Gringos see on the 6:00 news: that world of wars and quakes and starvation and little brown people with desperate eyes who were born to be part of Dan Rather's script. I could remember the old lady's black warts, her golden face above the fire, the foreign sounds she made, her veiled, questioning eyes, her wrinkled hands. Yes, she was from the world that ends when "Wheel of Fortune" begins. El Salvador itself was part of that world, as much as Viet Nam had been before its ex-warriors began standing around, life-size, in California refugee lines—back when they could be shrunk to fit inside a television and made to seem stoic and brutal. This whole Izalco travesty was a part of that other world. I recognized Cordelia's grief as part of it, too, and was surprised to find it so real, and to find that I cared about it and about her so much.

We had dinner in the open air; Cordelia made a fire and cooked tortillas. Most of the conversation was in somber Spanish. The wind was mournful and cool as we ate.

We slept uncovered; the rain didn't start until dawn. It was not a downpour here but a drizzle. Most of the serious moisture seemed caught behind the dust. When we started getting wet, we moved inside the jeep and cranked its cover up.

Cold tortillas were our breakfast. Cordelia passed them out ritually, taking her mother's place.

Johnny decided we needed to stay and do the work of reconstruction. God had told him things would be fine in Zarahemla and Belen till we got back. The next few days Cordelia and I spent much of our time gathering bamboo stalks. The men made them

into simple frames to brace the adobe. These would be the Indians'
new houses.

To Cordelia, this was duty, life. To me it was great charity. I
loved the bigness of my work. I was significant, competent, adored.
A white saint, a savior with a sunburned nose, re-creating a world,
making sense and shelter where there weren't any. It was sadly
romantic.

The places where we found bamboo were like gothic cathedrals.
The stalks would arch and come together above us like praying
hands. All around us was an almost heretical beauty: flowers like
red bottle-brushes; butterflies whose wings were as blue and shiny
as peacocks' necks; Salto Blanco. I felt I had earned the waterfall
and the sulphur pits and every orchid there. Wherever I went, I was
taller than my hosts, as though I were elevated. I was highly
regarded, sometimes adored.

This is what I had wanted all during my marriage. Adoration.
I had wanted to transform my husband and to have him say in
some future testimony meeting, "And to my wife, to her I owe
everything I am or ever will be." Weeping. Tears dripping onto the
microphone and making static. "She has saved me. Loved me when
I was past loving. When I was a brute and a bozo. Loved me
through all my anger and tragedy. Made my home a haven when
I had it ruined. I adore her with my soul. I worship the ground she
walks on." Etc. Etc. I wanted to be making radiant, sparkling tears
while he detailed my grace. I wanted to sit in a pew, growing glass
from my eyelids, living a miracle.

So now I was living a miracle. Getting off on it too. The smell
of bamboo. The sweat on my eyebrows. The blisters on my palms.

Cordelia just worked.

It took a full day to put a house up. Four weeks to accomplish
the basics of the reconstruction. Then we worked on the chapel—
which had also been made of bamboo and adobe and had also
been destroyed. This would be our Grand Finale. Johnny said that

when we had it finished, Alberto and I would do a concert of rededication. It would be our great missionary effort.

"We've got to do something," Johnny said, "to bring these people back. To remind them of God again. Some have lost faith, you know. Nature, kiddo. Nature, you see, is a witch with a capital 'B'. Acts like she's going to give one nice harvest and then she ups and splits open. A real bitch."

Nine

We finished the chapel three days later. Late that afternoon, all of us, including Primitivo, Alberto, and Cordelia, went to Salto Blanco to wash off our sweat with sulphur water.

Primitivo had a new-woven blanket to clean, which he did a few feet from our bath. He stepped on the blanket, turned his foot, stepped, turned, danced like Fred Astaire in a box. The Indians called this blanket cleaning *batanando*. It looked ritualistic and fun.

Primitivo was dressed all in white. His clothes matched his tangled hair. His pants were rolled up around his bony, calloused knees. He grinned down at us and told stories. Alberto translated. The one I remember best was about Tecum Uman, the Indian prince who was killed by Don Pedro de Alvarado, during the conquest.

"Tecum Uman," said Primitivo, drawing the vowels out like he was summoning the guy's ghost, "he came ready to fight. He held his spear and his rope. He was naked." The old man gestured to his swaying hips. "Then comes Alvarado" (this name whispered disdainfully), "Alvarado in armor" (hands circling his body), "riding a horse in armor" (his hands around his face now, fingers moving rapidly to indicate how the gold and silver shimmered on the conqueror and his animal.) "Tecum Uman, he thinks the horse and the rider, they make one war machine." (A wide-armed circle, his feet still working the wool.) "Tecum Uman, he comes with his spear and aims where the heart should be in the machine. The horse, it falls. But the rider is unhurt. The rider, the Alvarado, he slits the throat of Tecum Uman." (A quick motion to the neck.) "That's how the conquest was. People, they were not prepared. We are prepared now. We have help from many enemies." He grinned again, then watched his feet, pointed to them, showed us how nimble they were, how perfectly they softened and cleaned the blanket.

Cordelia laughed at her father. It had been a long time since I had heard her laugh. Her hair was still unbound. It came to her hips like giant crow's wings, half-submerged in the water. The steam rose around her. She was something glorious in the midst of that steam. There was a beauty and dignity in her, a straightness of back, an anomalous, unconscious, spectacular joy. The steam was circling her face, making a halo. The waterfall was directly behind, like pure, roaring light from God.

She held my hand as we returned to our new hut after the bath. She spoke to me in dialect now, not even Spanish. I answered in the two or three dialect words I had learned: "hah" (yes), "neh" (no) and "hoh-Bah" ("let's go"). She thought I understood her.

She was still grief-weary, and cried privately on occasion, but the sign that she had returned to herself was given on the last day of our stay in Izalco. She braided her hair down her back, put on a fresh *huipil* and took me with her after lunch to see *Dinastia*. Afterwards, she indicated that she wanted a reading lesson, which I gave her. Then she wanted to write—or rather, she wanted me to write for her—a letter to the cast of *Dinastia*.

Alberto helped. He translated her sentences to me, looking at her with disapproval, even scolding her at one point, with angry, incomprehensible sounds.

"It is a waste," he complained to me.

Cordelia, wearing a sweet, childlike smile, shrugged helplessly, just as her father had done in answer to his wife's death.

"*Dios mio,*" Alberto said.

Cordelia spread her hand over her mouth and nose. Her eyes glittered.

"Stuff as dreams are made on," Alberto said.

I gestured for Cordelia to continue. She gave me the words in Spanish: "*Queridisima Linda Evans y Joan Collins: Ustedes son muy lindas, y les amamos mucho. Para sevirles, yo soy Cordelia Santos Chaves.*"

Alberto, rolling his eyes, translated. "Dearest Linda Evans and Joan Collins: You are both very beautiful and we love you very much. At your service, etc. etc."

I wrote the words out. Cordelia copied them carefully onto another sheet of paper. It took her twenty minutes to do this, because every letter was done slowly and re-traced at least twice. Three times she was dissatisfied with the looks of her work and started over. But when the letter was done, she beamed, holding it up, showing us how well she had imitated me, and kissed it. Alberto finally laughed, put one arm around her and one around me and brought us both into his chest. We huddled there and swayed in each other's arms like a celebrating family.

In the evening there was an extra guest for dinner: a marimbist from a nearby *aldea.* Johnny had paid him to join us and play the accompaniment to our concert that night.

The marimba he had brought with him—probably tumplined to his forehead, the way I had seen so many peasants carrying their burdens along the road—had been made by his great-great-grandfather. Petrified gourds were lined up under a wood frame and unevenly arranged to approximate a scale. The marimba man had never studied any sophisticated version of music, but had been taught by his father, who had been taught by his, who had been taught by his, and on down the ages—even before the conquest. Here was a man who carried his heritage on his back.

He was shy and hungry, a high-cheeked guy with oriental eyes and a creased forehead—the perfect image of the third world. But when he played his instrument, he was a wizard of motion, intent and dedicated to sounds. He raced his mallets over the gourds, hitting them so rapidly that his fingers disappeared. It didn't matter what we sang; he could improvise accompaniment. Being *Evangelico*, he knew no Mormon hymns, but he faked something beautiful. We practiced for a half hour, until he was sweating like a horse, wiping his forehead and cheeks in a shy, sleepy, self-effacing way.

Finally we went to the church, Johnny leading us, holding a kerosene lantern. By the time we arrived, we were the beginning of a parade. It seemed everyone in Izalco—Mormon and non—knew about the concert and was coming to witness it. Johnny told me this would be the first time for most of them to hear "real music."

Johnny turned up the wick of his lantern when we were inside, and light filled the chapel. I looked around me at all that bamboo Cordelia and I had gathered, at the adobe we had laid, at the roof Alberto and Johnny had nailed down. It was marvelous.

There were no chairs. The audience sat on the dirt floor, which was soon overcrowded. Everywhere were brown faces with bronze cheeks and eager eyes, looking at me.

"Give it your best shot, kiddo," Johnny said. "Ham it up, make it fancy. Make this an evening nobody is going to forget forever. You can become a legend, you know. Legend in your own time."

We started with a Martin Luther hymn: "A Mighty Fortress." The marimba man beat pitches of hollowness behind our intuition. Alberto and I made harmony.

> "A mighty fortress is our God,
> A tower of strength ne'er failing."

We were molding the fortress, kissing the strength. The audience had gasped with our first chord. Now they watched us in awe.

"He overcometh all;
He saveth from the Fall.
His might and power are great.
He all things did create."

Some of the old ladies were weeping. Even the little kids were quiet. This was a sacred experience we were making, and they knew it.

"And He shall reign forevermore!"

I hit a high "C"—or an approximation of one—and the marimba gourds vibrated like the Spirit was crackling out of them. Alberto bellowed his harmony. And those last notes—those triumphant notes—did not stop when we closed our mouths, but broke free from us like they had their own eternity, and moved directly into the night. You could feel them the way you can smell flowers from paradise when the wind is just so.

Alberto looked exhausted. I closed my eyes and breathed in the leftover streaks of our music. There was an uproar of applause, as loud and intent as Salto Blanco. The little chapel we had reconstructed ignited with clapping and with the Holy Ghost. I imagined us to be the only piece of light in the whole village. The center of the world.

We sang for two hours, sometimes with the marimba; sometimes a cappella. We performed each song at least twice. Even then, the audience demanded *otro, otro*, and stood to show their determination.

Johnny explained to them that we needed to return to Zarahemla; there was no more time for songs. The jeep, he said, was right outside. We would be going back. "*Ven a despedirnos*," he said. "Come tell us good-bye."

We left the chapel and the audience poured out behind us. They stood around the jeep, still clapping. All around us was the magic of heaven. The dust was clearing, the rains had not yet started, and everywhere—perhaps attracted by the kerosene lamplight—were fireflies. Droves of fireflies. They were in the bushes and in the air, like shooting stars. It looked like it must have looked for the inhabitants of the City of Enoch, when the whole place was lifted into the sky. Those Enochians must have seen the stars around them like emblems of their reward, sparkles of grace.

I made my way through the crowd and, waving, climbed into the jeep. Even as we started down the road, the people followed us, clapping, shouting. A mile into the journey there was still a woman jogging behind us, striking her hands over her head like she wanted them to make fire.

I recognized her as Marta—the one who always knelt when she saw Johnny. Johnny was waving back at her, his hand hanging out the jeep like a lily in the wind.

Ten

I must have gone to sleep almost immediately; I have no memory of the trip. When I awoke I was in my bed at Zarahemla. I could smell eggs and tortillas. Luisa was waiting in the kitchen. There was a letter for me on the table, from Mom and Dad. It thanked me for my one letter (I had written five), asked me to write more frequently (!), then told of all the marvelous things they were doing—in Mom's handwriting, of course. She claimed Dad was becoming "Mr. Sunshine," which I seriously doubted. No mention was made of Luisa's pregnancy, or my trip to Izalco, or of Manuelito. And no mention was made of when we might be returning home. We had been in El Salvador three months already, though time wasn't the same here. You lost track of days and weeks; you judged hours by the sun. Space was time. America and all the outside world were years ago away. World events were unheard of and too distant for concern. Local events were blown up by the yellow press.

"How are your parents?" Luisa asked. Her voice was weak.

"Fine," I said, kissing her cheek. Then I lied: "You're looking swell."

"I'm having a good day," she answered. "Every now and then, I have a good day. I need to *aprovechar*."

"How's that?"

"Take advantage."

I finished my breakfast and helped her wash the dishes.

Luisa said, "I understand you were a great success."

I looked at her with questions.

"You did a concert, yes? I heard you were successful."

"I guess I was," I said. "Well, not alone. Alberto sang too."

"I'm happy for you," she said. "Once in a woman's life, she should be a great success."

"Miss San Cristobal speaking, right?"

She gave a strained, feeble laugh. "Miss San Cristobal, yes." She moved her hands above her head as though presenting herself the crown. She wavered, looked like she might faint. "I'm fine," she said when I reached for her. "Self-mocking can be too much, no?"

"There's nothing about you to mock," I said.

"Oh but Julie, there is. Of course there is. In everyone's life are terrible jokes. Even in yours, yes? You married the one person who could hurt you so much. Yes?" She smiled. "Oh, Alberto was looking for you. I told him you were sleeping. Now he'll think you're a *dormilona*."

"Has he milked the cows already? I suppose he has."

She nodded.

"Embarrassing to sleep in like that."

"*Tranquilo*," she said. "A woman who has her great success deserves to sleep in the next morning." Her voice was accented, mellifluous, weak. Weaker by the moment.

"Where is he now?" I said.

"Alberto? Gathering eggs. He did want to talk to you. I'll take you to him, if you'd like." She rubbed her stomach.

"Does it hurt?" I said.

"It's kicking. Yes, it hurts a little. Not much. I like the kicking. Baby is alive." She sat down. "Maybe you were right. I can't stand so well now. I'm faint."

I asked again if she was all right.

She stood, as though my question were a challenge. "Yes. Fine. I can take you to Alberto."

"No, you should rest. I can find him."

"Alone? No. I know you have been frightened by some things at Zarahemla."

"Not lately."

"The mango trees have scared you."

"No—really—I'm all right."

"I know. Please, let me accompany you. Baby loves exercise. And there is something else I wish you to see."

We left the cabin and began walking towards the mango trees.

"I promise," Luisa said, "there will be only mangos there this morning. With perhaps an iguana or two."

Of course she was right. There were mangos, and there were iguanas—seven iguanas, some bright green and some grey, walking on the limbs.

"I make jam from these mangos," Luisa said. "It is good for the children. It has vitamin A. Do you know how to make jam?"

I said I had made it once before.

"You should know," she said.

She stared at a long grey iguana trying to camouflage itself on the bark. "I know that one," she said. "He was here when we first came. But he was very small. Look at his size now. I named him Gomer," she said. "After Gomer Pyle the TV show. I loved Gomer Pyle when we lived on the Other Side. Do they have Gomer Pyle anymore?"

I told her I thought they did.

"I don't think I will ever see Gomer Pyle again. And my grey Gomer—no, Gomer, you cannot hide from me. I see you. I know where you are. I have lived here too long to be fooled by you." She turned to me. "Silly iguana. I will miss him."

"When he dies, you mean? Is he that old? Will he be dying soon?"

"I don't know when he will die." She smiled. "I mean I will miss him when I die." She picked a mango. "You have tasted mango, haven't you? This is what I wanted to show you. Don't pick the mangos before they have blushed. Then peel from the top of the fruit. You see how easily the skin comes off? You must be sure to save the skins. If you soak them in sugar water, they make good juice. Then when their color is gone, put them under the gardenia bushes. Gardenias love mango skins. That is how I bribe them to grow for me. I want my gardenias to grow well. I have taken good care of them. You won't let them get small, will you."

"Well no, not if I can help it."

"I want you to care for them when I am gone." She was growing visibly paler. I suggested she return to bed. I could find Alberto, I told her.

"He's there." She pointed to the barn. "Yes, perhaps I should go back to bed. My good feeling is leaving me." She turned and walked slowly towards the cabin, stopping twice and hugging her womb. I waited until I saw her enter. Then I went to the barn.

Alberto was behind a bale of hay.

"What are you doing?" I said.

"Discovering chicken eggs."

"Luisa said you wanted to see me."

"Yes. With bad news, alas. Now you will learn what it is to be under President Piggott. Read this." He took a piece of paper from his pocket. The letterhead said "*Presidente* David Jorge Piggott; *La Iglesia de JesuCristo de los Santos de los Ultimos Dias.*"

"Read," Alberto urged.

The letter said: "I know your intentions were only the most noble, but I was not notified of your lovely radio program. I am certain you understand my position. I must know what's happening in my district as regards the Church. Please desist from making further tapes. They are lovely, but the time is not right. I have taken the liberty of contacting the station and requesting that the tape be turned over to me. I have it in San Salvador. Should you so desire, you may come to pick it up from me—on the condition that you use it for strictly personal purposes, with no Church connections. Thank you."

It was signed by the president. He had stolen our tape from the radio station. I couldn't help myself. "That pig," I said.

"You see, Julita," said Alberto, "what fools these mortals be."

"That pig!"

"Why don't you take him up on his offer? Go talk to him in San Salvador."

"With you?"

"No, he doesn't trust me. And I feel uncomfortable in his mansion. He dresses his maids in identical costumes, you know. Blue uniforms."

"Yes, I've heard about that," I said.

"I feel uneasy there," he said. "*Presidente* makes me nervous. He makes me think things I don't like."

"I won't go alone."

"Yes, you will go alone, Julita. I will put you on the bus. I will telegraph your father and tell him to meet you at *Avenida dos*."

"He doesn't get his mail."

"There are ways," he said. "He will get the message."

"I'm not thrilled about this idea," I said.

"Then do it out of duty."

He handed me an egg and kissed me under my chin. I agreed to do what he wanted—to go to San Salvador out of duty.

Johnny was not so sure the trip was wise. After dinner, I saw him talking to Alberto by the lake. When I joined them, Johnny said, "Well, kiddo, how strong are you anyway?"

"Oh," I said, "you'd probably take me in an arm wrestle. And I suppose I'd die if I got shot."

"Oh don't worry about that," Johnny said. "I've already prayed your protection. Physically, you'll be fine. God's given his word on that, and if you can't trust God's word, whose can you—right? Naw, that's not what worries me. You're going to see things at The Pig's, though. Rich things. Maybe things that will make you miss the States. Maybe you'll hear things. Julie, how strong are you?"

"Johnny," I said, "Are you afraid I'm going to shack up with Piggott or what?"

"He'll try," Johnny said, "to convert you. He may tell some heavy-duty lies about me and then feed you some rich American dessert and have you sleep on a feather bed. He may be just pretty hard to resist."

"I hate him," I said. "I don't even know him and I hate him, okay? Trust me. Don't worry."

"Aw, don't hate him, kiddo. He's a good man, just a little messed up is all. Too rich for his own eternal good. He was a fine missionary. We were great friends on our missions. Piggott and your Dad and me, we were pals once. Had great plans to come back. I've told you, right? Aw, it's so ironic. We're back here, just like we said. And Piggott's gotten rich and spends his time serving Mammon, and your Dad—no offence—he's gotten himself exed and joined the army of this world. It's just me, kiddo. Just me. This isn't how I wanted things. Not by a long shot."

"I won't even eat his food," I said. "I'll get the tape, give my little speech, and come home."

"And you'll be seeing your parents. I guess you've missed them."

"Some."

"Suppose they want to go home now? Are you strong, Julie? Really strong? Because I want you back here, you know. You're doing good things. I want you back."

"I'll be back," I said, and he asked me to kneel before him.

You don't realize how strange it is to kneel until someone asks you to do it. There's something absurdly vulnerable and archaic about the pose. I almost giggled as I obeyed my uncle and went to my knees.

Johnny put his hands on my head, then had Alberto put his hands there too. Johnny spoke.

"Julia Suzanne Albertson," he said, "by the power of the Melchizedek priesthood which I hold and in the name of Jesus Christ, I bless you and give you direct from Heaven the words of God to you." Then he waited. It seemed like a full minute of utter silence, as though this was the time it took for God's thoughts to make it to Zarahemla. When he spoke again, his voice had changed, become lower and softer. There was new power in his hands. They trembled on my head as though electrified. Waves of warmth came through my scalp. "Behold," said this new voice, "I am your God. You shall worship me. I will be on your right hand and on your left, and though enemies conspire, you shall not be lost. My angels will stand in your path and protect you, even save you if need be. You shall go to the mansion of my former servant, David Piggott, and you shall say to him that I am not pleased with his actions. You shall have the spirit of discernment and shall not be led astray by the glitter of this world. You shall say to your father and mother when you see them that the work they are doing is good, and they must remain in Belen to do it. And you shall return, in the arm of my power, to this land I have accepted for mine own, even Zarahemla. Behold, remember me and forsake me not. I am God, even Jesus Christ." There was silence again; the Spirit, I supposed, was ascending.

Johnny's hands stopped trembling. He lifted them from my head, but kept them just above me, as though there were little bits of heaven still dripping from his fingers and he wanted me to get them all. I imagined glitter in my hair.

Finally he sighed and put his hands in his pockets. Alberto backed away from us, tears in his eyes.

"Well," said Johnny, "it never ceases to amaze me how God speaks to everyone differently. He used a hefty vocabulary for you, didn't he kiddo. Fancy speech. Actually, some of those words I spoke I don't even know. And if that isn't remarkable I don't know what is. Well, I feel better now about you going. God will be with you, and you'll come back, won't you. Nobody's going to pull any wool over your eyes, kiddo, nor silk neither."

Eleven

Salvadorans call them Chicken busses. Named, I assume, for the crowds—like nervous birds in a coop—and for the squawking of the passengers and the ancient bus parts. You hear the jam of metal as the motor turns. The wheels hit their fenders and you feel every bump on the road. The paint has peeled from the exterior years ago. There are only hints and splotches of the bright blue it used to be. The bus is mostly grey now, and full of graffitti like "*Viva la Revolucion,*" "*Viva la Gente,*" and "*Cuna de Abuela.*" There is spray-painted sex between the headlights. The seats are mock leather, spilling their foam rubber guts. Most of them are also autographed by ambitious teenagers who have left their initials and their world view. The seat I shared with two old men said, "*Vivir es morir; morir es vivir.*"

The ride was bumpy but uneventful until we were nearly at San Salvador. Then, in the middle of the road, a grey army jeep was parked sideways, two militarized teenagers standing with shouldered rifles before it. When the bus stopped, the two kids boarded, and behind them four more who had been in the jeep. The old men beside me gasped. Mothers gathered their children and held them tightly. The soldiers asked the driver some questions, which he humbly answered. He produced his papers, and immediately everyone was reaching into purses or backpacks for their sedulas. I took mine from my wallet and held it discreetly in my lap.

Whenever the soldiers talked to anyone, they used sharp, staccato—but still very young—voices. Those answering sounded like beggers, though I couldn't understand most of their words. I thought, I am the only *Gringa* on this bus. If anyone is killed, it will be me. I remembered that the three American nuns who had been murdered were raped first. I did not want to be raped.

Their guns, I thought, looked like toys. I could not keep my eyes from the triggers. Loaded toys. If they shot me, would I feel anything or just die before my brain could interpret the pain? But I would not die. I would not. Not after Johnny's blessing. I was under official protection.

One of the soldiers reached down a girl's dress to find her *sedula*. An old widow jumped from her seat, two rows behind the girl, and yelled at the soldier to stop. She came forward and took hold of his ear, lecturing him (as far as I understood) on *la castidad* and the shame such actions would be to his mother. His ear in her hand she led him, still scolding and giving no time for response, out the bus, where she shoved him away, pointed to heaven and then slapped both his wrists.

The other soldiers watched the scene, amazed at first. Then they laughed, and everyone on the bus laughed with them. They left, signalled the driver to move on, and waved at us like friendly relatives after a nice garden party, as we drove away. The old woman came running behind. The bus stopped for her. We all clapped when she boarded.

I wondered if she was an angel—one of my guardians. When I clapped it was not only for her performance, but for God's, and Johnny's too.

I thought the incident had left me unfazed, but my eyes clouded when I saw the statue of El Salvador del Mundo—Jesus with one arm raised, standing on a stone globe—and knew we were entering San Salvador and that (provided they had received Alberto's telegram) my parents were minutes away. The bus rumbled over chuckholes and loose gravel. We passed through a ghetto of drab buildings, then the marketplace, where hundreds of people congregated like ants. Most of the men wore cowboy hats. The women, many of them, wore scarves. There were sounds of industry: the hiss of a bus, a distant siren, the throb of a traffic jam. San Salvador was a dilapidated hornet's nest. Unlike Zarahemla, there were no flowers here. Just dirt, cracked roads, old paint, noise.

I read the street signs. *Bolivar, Asuncion, Avenida una.* At *Avenida dos,* I saw Doodle Dan Van, with Mom and Dad inside it. I stuck my head out the bus window, waved with both arms and yelled "Here! Here!" like I was afraid I'd be marked tardy. Mom saw. She waved back and looked like she was doing a jig in the front seat. She flung Doodle Dan's door open.

When the bus stopped I leapt from the door to their arms, hugged them both together, and sobbed. Dad helped the driver retrieve my suitcase, which was strapped on top of the bus with all the other baskets and foodstuffs the natives were bringing to market.

Dad was furious with Johnny for letting me come alone. There was no excuse for that, he said. I could have been killed.

I told him I couldn't have been killed, but did not elaborate on the why.

Mom's first words to me were, "How in the hay-ell is your sweet little gizzard?" She was wearing a Hunter Orange dress that could have been seen from a mile away.

"Should we go out to eat before visiting President Piggott?" she asked. There was so much she wanted to tell me about their work. She could understand why Johnny and Dad had loved their missions. What a land this was, she said. Paradise!

"We can talk at Piggott's place," Dad said, still fuming at Johnny.

Mom said, "This is the first I've seen your Papadopoluos mad in weeks, Digs. Isn't it, Chuck. He's been having such joy. And he'll get over this. Chuck, you'll get over this. Johnny meant well. Nothing happened."

Dad grunted and turned the ignition. He looked at the address in his wallet, turned a couple of corners into ridiculously skinny streets, honking as he did, then parked the van and pointed. "That's it."

Yes, a mansion. A black fence around it like thin, upraised spears. Jagged glass sparkling blue and green all over the roof. A satellite dish, a garage bigger than most houses in the neighborhood, three blue chevrolet sedans in the driveway. Next to the door, a brass plate with the name "Piggott" in gothic calligraphy.

I said, "Get a load of this."

"How about that," said Dad. "I can still find my way around the maze."

"Now put on your best smile, Chuck," said Mom. "You haven't seen Dave Piggott in a long time. You don't want him to think you've gone sour."

"I suspect he's heard. But I'll smile, Dear, if it's what you want." He bared his teeth at her and rang the bell. An Indian girl answered, dressed in a blue uniform, blue cap, blue anklet stockings, blue shoes. She curtsied.

"*El Presidente,*" Dad said. "*Somos los Albertsons, Julia y Carlos y Emilia, a la orden.*"

She curtsied again, showed us into a huge parlor with a red Persian rug and a chandelier that looked like it was being reserved for some temple's Celestial Room.

I conjured a picture of The Pig: a man about six feet tall with hard black eyes, a sharp nose, thin, bloodless lips, a lawyer's vocabulary, a pin-striped suit. When the door opened, I was stunned. Before me was a blue-eyed fat man. He was a giant—maybe three hundred pounds. He had silver hair, Santa Claus eyes, clean fingernails, the biggest smile I had seen.

"Well now, for golly sakes," he said. He rushed over to Dad with an outstretched hand. "I heard you folks was here, and I wondered just when you'd take and visit. Well now, this isn't little Julie, is it?"

"Hello," I said.

"Well now, look at you. Welcome, welcome. I hope you can stay the night. I get visitors too rarely. And this is your wife, huh, Elder Albertson. I think I met you once or twice back at one of them reunions, didn't I?"

"I think so," she said. I knew she wanted to tease him about the size of his gut. She was restraining herself admirably.

"Elder Albertson," Piggott said, turning to Dad again. "I can't believe it. Boy it's good to see you!"

"Good to see you too," Dad said. "The name's Charles, now. Chuck."

The Pig made a great laugh. "Isn't that a joke? You know, Julie—and what was your wife's name?"

It was another open line for Mom. I knew she wanted to say something like "It was Pippi Longstocking till I had it changed" but she gave a straight answer: "Call me Em."

"You know, Em," he said, "on your mission, you never use first names. That's because you just don't do it. You're 'Elder' when you're a missionary. I'm not sure your hubby knows my first name—do you?"

"David."

"My friends call me Dave."

"Did you know mine?" Dad said.

Piggott laughed hugely, "Maybe once, but I couldn't of remembered to save my hide!" Piggott slapped him on the back, laughing like he was the funniest man on earth. "Chuck," he said, "Chuck, you're in luck. We're having my favorite tonight: stroganoff and banana cream pie. How does that hit the old gullet?"

"Sounds like real food, Dave."

"Any more real and it'd bite you back." He laughed again. "How about you, Julie? You ready for something more than tortillas and beans?"

"To be honest," I said, "I think anything fancy might make me sick. I've gotten used to simple foods." I didn't want his hospitality or his calories. "I've been a little sick," I said.

The fat man was instantly serious. "Well now, Julie," he said, "there's one of the best clinics in all of El Salvador just down the street. Is it diarrhea, sweetheart? Everybody gets it sooner or later. Remember, Chuck?"

"It's colitis," I said. "I've had it for a long time. It's not bacterial."

"Well they can treat anything at that place."

"It's okay, President. That's not what I came for. I came—"

"Oh I know, honey. About the tape. I'm so glad you did come. I wanted to explain to you about all that—oh for golly sakes. We'll need to have a heart-to-heart, I think, won't we. After dinner—oh no, it'll have to be after breakfast. I got a meeting after dinner. But after breakfast, we'll have our heart-to-heart." He winked—the kind of wink that on a thin blonde guy in swim trunks would be cute and sexy, but that on a fat guy was obscene. "And then, afterwards, you and me can take us a little trip over to the clinic and I'll pay for an exam of your whatever-it-is."

"I've been examined," I said. "I just have to be careful is all. It's not bacterial."

"Well then, that's just fine, Julie. What would you like for supper? You name it and you'll get it."

"A couple of tortillas would be fine."

"Corn or flour?"

"Corn, please."

"I feel like a waiter," he said, laughing again. "Now Julie, I have a bed for you too. It's the softest thing you'll ever sleep in. A feather bed. They don't even make them anymore Stateside. Got one for this old married couple, too. My golly, it's so good to see you." He punched Dad in the shoulder. "Come on, come on, let me show you your rooms—I feel like a porter."

Yes, they were beautiful rooms. Irresistible. Mine was done up in pink and purple. The wallpaper was coordinated with the bed:

pink stripes on the walls and the dustruffle; apple blossoms on the top quilt.

"Now if you're tired, Julie," said Piggott, "you just rest now, and I'll have a maid call you when it's dinner time. How does that sound?"

"I'm not tired," I said.

"You like the room?"

"Very nice."

"Now, if you're tired—"

"I'm not tired. Thank you, President."

What I wanted to ask was who the heck had written the letter for him—that articulate, lawyer-perfect, sterile letter? Because The Pig was a hick. Someone you'd meet in Sigurd, Utah.

Before supper, Dad and I had a talk in the parlor. We sat on the velveteen chairs and closed the French doors. Mom was to have joined us, but one of the Indian maids was teaching her how to get to the coconut meat without hammering the shell to bits.

My letter about Manuelito had never been received. Maybe that was lucky, Dad said. If he had known, we would have been out of here like that. (He snapped his fingers.) "We were told," he added, "that there was no more violence down here. We wouldn't have come—especially not with you—if we had known that was still going on."

"It's okay," I told him. "I'm not spooked by the memory."

"You've worked through it, have you?"

"Yeah. I have. I've worked through it."

"Good. That's good." He raked his fingers through his hair—what there was left of it. He seemed to be talking to himself, and glanced at me only occasionally. This was Dad's way. "First time I saw something like that, it undid me. And it's natural to cry or upchuck or do whatever your insides want to do. You shouldn't fight that."

"I'm okay."

"Fine. Like I said, that's good. But if you need to do something—even if you need to go home—you tell me. Don't hold back. I've seen guys go crazy holding back."

"Don't worry, Dad. It was hard at first. I'm okay, though."

"One thing's pretty clear: there's still a helluva lot of unrest here. I guess you felt that on the bus today, didn't you—damn that John-boy. Damn him to hell."

"Dad—"

"Sorry, Jewel. But putting you in danger like that!"

"That's not how it was, Dad. If you want the truth, he *saved* me from danger. Never mind."

"Saved you, huh." He crossed his legs and scratched his foot. He was wearing jeans, a sweatshirt, and the rattiest looking green socks I had ever seen—all his clothes dirty from the drive. He looked ridiculous in that velveteen chair.

"So," I said, "is it like Mom says? You're becoming Mr. Sunshine? I reckon she thinks you'll end up getting baptized back in the Church after all this charity."

"Reckon she does."

"Not much chance of that, though, is there."

"Not much. I love your Mom, don't get me wrong. One hell of a lady, there. If it were something little she wanted—anything little—I'd do it, you know that. But the Church! Hey, the Church is not little, Jewel. I helped make it bigger myself, all those fifty-three Salvadoran converts I baptized. The Church is huge, gigantic, and your mother wants me to swallow it like Tylenol. Do you understand what I'm saying? I can't do it."

"I understand," I said, and we looked at each other for a long moment, which seemed to embarrass him.

"I love your mother," he repeated, "but I'll tell you a secret if you promise not to repeat it."

"You got it. Brownie's honor."

"You're still a Brownie scout?"

"I guess so. I never got promoted. What's your secret?"

He looked at me with his crooked, mischievous grin. "I hate orange," he said.

We both laughed big. "Criminy," I said. "You must be going bonkers."

"Maybe so. Now you keep that quiet or you'll be de-brownified."

Mom appeared at the French doors then, holding two perfect halves of a coconut.

"It's the easiest thing in the world," she said as Dad let her in. "I should have figured it out myself. And you'd best know you'll be eating the fruits of my labours tonight. This coconut goes right in the pie. My hay-ell, you two smell like a barn. Let's get cleaned up so Piggott doesn't rent us out a sty. Come on you bozos, hit the showers!"

We hit the showers. We both liked to make Mom happy.

I had rice and beans with my tortillas for dinner. Mom and Dad and Piggott ate stroganoff.

"You know, folks, Julie might have something over on us," said Piggott. "Rice and beans makes a complete protein."

"Is that right?" Dad said.

"I practically bust my suspenders laughing when I think of them BYU kids coming down here to take and re-educate the Salvadorans—before the conflict, of course. Them kids. Figure they're saving the world if they get people to eat eggs." He bellowed. "One time, a group of them come down here and had the natives digging up all their medicinal herbs so's they could plant radishes." He laughed again. The table shook in the aftershock. "I still can't believe you're here, Chuck. I look over at you and I have to squint my eyes. You're lucky I haven't pinched you. Ought to pinch myself, I guess."

"I'm really here," said Dad.

"You know, Em, your hubby and me went through some pretty tough times together on our missions. Your brother too, of course. The worst—you'll agree with this, Chuck, was when my companion, Elder Zarate, got hisself killed. We was on a bus, and—oh they drive crazy in these parts, isn't that the truth. Anyways, there was these two buses—I hate to remember it—and they took to racing up a hill. Elder Zarate, he stood right up and told the driver to cut out the drag racing, and right then the driver slams on his brakes and Elder Zarate goes flying through the window. Anyways—well now, Chuck, you can tell the story if you want. I'm sure you remember it good as me."

"You're doing fine, Dave."

"You want me to tell it? Well, Elder Zarate was killed, as you might expect. Elder Albertson—your hubby here—and Elder—your brother, John—they was on the bus too. We got out, all of us did, and Chuck here, he wanted to put his hands on that poor kid's head and take and raise him like the daughter of Jairus, you know? And he was about to do just that, and then him and me—Chuck, you'd do better explaining this yourself."

"You're doing fine. I don't remember it well."

"Oh golly. Golly sakes. I remember it like yesterday," said Piggott. "We was ready to raise him and then all of us had this sort of a vision, where we knew that this Elder Zarate, he was just finishing his mission up on the other side. We knew we shouldn't bring him back. Chuck, you remember that, don't you?"

"I think I didn't feel it like you did," said Dad.

"No, no, you did!" he said. "You felt it more!"

Dad gave a shy laugh. "Afraid not, Dave. I lied about a lot of things back then. That was just one of them."

"Did you, Chuck?" He served himself more stroganoff. "I see." He offered the meat to Dad.

"I'm full," Dad said.

"Julie—don't you want to try just a little bit?"

I said no.

"Well, then, I guess we'll have us some leftovers tomorrow!" He laughed. "But I hope you've saved just a little room for the banana coconut cream pie. Oh, it's good. It is goooood." This was Mom's cue. She announced she was helping with dessert, and went into the kitchen.

Piggott shoveled his food into his mouth. When he finished, an Indian maid appeared and cleared the table. Another maid brought plates. Mom came with the pie like it was a crown for someone's coronation. Piggott made the "A-OK" sign.

"Fresh coconut," Mom announced. "Fresh." She served us, then returned to the kitchen to eat with the maids. We could hear them giggling. I wanted to join them—that seemed my place much more than this well-appointed table. I waited for a break in conversation to excuse myself. But conversation got heavy fast.

"Now, Chuck," said Piggott, "I hope I'm not interfering with your life," he said, "but I notice you don't seem to be wearing your temple garments. Are you—have you—"

"I'm excommunicated, Dave."

"Oh. Oh. I'm sorry to hear that. It's a little surprising. I guess things happen. I won't ask you—shoot, I shouldn't have asked you anything. That's your business. Shoot. But of course, I've known a lot of people who was excommunicated and they come back stronger than ever."

"I don't think that will happen," said Dad.

"No?" Piggott held his fork two inches from his mouth and gazed at Dad with those awful blue eyes.

"No."

"Well," he said. "You know I'm divorced. Has John mentioned it?"

"I had heard," Dad said.

"I don't want to talk about it, really. Don't know why I brung it up. Worst thing of my life. Anyway, so. How's the pie?"

"Wonderful," Dad said.

"Isn't it? And fresh, like your wife said. You can't find fresher bananas. They got picked in the back yard about fifteen minutes ago. How about that?"

They talked about the pie: texture, taste, sweetness. Like a couple of gourmets.

When Mom came out, I half expected her to be wearing blue. She was still orange. She said, "Well, well, well, you never can tell. You might go to Heaven and you might not." From all appearances, she was back to normal.

Twelve

I was tempted to sleep on the floor, but the feather mattress was too soft. I collapsed into it without undressing. When I awoke a few hours later, a clock was glowing green on the bedtable, displaying the date and the time, of which I had lost track. It was three minutes past midnight, July 28. I was legally divorced. Somehow, it had slipped by me that the date was so near. But my intestines knew; they woke me up at the appointed time and radiated a dull pain into both my thighs.

I stared at the clock and began to cry. My intestines, my eyes, my stomach ached. But the tears weren't for me. In my head was the question: "So now what's going to become of him?"

Not that I loved my husband—my ex-husband. I didn't. I ached for him is all. That pain in my intestines was just getting him out of my system—bleeding him out, if that's how it had to happen. I would be fine, unhampered, but who would take care of him? He was so pathetic. I wouldn't have married him if he hadn't been so pathetic—if he hadn't needed me desperately. There was a time I almost called the wedding off, in fact, but his pathos was too great.

It was a friend of his, a university professor who claimed to be a real socialist, who almost broke us up. We had gone to meet him because my ex wanted to introduce me to all of his friends. There were three; this prof was the third. Professor Cummins.

"This fellow," said Professor Cummins, putting his arm around my fiance like a defiant fag, "this fellow understands socialism better than anyone I've ever met. He also understands that the Mormon church is crock."

I got stiff-backed and sassy. I pulled out my best college vocabulary. I said I could smell a non sequitur a mile away.

Professor Cummins hated me. I considered this a convenient test of my fiance's love: he would have to choose between us.

"The Mormon church," said the prof, his arm still around my man's shoulders, "is overpopulating. The world can't tolerate that."

My fiance said he had forgotten about overpopulation. Yes, the Mormon church was overpopulating, he agreed. That was true.

"The Mormon church," said the prof, "is a capitalist plot. It imprisons its members with superstition and then robs them blind."

My fiance said that was correct.

"The Mormon church," said the prof, "is no place for thinking people."

My fiance said that was right. His mentor squeezed his shoulders.

I tried to defend the Church's position on overpopulation. It was a lame defense. The prof said to my fiance, "Explain it to her."

He did. He gave statistics and proofs, quoted a few anti-Mormons, looked at me with hard, hateful eyes (one dilated, the other a stone), and told me I was being an ass. The prof looked at him affectionately.

I said, "Take me home."

The prof said, "I'd think real seriously about this marriage, boy. Real seriously. She's not what you suppose." As though I were not there.

I offered my hand to Professor Cummins. I said, "Good to have met you."

He didn't answer.

I was staying with my fiance's family. We drove there not speaking, looking straight ahead like we were on an unpredictable railway. His glass eye was monstrous.

My fiance said, "I had forgotten about all that."

I didn't reply, and I didn't sleep that night. At 3:00 in the morning I called my mother and said, "We've lost him."

Those words. "We've lost him." Why "we"? Whose life was this? Mom had failed in her miracle-making with Dad; was she giving herself a second chance through me and my man-in-need-of-grace?

Mom said, "Hang in there, Digs."

I told her I would hang in there, and then I put the phone up and sobbed. In the morning I looked hideous. My fiance took me in his arms and said, "Hey, it's not the end of the world."

In retrospect, those are the kindest words I ever heard from him.

I told him I loved him, loved him, loved him. I poured love over him like a great anointing.

He said, "Maybe we should get married anyway. Without you, I'd drift."

That was true. I knew that. I made him promise to never see the prof again. "He is a hole of an asp," I said.

He promised, we got married, went to a Motel 6. He loved me then. We had just been eternally tied in the temple, and he was repenting of his anger and savagery and getting Professor Cummins out of his system. He was pouring his past into me, and I was so silent, not opening my mouth but to kiss him. I was loving him away from his sins.

For two weeks, there was no anger. Then I asked a fatal question, not realizing there was not enough trust between us to handle the implications. I said, "Is there any chance your Dad committed suicide?"

It was as good as blasphemy. You could see the color drain out of his cheeks. His good eye ignited. He said, "Holy crap, woman."

He thought it was true, that was obvious. People don't get so angry at an innocent question unless it threatens some ugly truth they're protecting—some awful secret as precious to them as love. When he looked at me, he knew that I knew. He said the only thing he could have said, given the state of things: "You are totally incompetent."

Incompetence was my secret. I said, "Don't talk to me like that."

"The plane engine froze and he didn't see the telephone pole."

"And his business was falling apart and your mother was torturing him for money, right?"

He told me to go play on the highway. I said that was a weird thing for a husband to suggest to his wife.

He repeated himself.

I said, "Well didn't your mother torture him?" I had never seen myself like this. I was too embarrassed to shut up. I hoped I'd find some ultimate truth, something so significant that it wouldn't matter how low I had gone to get it.

He pulled the Church in on top of us then, said I and all Mormons were asses and that if he learned someday that Joseph Smith had made up the whole thing, then after he died he would personally strangle "Old Joe," and Brigham Young too.

I said I didn't think strangling affected a spirit.

He repeated that I was totally incompetent—a phrase that became my appositive during the rest of our marriage. The next morning, he went to Professor Cummins.

Those two were a pair. If Mom and I and our female ancestors were in this marriage together, then so were my husband and his prof and all the anti-Mormons who had ever lived. Maybe including my dad. We were all of us aligned against each other and set to act out the contest again and again and again, one side waiting for the miracle; the other side scratching away at whatever it was that divided and bonded us.

Of course, in the final analysis, their side won—at least as far as I was concerned. The divorce was final. The green clock proved it.

I prayed. I said to God, "Bless him. Bless that S.O.B. He won't have me anymore."

I tried to sleep some, and couldn't. I washed my face three times before breakfast, then kept my eyes averted as we ate.

"So Julie," said Piggott, sponging the last of his egg with his toast, "so, let's have our chat." He licked his fingers, wiped them with a napkin, stood.

His "office" was done in azure and over-filled with plants. He gestured for me to sit. I found the armchair the kind of thing Goldilocks would have traded for a nice board. I sank like it was a padded toilet.

"Now Julie, honey, let me explain my position. First off, I want you to know I think you're talented as all get-out. No, I mean that. You have a voice to make a meadowlark cry tears. I mean that. It's just that right now, there's what you might call turmoil around here."

"You mean the war?"

"Oh it's not a war. Well, a mild one, maybe. The real thing is long over. Anyways, the Church is strong. But there's some leaders of the government thinks the Church is messed up with the CIA or some such hogwash." He wiped his face with a hanky; his last word seemed to have reminded him he was sweating. "We've had troubles getting Church supplies across the border, and, frankly, John is a little too political to be safe."

"Uncle Johnny is?"

"Listen," said Piggott, "there's more than farming going on at Zarahemla. If you want to know the truth, I've been kind of put on alert by the Church to keep watch on him. And I have my own reasons—that's beside the point. Put it this way: suppose that Alberto kid turned out to be a *guerrillero*, and then him and you have broadcast these tapes—beautiful tapes, I grant you—in the name of the Church. Well now it sounds silly, I know, but it could close up the whole operation. People who've lived on tortillas and water for two years just so's they could go to the temple, they lose everything they own, maybe even their lives. Sunday school teachers don't get their manuals, missionaries don't get their scriptures, people who've been endowed don't get their garments or temple clothes to be buried in. Now, do you understand my position?"

"Alberto's not a *guerrillero*," I said.

"Well now, I'm sure he's not. But there's other things. I don't want to make accusations, Julie. The Church has told me to be on the alert. That's all I'll say about it. I can't let the Church's name be used on your tapes. That's just all there is to it." He smiled a big, fake, Cheshire cat smile.

"All right," I said.

"You sing so pretty, Julie. If I had my way, I'd have you do a little concert right in the plaza here. Turn these people away from their daily routine and give them some music. I've always loved music myself, you know. And not that country stuff neither. I was raised and reared in Spanish Fork, Utah, and I'm thankful and grateful for it, because I've used everything I learnt there, but I never listened to the same radio stations my buddies did. Is who I love is Mozart. That surprises you, don't it." He laughed and wiped his face.

"I like Mozart too," I said.

"Well now, you see? That don't surprise me, since I know your papa is from cultured stock—California—but I bet your friends loved the Rolling Stones and the Partridge Family, didn't they? I bet they thought you was a weird duck for listening to old Wolfey."

"Not really," I said. I didn't want to look at him. Last night's tears were too close.

"Julie." He leaned earnestly over his desk, his hands clasped in front of him. "Julie, I know maybe you've heard bad things about me. What I ask—all I ask—is that you be patient till you know the whole truth. I'm here because I love the people of this place and I want to help them."

"You work for Westinghouse, don't you?" I said.

"Well now, that's how I make my living. But no, I work for God."

"Westinghouse isn't God's company, as far as I know, President. I don't think God likes what you're doing. I think God isn't pleased. Not pleased."

"Well, I don't know. God knows I'm nothing holy, that's for darn sure. He knows my struggles. But I think He loves me, honey.

And—now I don't want to go on defending myself. Listen, why don't you and your folks and me go for a spin and I'll show you some of my projects. I'll show you the place I call Bountiful. Would you like that?"

"Is our 'heart-to-heart' over?" I said.

"Well no. Not if you don't want it to be."

"I just wanted to say one thing."

"I'm all ears, honey."

"Just this: I came here to do a good work, and I want to do it. I just want to know if you're going to stand in my way wherever I turn."

Piggott looked at me with a good-natured twinkle, his face puckered into a crooked smile. He started chuckling. He said, "You are definitely your Mom's kid, arncha. Well, I admire your spunk. You bet I do. Like I say, Julie, if it was up to me, you'd be performing on the best radio stations in this place, and on TV too. But it's not up to me. I get my orders" (he pointed to the ceiling) "from higher up."

"Can I have the tape back?"

"For your own use, yes. But—and I regret this, honey—not for the radio. You understand that, don't you."

I held out my hand. I was almost crying again. It made me mad I should cry. The tape wasn't that big a deal.

He took it from his desk drawer and laid it across my palm.

"Now let me take and show you around the city," he said, patting the tape like it was his magnanimous gift.

Thirteen

The big cities in Central America are similar, from what I've seen. Rats crawl in garbage bins, undulating like black caterpillars over watermelon rinds. Flies make little whirlwinds wherever vendors cart their wares. Buildings are big and brick and dirty and labeled with spray paint graffiti. Naked children play in the unpaved streets. Bony dogs with hungry, yellow eyes sit outside meat shops. Drunkards drool in gutters. Grim boys who look barely old enough to be sluffing high school parade importantly in front of banks and office buildings wearing blue uniforms and slinging machine guns.

Piggott took us to Plaza Libertad, showed us the statue of a woman holding two wreaths. "There was a little massacre here back in seventy-seven," he said. "And right there," he pointed to the cathedral directly ahead, "that's El Rosario Cathedral. Oscar Romero used to do mass there. You've heard of him, of course."

"Of course," I said. Oscar Romero—the outspoken priest who was murdered while administering the eucharist—who hadn't heard of him?

"He wasn't actually killed here, it was in the chapel of the Divine Providence Hospital a little ways distant. But the way people talk, it was right in there, while he was praying. That event, that one event, it started more bloodshed than anything gone before."

We went inside the cathedral. It was arched, dark, spacious. An imitation universe. Dimly glowing globes hung from the ceiling like a row of planets. The walls had unlit electric candles spaced throughout, in pockets intended for torches. There were bright statues at all the stations of the cross, portraying some event of Jesus' life. Near the altar was a tapestry with the inscription: "*Loor a monsenior Romero. Comite de Madres y Familias de Presos, Desaparecedos y Asasinados Politicos de El Salvador.*" Praise to Monsenior Romero, from the committee of mothers and families of the prisoners, the missing, and the murdered of El Salvador. I wondered if Luisa's mother had helped with this offering.

"Quite a guy, Romero was," said Piggott. "I met him once at some dinner. A sweet fellow. Wore glasses, had a real soft voice. Sweet. You wouldn't imagine him being a hero. But during the worst of things, he still spoke against the government, accused it of repressing the people, taking advantage, killing innocent kids—which was true, let's face it. Anyways, Romero said whatever he wanted to, about religion or about politics. You've got to admire gumption like that. Me, I didn't say a thing back there in the bad part. Locked my doors. Locked my windows. Somebody tried to break in once, but the alarm went off and scared him. I tell you, it was a bad time. There was a month there that I took to hiding. Had to, to save my skin. Some Indians put me up."

"Where?" I asked.

"Tiny place called Izalco. One of the finest members of the Church lives there."

"Primitivo."

"Primitivo, yes," he said slowly, almost suspiciously. "How do you know him?"

I shrugged.

"John—he took you to Izalco? Is John doing something there?"

Mom answered. She went on and on about how John was rebuilding the whole place and saving everyone there. (This was the content of one of the two letters they had received from me.)

"John's there, is he," Piggott repeated thoughtfully. "Well. Primitivo's a good man. He's—"

"I know," I said.

"I woulda starved if it hadn't been for him." He looked at his stomach and pounded it, laughing again. "Course I compensated for what I missed. I do love to eat, guess that's clear. But I was starving there for a time. I was holed up in a little cave actually— just like Moroni was when the Lamanites was after him. I thought about that a lot. Well, it was Primitivo kept me alive. Brung me food, scriptures, water. Course, for him to let anyone know where I was, well it woulda meant death for us both. So there was days he couldn't come. Seemed like weeks at times. There was once—hope this don't make you sick—once I took to eating bugs, mosquitos and fleas mostly, just for the protein. And then he'd be there, the old man would, like God had told him I was at my limit. He'd have tortillas or bread. Once he brought me a jar of strawberry jam one of the missionaries had give him." We sat on the cathedral's front steps. Piggott looked at me like he was giving his gospel witness. "I love that guy," he said. "Jesus is going to have something for him after this life, I'll tell you that for sure. That old guy's going to have a bigger place than mine. A solid gold mansion. You watch. Saved my life, he did. Him and God." He sighed. This had been his great speech. About food and mansions, I reflected.

He told us more about the cathedral, and some about the Spanish conquest. He figured he was filling us in on all the details of history we had been longing to hear. Some of his information wasn't quite correct.

He drove us, then, around a mountainside, through a couple of pastel *barrios*, a cemetery, and finally to his project. He announced: "This here, this is Bountiful."

Before us was a little America. White pre-fab houses with clover lawns and volkswagens were lined up in neat little rows, separated by palm trees. It looked like somebody had misplaced a subdivision of L.A.

"Some folks call it Mormon Row," said Piggott. "But there's non-members here too, though most of them convert before too long." He sighed. "It's the one thing in my life," he said, "I wouldn't change."

Mom looked at the houses. She said nothing. She had been unusually quiet during the whole tour. I said that "Mormon Row" looked to be very nice.

"Yes," said Piggott, "yes it is. And the tenants, they take good care of it too. You lift them up and they find out they like the view."

Dad said it was really something.

"Why don't you come on down here, Chuck," said Piggott. "Come on down and live here. You're young, and you have a lot of expertise, doncha? Come on down here and live. You know, these houses have disposals and septic tanks. You can live the way you're used to."

Dad laughed like the invitation was a good joke. Piggott laughed too.

What I wanted to ask was if a person had to wear blue to get one of those pre-fab houses on Mormon Row.

Dinner that night at the mansion was lasagna and pumpkin pie. Piggott had three servings of everything.

Afterwards, Mom helped the maids wash dishes. I was going to join her, but once again the conversation got interesting. Dad asked about politics.

Piggott said, "Well, Chuck, if you want to know the sad truth, this place is ripe."

"For communism?"

"That's right. The other day," Piggott said, "there was three bodies found in a gulch. Now it's not so bad as it was back in seventy-nine, eighty. It's never been that bad and I hope it never will be again. I remember seventeen bodies two weeks in a row, back there a few years ago, all of them beat to a bloody pulp. You never knew just who was doing the killing—could be the Right, could be the Left. They'd dump the bodies off *El Porton.* Anyways, things have calmed down, but you still feel the fear. You get the idea there's commies crawling in the cornfields looking for spies. And then the government's running scared. This here is violent country. There's quakes and volcanoes and communism getting ready to burst any second."

"Are you in any danger?" Dad said.

"Naw. I'm protected. Too many people on both sides work for Westinghouse. And I have the Lord. Back awhile, one of the Church members had a visit from rebels. They told him—Hermano Garcia is his name—they told Hermano Garcia to spy for them or they'd kill him, and they left him a knife as, you know, a kindly reminder. Next week come some government guys—the *Guardia,* right? They tell him to spy for them or he's history, and they leave him a couple bullets to remember them by. So Hermano Garcia, he comes to me and he tells me the situation. So what do you think I told him?"

"What?" said Dad.

"I told him, I says, '*Hermano,*' I says, 'pay your tithing and keep the commandments, and nothing will happen to you.' And it hasn't. The Lord protects his own."

"Wow, Dave," said Dad. "You could sell that story to *Especially for Mormons.*"

"Maybe so."

Dad pushed his plate away. "Maybe so," he repeated. "You know, Dave, when I was in Nam, the hardest thing was not knowing who the enemy was. The country was seething evil, and you just had to make your best guess where that evil was. Sometimes we made good guesses; sometimes we didn't."

"Well now," said Piggott, "these people around here, most of them, why they're poor as church mice. Well you know that, Chuck.

You lived here two years! Think about it: what starving guy in his right mind wouldn't want a government that guaranteed him something to eat every day and told him the rich fellow up the street would be his equal? It's clever, this communism is."

I looked around the dining room. The walls were papered in a satiny fleur de lis; the chairs we were sitting on were blue velveteen; the chandelier above us was weeping crystal. And we were talking about how communism tempts the poor.

"There was one time," said my father, "when I barely escaped ambush. I was running like hell, and I ended up in a sort of thatched barn—the kind you see around here a lot. There was a kid in the barn. Maybe a sixteen-year-old kid. I looked at him, and I thought—well, are you the devil? I had no idea who that kid was or which side he was on. You don't."

"That's how Satan works," said Piggott. "You never know for sure."

"No, you don't," said Dad.

I wanted to know what had happened in the Vietnamese barn. Dad didn't talk often about what he had actually done in Viet Nam, just about the politics behind it. I said, "So what happened?"

"What?" Dad said.

"In the barn."

He looked at his hands, lifted them like they were heavy and foreign. He said, "I'll never say war is good. I'll never say that. But there are worse things."

Nobody spoke for a minute, until Piggott said, "You know, Chuck, when you take and remember back to when we was missionaries, oh was we naive. We figured if we could just take and get the Latins into the water, everything would be solved. Politics wasn't in the picture back then. I didn't even know what communism was back then. Boy, I know now. Do I ever. Is what it is, is the devil's plan. God's told us that."

There's not much you can say in answer to God. I took a last bite of my tortilla, feeling it like a rock in my throat.

Fourteen

Mom and Dad wanted me to see Belen—just thirty-seven kilometers away—before they returned me to Zarahemla. I agreed, on the condition that the visit not take more than a day. There were things at Zarahemla, I told them, that I had to get back for.

"Things?" said Dad after as we left Piggott's mansion.

"Things," I repeated.

"Do these things have names?"

"Oh Chuck," Mom said, "mind your own business, for goshsakes. Digs isn't a baby."

Dad stopped the van. I thought he was going to keep it dead until he had dragged some kind of confession from me. He had stopped, though, for a Catholic parade just before the statue of "*Cristo en el Mundo.*" We watched, not talking.

Solemn men held statues of the Lady of Sorrows and her bleeding son and marched slowly down the street. The statues seemed to be floating above the procession. The men were moving the images from one church to another. I sat looking at the sad, ethereal eyes of The Virgin. The artist had painted white stars in them, so her tears seemed to be perpetually gleaming. Beautiful tears, and her pink-cheeked face so calm and serene it made you think true peace and true beauty isn't attained until you can keep tears like that in your eyes. The way the old-time movie stars—Greer Garson and Donna Reed and Ingrid Bergman—did, with their faces haloed and their tears brimming, glistening, shining like their brains had been doused in moonlight.

I never cried like that. When my ex hurt me, I bawled myself into a red, snotty nose and eyes that looked like they had been scraped on a whetstone. I looked hideous when I cried, he said. I was never like Greer Garson or Donna Reed or Ingrid Bergman or the Virgin Mary.

Well, I imagine in real life, Greer Garson and Donna Reed and Ingrid Bergman could cry like the rest of us. I imagine when her son was crucified, Mary didn't just stand there with her hands outstretched and her half-closed eyes full of beautiful tears and peace. I imagine she sobbed till her eyes were bleeding. But you can soften anyone up with low lights, a filmy lens, some imagination, a nice soppy script.

Of course the Latin men holding the statues have bought into the whole lie. They figure they're holding history in their overworked hands. No wonder they're famous lovers. Tender and gentle, like the woman's body they're exploring is thin glass and touching it too hard will either break her or bring out those terrible, beautiful, static tears and that tormented half-smile. No wonder the Latin woman's prayer to the Virgin finishes with a plea to keep her husband from harlots. That macho search for a living Mary predicts roving eyes. Those men want to keep holding onto the motionless, the pitiful, the pitiable woman. Caress her plastic feet. Pray into her eyes. Lick the dirt from her hem. The women just have to keep practicing the pose and praying for a miracle.

The men did not look anywhere but straight ahead as observers tossed white carnations onto the statues. When the procession ended, the crowds surged into the space where their sacred images had just passed. Cars honked; children shouted to us "Goose bite my lung" (their attempt at "Goodbye My Love"); the cathedral bell tolled three times, signaling the arrival of the gods.

Dad started the van again. We passed "Cristo en el Mundo" and rounded the bend at the suburban ghettos, then drove into the tropical wilderness.

Belen was a haven for grapefruit. It had one Catholic church, a flock of green parakeets flying around, little adobe houses, and grapefruit trees. There were more grapefruit than people.

Most everybody wore white—except widows, who wore black. Girls wore white cotton dresses; boys wore white cotton shirts and pants and cowboy hats. Black hair, brown skin. Most of the color in Belen was in its flowers and parakeets and grapefruit. It smelled of citrus. There was a heavy, moist fragrance around us that transcended Doodle Dan's frame and glass.

"We've found Eden," Mom said, and rolled down her window to wave at everybody in the plaza. Everybody waved back. "Or, I should say, John found it for us."

Mom detailed their work: they were farmers, musicians, teachers of literacy, examples of Mormonism ("at least one of us is"), feeders of the hungry, helpers of all in need. "Such a joy," Mom said.

"Such a joy," Dad repeated wryly.

They lived in an adobe hut without running water. "Makes me feel like a real woman, Digs," Mom said. "Like my grandma. Grandma used to go to a well for the drinking water. Worked her little buns off, Grandma did. No dishwashers or food processors or McDonalds back then."

Dad parked the van by a huge grapefruit tree. Before us was what I assumed to be their house. A bunch of little kids were waiting in front of the door. They held open their arms as Mom got out. She hugged them and produced—from the same kind of miracle that made fish and bread loaves in Christ's time, I suppose —a caramel for each. There were ten kids. They ate their candy, chattering Spanish to her which she answered with, "Well, the same to you, sweety," or "I feel exactly that way, yes." Then they hugged

her again and ran or skipped or hopped away. It was like something from a fairy tale: you enter an enchanted forest and have to
pay your sweet dues before the trolls and fairies and rabbit children
will give you passage. And who, you might wonder, has charmed
whom?

Mom and Dad unloaded the van. Mom talked to me as she
worked. "I do all sorts of domestic things here, Digs. You'll be real
impressed. Of course I'm not as good as my own mother. I don't
make whole wheat bread from scratch. Have I ever told you about
mother's homemade toast and tomato juice? Here, take this." She
handed me a basket of avocados. Apparently, she had visited a
marketplace in San Salvador. I have no idea when she did that.

"Wonderful avocados, you'll see," she said, and put another box
inside my basket. "Mother's toast. Oh Digs, you missed out on
something wonderful. I remember getting up on winter mornings
and coming into the kitchen in my pink doggie slippers, and Mom
would hand me a cup of hot tomato juice and a big slice of bread,
fresh from the oven. I'd dip the bread in the juice. Best breakfast
in the world. Too bad your Mom didn't do stuff like that, Digs."
She had loaded herself with other boxes, up to her neck. We
started for the door.

"I always liked your poached eggs," I said behind her.

"Did you? I remember once I gave your Dad creamed eggs over
soda crackers for supper. He threw a fit."

"No I didn't," came Dad's voice behind us.

"All right, not a bad fit. You just said you'd prefer something
red—yes you did say that. Anyway. I wasn't much for domestic
jobs." She kicked the bamboo door. It opened. "When it gets right
down to it, I wasn't as good a mother to you as mine was to me,
Digs. I didn't do all those Molly Mormon things." She put her
boxes on the floor and told me to do the same. There was no other
choice. The hut was completely bare save one mat in the middle
and three large suitcases alongside one wall. "But then," she
continued, "I think my Mom wasn't as good as hers was either.

Here, Digs, a mango." She reached into one of her boxes and tossed me a tiny red fruit. "The smaller the sweeter," she added.

I peeled it and ate. The fibers stuck between my teeth. I picked them out with my fingernails. I said, "I guess it's a good thing I never had kids."

"What?" Mom answered, her mouth open for another bite.

"Well it sounds to me," I said, "like we're just going steadily downhill."

"Downhill? Oh, you mean because I never made bread. But I'm repenting, Digs, I'm repenting. I not only get our water from a well, but I go to the center of town for it. And I've learned to grind corn and make tortillas. Haven't I, Papadopolous." She threw him a mango.

"Yup," he said, catching it.

"No, Digs—you've got to have children. Oh I hope you do. Get married first, of course. Remarried. But children are a delight."

We sat on the mat, eating our mangos. We put the peelings in another of Mom's boxes.

"A delight! Mom," I said, "we wore you out."

"You were a handful, that's for sure. And, like I said, I wasn't much of a homemaker. That's no secret."

I laughed, remembering another of her cleaning songs. I started singing it. Mom joined in:

> Oh say can you see
> Any dirt on the floor?
> Then we'll sweep and we'll mop
> And we'll wipe down the door . . .

Dad rolled his eyes.

"You know what you should have been, Mom?" I said. "A stand-up comic."

"Naw," she said. "Nobody would have enjoyed me as much as you guys did. Oh Digs, you had the cutest laugh when you were little. I'd sing you some stupid song and you'd squeal—wouldn't she, Pop. You'd squeal and laugh until your tonsils practically blew out. It was so fun! I adored you. But it was very hard for me to wash your dishes and keep your clothes clean. Things were just changing for women back then, but they hadn't changed yet. I was sort of caught in the turnstile."

"We came out okay," I said. "Only one divorce in the family."

"Hang loose about that, Digs," she said, and bit into her mango. "Just hang loose."

There were little holes in the adobe walls and thatched roof where sunlight pored in. There were beams of sunshine all around us, some of them criss-crossed, and white dots on the floor. I looked at the web of light and thought how I loved my family.

The next day—my last with them in Belen—Dad asked me if I wanted to go egg hunting with him. There were scads of chickens around—uncaged—and egg hunting was fun, he said. Ask any kid at Easter. He put on a ridiculous straw hat—the kind scarecrows wear.

I suspected the "egg hunt" would turn into one of those father-daughter talks. I was right.

He said little at first. We found five eggs in some thick grass behind the hut. Dad stood there, wiping two of them on his rear pocket. "Jewel," he said, "these things you have to go back to Zarahemla for—is one of these 'things' Alberto?"

I had known it was coming. "Alberto's okay," I said.

"You two have become—shall we say—buddies, haven't you?" He took off his straw hat and put the eggs in it.

"Yes."

"Maybe more than buddies?"

I loved the way he introduced the subject. He had never been a talker, but he had never been subtle either. He could polish off a non sequitur with the same finesse that Piggott could polish off beef stroganoff. ("How are you liking the weather? You still a virgin?")

I said Alberto and I were close.

"So," he said. "So."

His thin hair was mussed from the hat. He looked poor and sweet in his jeans and T-shirt, holding the hat before him like a begger. We were peers. I wasn't so much younger than he was. We had both been through our little wars.

"Alberto's a good boy, Dad," I said.

"Uh huh. Is he a communist?"

I thought about it. "I don't know."

"It would be easy to be a communist around here."

"I guess it would."

"Sure it would. It's beautiful stuff, communism is. Idealistic, fair—beautiful. If human beings could really be free and good like that—if we really could have equality—I'd be the first one to vote for communism. But we're selfish mutts, Jewel. We're greedy and competitive and full of lust. That's why no communist has ever taken power without putting on a massacre."

I said, "Maybe that's true." What I was thinking was that he used to call me "Jewel" when I was a baby. Hearing it now made it seem almost like nothing had changed.

"Communism is evil. Devil's counterfeit," he said.

I grinned. "You're sounding like my seminary teacher."

"Am I? Your seminary teacher. Well, that's ironic. Isn't it."

"Not really."

We climbed a hill to another site where he often found eggs. Another adobe hut had been there once, but it was in ruins now. The chickens laid their eggs around the remains of the brick and the mossy bamboo. "I'm no seminary teacher," he said, lifting a nearly disintegrated adobe brick. It crumbled in his hands. "Do you think you could teach seminary, Jewel?"

"Me? I don't think they let divorced people do it. Isn't there some sort of Church rule against having divorcees teach the kids?"

"I've been out too long to know. If there wasn't a rule, could you do it?"

I knew I couldn't, but I said, "I don't know."

"You've seen some pieces of hell, haven't you. Still makes me mad to think about something like that happening just outside your door. I mean to have some words with John when we go back."

"Dad—"

"Never mind. I'll be diplomatic. Maybe bang my shoe on his head, I don't know." He found three more eggs under some mossy leaves. We started back to the hut. I told Dad that my seminary teacher was a geek.

"A geek?" he said. "That's a new word for me. Well, any fanatic can sound like a seminary teacher, can't he?"

"Probably can."

"You know, Jewel," he said, glancing back at me then holding my hand down the hill so I wouldn't slip. "You know, a divorced person probably has some big needs for love. It would be easy for a divorced person to do a big 180 degree rebound."

"And you don't want any communist sons-in-law, is that what you're saying?"

"I'm not sure what I'm saying, actually. Just be careful. Intercultural romance—it doesn't work a lot of times."

I wanted to ask just how much he knew about intercultural romance, and where he had learned it. (Viet Nam, maybe?) Instead, I said, "So what if I did? If I married Alberto, would you bring a shotgun to the wedding and stand in front of the temple door?"

"No. Is this an announcement?"

"No." I slid down the last foot of the hill. He gripped my hand to keep me up, then let me walk before him.

"Dad?" I said, turning to him. "That kid in the barn—"

"What kid?"

"The one you told Piggott about?"

"Oh."

"Did you kill him?"

He looked away, inhaling deeply through his nose, then looked at me again. "Why are you asking me this? Punishment for my invading your privacy?"

"Did you kill him?"

He gazed at me, then nodded. "Yes," he said, and sighed like the word was a great relief.

Mom waved her orange scarf at us from the bamboo door. She was doing Gypsy Rose Lee again.

Fifteen

Zarahemla was misted when we arrived. It looked like something out of *Star Trek*—a city on a cloud or a some quaint village guarded all around by ghosts. I had slept through most of the return trip, and awakened with Dad's terse words to John: "Got a bone to pick with you, buddy."

"Well what a surprise," Johnny said. "I didn't think you'd *all* come back. Things slowing up in Belen?"

"You thought we'd send our daughter back to you by bus, did you John?" Dad said, getting out, slamming Doodle Dan's door. "Not a chance. And that's the bone. Don't you ever let her leave this place alone, you got that?"

"She didn't go alone," Johnny answered soberly.

"Oh you sent an angel, is that it?"

"I don't expect you to understand, Chuck. Don't let it ruin our relationship, huh? She's back safe."

Mom got out of the van and kissed Johnny on the cheek. "I hear," she said, "your wife is P.G. How's she doing?"

"Not so good." He motioned to the cabin. "Why don't you go see her."

When we went inside, the silence was palpable.

I called "Hello." Luisa's door opened. She stood there, thin, pallid, feeble. I was shocked by the change in her. She had been sick when I left, and weak, but she was wearing death now. Her skin was still yellow, but there was a sheen to it, like what you see at a viewing. Her face reminded me of the makeup job I had once done on myself when I wanted to sluff school. I had put white goop over my cheeks and grey goop under my eyes. I looked convincing enough that Mom put me to bed. But this was no act for Luisa. Her voice was raspy, exhausted. Little blue veins were pulsing in her temples.

"How was your trip?" she whispered.

"Oh it was great," I said, my voice softening to complement hers. "Quite a place he has, Luisa. You ought to see it."

"I have," she said.

"Oh Cookie," Mom gushed, walking past me to embrace Luisa. "Congratulations! Oh, you look good! But you're tired. You shouldn't be up like this. Look at that tummy! You're doing it, aren't you, Cookie. Growing a kid."

Luisa smiled and put her hands over her womb.

"Let's put you to bed," Mom said. "Come on, Digs. Help out." She supported Luisa's right arm, I supported her left.

"But I want to hear," Luisa protested. Her accent was thicker than usual. She sounded like a sickly, foreign, whining child.

"We'll tell you everything," Mom said, kissing her ear, "but while you rest, Cookie, huh?"

We laid her down. Dad closed the door and went outside with Johnny. They continued their argument, largely inaudible to us but for the rise and fall of their voices. Dad's voice rose the most.

"I suppose," Luisa said, "there were no messages for me— from San Salvador?"

I told her we had received no messages.

"It's all right," she said, and let her eyes close. "Tell me about it."

"I got the tape," I said. "And I got divorced. It turned final at midnight, night before last."

"Oh yes." We were still whispering. "A letter came for you from Jason."

"Jason?" My insides tightened. Automatic intestinal shutdown. I expected the cramps and aches to begin any second. "From Jason?"

Luisa nodded and motioned weakly to the bedstead. "Top drawer, under my etchings. I put it there for protection. Too many *desaparecidos* in El Salvador." Mom took out the pencil etchings. She said, "Luisa, I didn't know you could draw," as she handed me the letter.

So there it was, smothered with cancelled George Washington stamps. A letter from Jason, my ex.

I hadn't thought of his name in a long time. When we were married, he had been "Honey." After I left him, he became a pathetic face with a black "X" through it. The name itself was so personal and innocent. You could imagine a baby with the name, its parents calling after it, "Now you come back here, Jase. Be a good boy."

The envelope was tightly sealed. I sliced through a couple layers of finger skin opening it. The letter itself was typed. It said: "Dear Julie, you left some things for your hair. Electric curlers and curling iron. I don't know what I should do with them. Maybe they're worth money, right? If so, you should have them back. What do I do? Do you want me to put them away for you? Love, Jason."

Those last two words stood out as the real message of the letter. Love Jason. Like an order. Like I should risk my guts again. What I wanted to do was smash his nose. I wanted to put his head between cymbals and play the 1812 overture. I wanted to cry. For me. For him.

My curlers. He wants to know what to do with my curlers. Crimany, what a jerk I am! It's not as if he meant any harm. He was a child out of control. He sobbed, sometimes, after he hurt me too much. He cried, "What is wrong with me? Help me, Julie. Help me, Jesus."

If Jesus did anything, I don't know about it. As for me, I was a flop. Lord Jim jumping ship. Abandoning hope. Exiting the pedestal, robes lifted above my ankles. Here I was, divorced in El Salvador. Spitting in the sinner's candles.

"These drawings are really good," Mom said, pointedly ignoring the letter. "This one—do you know who he reminds me of? Daniel Castillo. Remember Daniel Castillo, Cookie?"

"No," Luisa said, sitting up in bed, suddenly energized. "It's not Daniel. It's John, not Daniel."

"Just the eyes. If I'm remembering them. Daniel's eyes are softer, sort of, than Johnny's. The rest is Johnny, I guess. But these are soft eyes. Don't you think so, Digs? My hay-ell, how long since I've seen Daniel Castillo? I might have married him if he hadn't gone back. Of course, I'm glad I didn't now." She laughed. "Well, I guess I'm glad. Do you ever hear from him?"

Luisa fell back on her pillow. "No," she said. "No. Never. Let me see the picture."

Mom held it up to her.

"It's very bad," Luisa said, glancing at it then turning away. "It is a very bad picture. No talent."

"No talent," Mom mimicked. "Bull-honkey, Cookie. After this baby is born, I think you ought to take this art stuff seriously. You've got a gift. You do. A real gift." She glanced at me, still pretending there was nothing portentous or even very interesting in the thin paper I held. "So, Digs, what does Jason have to say?" she asked. She continued to look through Luisa's etchings.

"Not much. He wanted to know where to store my curlers." A teeny crack in my voice. We had stopped whispering.

"Uh huh. You going to write back?"

"I don't know. I can buy another set of curlers. I never used them much. That's why I left them there. If I had used them, I would have taken them with me."

She looked at me. "It would be polite to write back. Finalize things, you know."

"Things are finalized. They got finalized on their own. That's the way the law works."

She gave me her grim smile and a ready-to-burst, pregnant pause. "Digs," she said, "Are you all right?"

I rolled my eyes. "Mother," I said. "I never felt better in my life." I crumpled the letter and tossed it into the bamboo bin. "Free throw," I said.

"Tell me more about your trip," Luisa breathed. The burst of energy had waned. "You met *Presidente?*"

"Yes, we met *Presidente. Presidente* must be the richest guy in El Salvador," I said.

"He is a good man," said Luisa.

I shrugged. "He may be," I said. "Let's hope the Lord has a big-eyed needle for him at the pearly gates."

"*Presidente* is very generous," said Luisa.

"Yes. We saw his Little America. The guy's filthy rich."

"You know," she said, "I grew up rich. It was Johnny who saved me from money."

"Bless his heart," said Mom.

"My parents had servants. Beef and rice for every dinner. Eggs for breakfast. Fried chicken in salsa for lunch." She gave a weak laugh. "I could have been very large if not for Johnny."

"That's one thing about living at Zarahemla: you'll never get fat. Anyway, you look good, Luisa," I lied. "Things must be going okay."

"The baby lives, yes. Oh Julie, such a miracle it is. You wait. When you feel life within you, you will understand. Suddenly your body belongs to someone else. Your body does things—things you never knew it could do. There is juice in your breasts. There is blossoming in your womb. You think—if my body knows to do these things, perhaps, then, it truly knows to become a god. Surely, it knows to die. Put your hand here." She guided my fingers to her side. "Feel." Yes, I felt a little pounding. "My child," she said. "Too eager to come."

"Listen, don't tire yourself, Luisa," I said.

Luisa closed her eyes again.

"You do look great, Cookie," said Mom quietly. "You're doing fine, just fine. Why didn't you say anything about this to me? You think I would have gone off to the boonies if I'd known? How far along are you?"

"Seven. Nearly seven."

"So, another few weeks and you're going to be bopping around the kitchen with a papoose on your back, huh?"

Luisa propped herself on her elbow with some difficulty. "Will I?" she said. Her hair swung down over her eye. Mom stroked it back and began to brush it with a half-bald comb. Luisa's head was tilted towards her elbow in that painful, half-sitting position. The hair came down the mattress, nearly reached the floor. Mom knelt to comb it.

"Will you go to San Salvador to have your baby?" I asked.

"No. Here. A midwife will come."

"No hospital? Do you feel all right about that?" I said.

She shrugged one shoulder. "You talked to *Presidente* about the music?" she said.

"Oh yeah. He was real apologetic. Gave me the tape and I gave him a promise."

"Yes?"

"He thinks Alberto is a spy or a guerrilla."

She laughed a little. "Alberto is not that," she said.

"He says the Church told him to be on alert where Zarahemla is concerned. I think he's jealous." I sat beside her on the bed. "He doesn't want Johnny converting too many people. It might show him up, right? He may be generous, but he's a despot. A territorial despot."

Luisa grasped my wrist. "He is a good man," she repeated.

What struck me then was not so much her words as the fact that we three women were at that moment linked: Luisa held my wrist; Mom held Luisa's hair. It was like we were roommates or sisters or entwined fates.

When she loosened her hold I said, "Hey, a lot of despots were good men. Brigham Young was a despot. But I can't believe God likes what Piggott's doing. I think God is pretty upset about the whole thing. I told him so, too."

"You sound," said Luisa, "like your uncle."

As though that were his cue, my uncle screamed outside.

"Oh crap," said Mom, dropping the brush, flinging the bedroom door open. "Digs, your father's murdering Johnny."

Through the kitchen window I saw my father lift Johnny in both arms and throw him into the lake. Johnny came up gasping and furious. Mom dashed for the water in desperate glee, and dived in with all her clothes on. "Splish splash," she sang urgently when she came up, her voice like Count Basie's. "I's a takin' a bath." She made a circle with her hand, splashing all the way around, making herself the center of the bubbles. Then she floated, kicked up a four-inch foam, made frog strokes with her arms. Johnny was treading water, glaring at Dad. Mom splashed Johnny's face.

"Don't do that," he said.

She did it again. "Get happy, Bozo," she told him. She squirted water through her fists, got him right in the nose, then squirted more through her teeth. Finally he gave in and dunked her. Dad just stood there, hands on his hips, like he was in charge of everything and disgusted by it. If Dad were God, I thought, he'd undo the rainbow and make another forty-day, world-wide flood.

And where, I wondered, was Alberto?

Sixteen

Luisa finally slept. Mom and I made spinach souffle for lunch. Dad and John kept up the fight at the table, though each pretended it was just a civil discussion, no hard feelings. Truth was, Dad didn't want to go back to Belen. He wasn't sure he wanted to stay much longer in El Salvador at all—not with murders happening outside his daughter's bedroom door. He had learned, he said, what he came to learn.

"Aw, you love it here," Johnny told him as we ate. "I can see it in your eyes. You're deceiving yourself when you talk that way, guy. Truth is, you miss being in your mission territory. You miss everything about your mission. What's happening is you're scared spitless, Chuck. These old missionary feelings are coming back at you and you're terrified they're going to take hold. You were a damn good missionary, you know."

"Please pass the *platanos*," Dad said.

Johnny sent the dish. "You were," he reiterated. "I think you made me a better missionary because you were so good. I had been a little wild, you know, back in my high school days."

"Uh huh. What does that mean, John?" said Dad. "You took a sip of beer at the senior party?"

"Aw, I kept marijuana in a little vase on my chest of drawers."

"Johnny!" Mom gasped.

"Oh I never smoked it, Em, but I liked it there because it was a felony. Stupid kid. Mother would roll over in her grave if she knew, wouldn't she. She thought I was so damn perfect."

"John was the saint," Mom said. "I was the vixen. I didn't keep pot in my room, though, John. Shame on you."

"I know." He looked sheepish.

The *platanos* were soaked in a pink cinnamon sauce and sprinkled with sugar, the granules like tiny diamonds, much bigger than sugar grains stateside. Dad held a *platano* on his fork in front of his face.

"And I'll tell you something," Johnny said, looking at him. "I went home after my mission, and I dumped that grass in the john. I was thinking of you when I flushed it away."

"You thought of me when you flushed, did you, John. Nobody's ever paid me a compliment like that before."

"You look like Pinocchio," Mom said.

"What's that?"

"Like Pinocchio, with that banana in front of your nose."

He bit into it. "My favorite dish," he said. "I'll admit I miss cinnamon *platanos* when I'm stateside, John. I'll admit that much."

"You miss more than *platanos*," Johnny said.

"Boy, thank God for you, John, to tell us how we feel and what we miss. What would we do without you?"

"Well maybe you wouldn't have the full truth without me, Chuck, I don't know. You want the truth? Do you? Here it is: you love this country, and you love the Church. Aw, you love the Church like a wife. But you don't want to be married to it because it takes so much out of you. You want to look at it from a distance and say, 'Lawdy, Lawdy, now that is cute.' You're a kid with a crush he never fesses up. I don't believe in your so-called apostasy anymore than I believe the devil has horns—anymore than I believe in the president of El Salvador—and believe me, that's not much. But this act of yours, it's breaking Emmie's heart. And you know it."

"I'm not a Mormon anymore, John. I don't know jack."

"Then take it from me. The truth: this stupid act of yours is breaking your wife's heart. Isn't it, Em?"

Mom shrugged awkwardly. "I guess so," she said. "I don't know, Johnny, I've learned to—"

"Don't you think I see what's happening to you, Em? Don't you think I see?" Johnny said.

"What'd you do, John," said Dad, "go and have another epiphany?" He bit into a tortilla like it was Johnny's face. "You want to know what I see? I see more heartbreaking here than what I'm doing, buddy."

"What the perdition do you mean by that?"

"John, if you know anything, you know what I mean by that."

"I do not know what you mean," Johnny said after a tense pause. "If you mean Luisa's unhappy, you're out of place."

"Am I?"

"Luisa's not your wife. You don't know her and you're not entitled to revelation about her."

"Maybe not."

"A man shouldn't judge another man's marriage," Johnny said.

"Why John, I think you've hit on something there. Must be inspiration. As usual."

"Listen, Chuck, I'm sorry if I've offended you. It's just I love my sister, and I love the gospel—and I love you, you bird-turd. I didn't mean to get fiery."

"Em," Dad said, "did you put him up to it? Promise him a commission on my tithing?"

"I've said these things," Johnny answered, "out of love. For all of you."

"Gee, what a swell guy you are, John," Dad said. "Pass the beans please."

*　　*　　*

After lunch, Mom and Dad went jogging. Mom wore orange sweats. Dad wore grey shorts, no shirt, the waistband of a jockstrap around his head—his sweatband. (The most significant part of it was sheared off so no one would think him anatomically confused; he just liked the feel of fruit-of-the-loom elastic, and probably wanted to show off his non-Mormon underwear too.)

Johnny and I were just outside the cabin. We watched my folks jog up the hill—a dot of orange and a dot of grey—and Johnny prophesied again. "Hate to say it, kiddo, but your father has brought the spirit of contention with him. There will be conflicts until he returns where God wants him. He can't run away anymore than Jonah could. God wants him in Belen, and your mother too. You've got to persuade them."

I promised I would try.

"I know you will," said Johnny, taking my elbow. "You came back, just like God knew you would. You resisted Piggott, and if your dad wants to take you away from here, you'll resist him too, won't you. You've passed God's tests, kiddo. Passed them with flying colors. Hey, let's talk, huh? Come on."

"Where's Alberto?" I blurted.

Alberto was in Izalco. "You've been dying to know that, haven't you," said Johnny. "You like Alberto."

"I'm divorced," I said to that, linking my freedom with Alberto's name.

"Congratulations. Help me pick some spinach?"

The nearest spinach patch was just north of the lake.

"This is our first time alone since you got back," Johnny said as we walked. "So, tell me, how'd it go?"

"Piggott's palace? It was everything you said," I answered. "And worse."

"The poor bastard's addicted," Johnny said. "What did he tell you? Anything interesting?"

"He gave me back the tape. Made me promise not to return it to a radio station."

"Did he talk about me?"

"Oh Johnny," I laughed, "he thinks you're dangerous."

We were there. We knelt for the spinach and laughed at The Pig. "Oh you know me—Big Bad John, right? So, what did Piggy say?"

"Oh, for instance, that there's political stuff going on here. That's not true, is it?"

"If the gospel's political, there's political stuff, sure. I know he might think I'm a socialist because I don't make the Indians around here wear blue uniforms. He might think there's something wrong with a guy like me who doesn't want money. Something un-American. Now, don't get offended, kiddo, but Jesus Christ himself wouldn't have been able to get a message on the radio in Piggott's territory. A man born in a manger wouldn't qualify worth beans in Pig Land. Piggott would have *El Salvador* himself shining shoes and living in a pre-fab."

We laughed and picked. Johnny took a handkerchief from his rear pocket. We put the greens on it.

"He's jealous of you," I said.

"Why do you think that?"

"He's paranoid you'll beat him in conversions. He's jealous."

"Did he talk about his wife?"

"No. He mentioned he was divorced."

"He didn't say more than that?"

"No."

"You've probably heard anyway."

"Heard what?"

"Well, it's a sad story, kiddo, and not one I want you to go repeating. You see, his wife fell in love with me. Hell, I don't know how it happened. God knows I was innocent. But Piggott blames me for her leaving."

"If I was married to Piggott," I said, "I'd probably fall in love with you too."

We picked a few more handfuls. I said, "Money must be the number one temptation in the world."

"Oh it is. It is. Harder to give up money than anything. For some people, giving up their money would be like giving up their identity. A man can't have his silver golf clubs and his wife can't have her mink stole. And the reason the Second Coming still hasn't happened is that man hasn't figured out how to share. There is enough in the world and to spare for all God's children, but rich guys hoard it and think they're saints when they give a few pennies to an art gallery. Hell, kid, it's pathetic. If the pioneers had lived the Law of Consecration, maybe no Jews would have died in Germany. If the pioneers had really done what God told them to do, they could have made Zion. Makes you think, doesn't it. Me, I've thought a lot. A LOT. God says this generation is cursed because we haven't remembered the teachings of the Book of Mormon—and what are those teachings?"

I had on my mind the story of Nephi and Laban from the Book of Mormon. I knew that wasn't what Johnny was talking about. Nephi chopped off Laban's head to get the history of his ancestors and the words of the prophets. God told him it was "better for one man to die than a whole nation to dwindle and perish in unbelief." What I said was, "Jesus is real."

Johnny smiled reverently. "Yes, kiddo, he is. Oh I know that like hot coals on my tongue. Jesus is real, and when he came here, he set up the Law of Consecration, where there was to be no rich and no poor, where everyone was to have all their material possessions in common."

I knew he was referring to the visit of Jesus to the Americas, but it sounded like he was saying Jesus had come right there to Zarahemla.

"That," he continued, "is the teaching of the Book of Mormon, and we're cursed for forgetting it. It's the Law of Consecration. And when someone finally remembers, why all hell breaks loose. Satan is right there, because he'd be bound if he couldn't buy off popes and priests and district presidents. Julie, you've seen it yourself. The jealousy. The—hell, I don't know—the sin! Don't go repeating this, but I won't be surprised when I die if I discover it was God himself planted love for me in Sarah's heart."

"Sarah?"

"Piggy's ex-wife. Oh, a beautiful girl. She deserved better than that. Much better." Johnny made a knapsack of the handkerchief and strung it through his belt loop. He took my elbow again and helped me up.

I said, "Piggott's maids gave us all sorts of fancy food, Johnny. I told them I wanted tortillas."

"Did you, kiddo?" He said the words with such gentle pride that I felt adored. Then abruptly his eyes took on a sort of holy terror. He took my other elbow, holding my arms like he could hoist me to heaven, watching me as if reading my thoughts, interviewing my soul. He said, "In the name of the Lord, I tell you God has a mission for you to accomplish in this part of his vineyard. There is work for you to do here, Julie."

I gazed into Johnny's blue eyes.

"Do you know that?" he said.

"Yes," I murmured.

"Say it then. Say, 'I know there is a mission for me here.'"

"I know—" My eyes teared. "My mission is here."

"Oh Julie, Julie," he said, embracing me quickly, then wiping my tears with his thumb. "if I could tell you the wonders God has revealed to me about this place! Why do you think I've called it Zarahemla?"

"It's a good name."

"It's more than that, kiddo. And you'll know someday. God wants you to know when the time's right."

"Does he?"

"Oh yes. I tell you, kiddo, your eyes are going to behold God's glory. You've seen Salto Blanco. You've seen Izalco, and Belen, and you've seen my place here. The fingerprints and toeprints of God are everywhere around you. You know that too, don't you."

I nodded.

"And when the time comes for God to reveal himself to you, you won't fight him. You won't say that riches are better than Jesus."

"No, I won't," I promised.

He squeezed me to him. "You'll be a wife again, Julie. That's a prophecy. God will call you to that again, and you'll do whatever God asks. You will feel such love—oh if you could only feel the love I have for Luisa, you would understand some of God's plan. I love her—" His voice broke. He let me go and pressed his eyelids, first with his fingers, then with his fists. Tears came down his cheeks and beard. "Oh Julie, I love her like my own blood." He sat down in the spinach patch, grief-weighted.

I knelt beside him, took both his hands in mine and stroked his thumbs. "You're worried about her, aren't you."

"Worried! You can't know, kid. You can't." He wiped his eyes and started to speak twice, but couldn't. He held his knees, buried his face in them. His body trembled with silent sobs. Finally he managed, "When I met her, I knew she would be my wife, and I knew she was an angel. She was the most beautiful girl I had ever seen. My Luisa! I baptized her, and she told me that when she looked up at me from under the water, she saw a halo around my face. It was God, Julie. God telling her I was her husband." He took two deep breaths and spoke more softly. "And she promised to give up anything God asked her to give up. She knew that if she failed, his judgment—" He broke off again. "We've been together twenty-three years, Julie," he said. "There's nothing about her I don't know. Nothing about her I don't love. Twenty-three years! Dear God!" He looked heavenward. "I want more time!"

"Johnny," I said, still stroking his thumbs. "Johnny, you don't know what's going to happen."

"Oh but Julie, I do," he said, returning his eyes to me. "I gave her a priesthood blessing, and I knew. Luisa is dying. Lord help her, it was her choice. She brought it on herself." Again he cried. There was not a thing I could do or say.

He wiped his face with his sleeve, apologized for being such a goon, picked a leaf of spinach and ate it. "I love spinach," he said emotionally, signalling that the subject had just changed. "Popeye was right, you know. Milk and spinach make muscles of steel."

I asked him who had been milking the cows, since I had been away and Alberto was in Izalco. He said, rising, slapping the dirt from his knees, "You know, it's a miracle how things get done. The people around here, they know when something needs doing, and they just appear and do it. It's either them or angels—and it could be angels, I wouldn't balk. But the cows do get milked. This morning there was a full bucket on the doorstep."

I didn't take a chance on angels. I milked the cows myself at dusk. I had missed the old bimbos. I think they had missed me too. They gave long mooos when I approached them, that sounded like affectionate sighs.

After milking, I helped Mom bedbathe Luisa, then went outside, walked around the lake, sang Alberto's songs, and thought what Johnny had said about Luisa dying. I said, "Father in Heaven," and looked into the night. "Don't let her die, God. Please, God. Please, if you're there."

Seventeen

There were nightmares for me that night, and the next one. The mangoes had faces again—not Manuel's this time, but Jason's. The faces were in anguish, screaming in hellish cacophony, using my voice. And somewhere, my seminary teacher was laughing.

I told no one about my nightmares. I didn't want to give Dad a reason to abandon our mission; I didn't want to be sent home over bad dreams. But I was grumpy from the sleepless night, drugged with unfocused fear and trembling. Mom accused me of having "the grumps."

She was right. I knew she was right. Later that day we had the argument which had been building up for years. So Johnny was right too: the spirit of contention had hitchhiked to Zarahemla with my parents.

In retrospect, I can see just how the fight happened. Mom, with her smile, her happy oblivion, tells me I have the grumps. I look at her orange lips, hear her jokes, all her wonderful lines and inspirational proddings ("You can make a miracle, Digs . . ."); I see her being everything I have ever wanted to be and am not. She sings to her orphans—she was ecstatic to see them when we arrived, more ecstatic than she had been to see me in San Salvador. I see her singing them a song that used to be mine:

> My baby should open his mouthie;
> My baby should open up wide.
> My baby should open his mouthie,
> So I can put spinach inside.

When I was the baby, it was oatmeal I had to open wide for.

So I am still a baby. I want attention. I complain to her about the brightness of her lipstick. She accuses me of grumpiness, cheerfully points out my incompetence. Then we go in to help Luisa.

Mom's entrance line as we enter the bedroom is: "Come come ye saints; no toilet paper fear." It's one I've heard before. It strikes me that I've heard most of her entrance lines before. She's getting old and redundant.

Luisa's eyes flutter open. She tries to make her mouth turn up. It merely trembles. But she's looking better than she was. When Mom is with her, Mom gets soft and Luisa gets strong. They have some kind of female empathy—symbiotic love—that I don't share.

"How are you feeling?" I say.

Luisa moves one shoulder.

Mom announces, "She's doing great. Another few weeks and voila!" She gives Luisa a kiss on her forehead. She says, "Isn't that right, Cookie?"

Luisa hisses, "*Si*."

"You've turned into a lifeboat, Cookie. That little papoose is floating around inside you like a turtle in a life-preserver. Everything's just perfect. You're doing great. Both of you are. So, should we rub you down?"

She nods. Mom gets the olive oil from the bathroom cabinet, lifts Luisa's nightdress and garments, and begins spreading the goop. I join in. The baby kicks at my hand as I oil its womb.

Mom hums the Primary song "Mother I Love You" as we work. Every so often she talks to the baby. She calls it "Boinky." She says, "How're you doing in there, Boinky? Doing all right? We're sure eager to see you, you little bumble tumble. I'm your Aunt Em. Your mom's the one you keep awake at night. It's her skin you're under, Boinky."

Luisa smiles, saved by this stupid humor, this orange-mouthed goddess.

"You're doing great," Mom repeats again and again and again. It's the second biggest lie she's told. When we finally leave, after seven songs and about twenty "you're doing greats," I tell her so. I say, "God could toss you pretty far for that one."

Mom, glancing at Luisa's door (yes, it's securely closed), motions me to follow her outside. She says, "What is this about?"

"'You're doing great,'" I mimic. "What a lie!"

"Digs, that's not only tacky, it's faithless. Where's your faith?"

"I gave it to Jason."

"Honey—"

"Why can't you look things in the eye?"

We are surrounded by gardenias. The rain starts its slow drizzle.

"Stop ranting, Digs. Just talk to me."

"Your whole life!" I say. "Santa Claus I could handle. That's a cultural lie. But Jason—"

"Honey, are you sick?"

I probably am. I know that. I am probably ready to have a nervous breakdown and see mango faces in my soup. But I say I am perfectly healthy. I say, "Do you remember what you told me?"

"When?"

"When I was trying to decide if I should marry that S.O.B. You said 'Women can work miracles.'"

"Honey, you're not making sense."

"'Women can work miracles.' That's a whole different can of Christmas candy. That's a piranha in my stocking. Mother, I wouldn't have married him if you hadn't said that. You told me to do it."

"I never told you to marry Jason—Digs, I thought he was the mayor of jerk city! I never told you to marry him."

"The heck you didn't. I asked you about it and you said 'Women can work miracles.' As good as a push. It was a challenge, for crying out loud. A Christian, feminist challenge!"

"What?"

"If I was a real woman and a true Mormon, I could make him change. Love him out of his anger. Be Mrs. Miracle. And now you're telling Luisa—who is sicker than a dog—that she's 'doing great.'"

"Digs," she says. "Aren't you sleeping well?"

Bingo. I say, "If I weren't sleeping well, then all this could be blamed on insomnia and cured with valium, couldn't it. Sorry Mom," I lie, "I sleep fine. I just want you to look tragedy in the eye. It's not fair you shouldn't have to."

The drizzle splatters my cheeks. Mom thinks I am crying. She wipes the rain with her hand.

"Let's go back inside," she says. The lake is boiling with rain now. Our hair is stringing. "But don't say anything about Luisa that she'd hear. Come on. This is no place for a talk."

A sheet of lightning whitens the sky. The rain bursts out of its clouds. Mom's orphans, who have been playing dolls in a cabbage patch (no kidding), run for the cabin door and get there at the same time we do. Mom says to them, "Gotcha!" They wail out gusts of laughter. I wait by the door, watching the children settle themselves under the table with their baby dolls. Mom puts her arm around my neck and pulls me in. We sit down. One of the orphans takes off my shoes and tickles my feet. I peek under the table. They run their fingernails across my arches. They tickle Mom's too. She gives them a monster roar.

"Don't let them inhibit you, honey," Mom says. "They won't understand us." She mouths "but she will" and points to Luisa's door. "Okay, Digs. Talk."

"It's your turn," I say.

"My turn?" She ducks her head under the table and roars. The gesture has the feel of someone throwing up. "My turn," she repeats, sitting up again as serenely as if there had been no interruption—as if she hadn't metamorphosed for the babies. "My turn. I'm not used to this. I figured we ought to talk sometime—I knew we'd have to. But—what do I say? Digs, I'm not a grim person. But I'm not naive either."

"No?"

"No. I've looked tragedy in the eye, Digs. I lost my mother, if you remember."

"It's not the same thing. It's not tragic when someone dies of cancer. It's sad and awful and reason for a week-long cry, but it's not like having your insides torn out by someone you love."

"You feel like I'm tearing out your insides?"

"No, Mom. Not you. But you put me in the situation. You encouraged me. I was falling in love or in crush or whatever it was, and you were right there, my model of womanhood and all that crap. You could have saved me but you didn't. What you did was yell 'Hey I've never told you this, but you're really a bird. You can fly!' You lied. I can't."

One of the orphans tickles my foot. I move it. Mom makes a quick peek-a-boo with the tablecloth. Again she talks as if nothing just happened. "You sound so bitter. Are you getting a period maybe?"

"No."

"Digs, one sentence from your mother shouldn't ruin your life."

"I worshipped you. If you had told me to marry Mohamar Qaddafi and save the world, I would have tried."

"No you wouldn't have."

"I might have. I took you seriously."

She shakes her head, amazed. "Imagine that," she sighs.

"I adored you. Whatever you said."

"Digs, Digs, you're blaming me for that? Blaming me for the divorce?" She still has to take a breath before she can say the word.

"Do you really believe in miracles?" I say.

"Yes. Of course I do."

"Did you plan on making a miracle with Dad?"

"At the time, I didn't know a miracle would be called for. But yes, eventually I did plan on it."

"So did it work?"

"Well, we love each other. That's a miracle isn't it?"

"Not really. Not a big one."

"Oh but it is. And Johnny and Luisa . . ." She leans across the table and whispers, "They love each other too, and look what they've done. Look around you, hon! We're right in the middle of Miracle County. Zarahemla! Isn't it a miracle? Don't you agree with that?" She roars at her children again and looks at me expectantly.

"Luisa is a skeleton," I whisper. "Where's the miracle?"

"Look at her stomach."

"Flies reproduce."

"Flies have flies. Human beings—look under the table, Digs. There is nothing more miraculous, nothing more beautiful or more perfect than a human child. Come on, don't be a grouch. Give the kids a good time. Play with them."

I lift the table cloth. The orphans are both grinning at me. Fat brown cheeks and chocolate eyes all twinkly. I peek-a-boo them twice, perfunctorily. They peal out measures of bouncing joy in return. My tears start rising.

"Don't you agree?" Mom says. She touches my fingers with hers.

"Do you know how much I wanted to get married?" I say, looking her square in the eyes.

"If you want to know the truth," she says, "I was afraid you didn't want to get married at all. I was afraid you'd be an old maid. Not because you're unpretty; I think you're beautiful, Digs."

"I'm a dog," I say. "A skinny dog."

"You're beautiful. I always thought so. Your looks weren't what scared me. What scared me was your hardness. My hay-ell, do you remember how you used to be? So gosh-damn intimidating. You loved to take some vulnerable, no-date kid and twist his heart up. I wanted you to quit that and settle down. If I did encourage you—if I did, that was why. A woman's greatest potential is realized in wifehood."

"That sounds like something a man would say."

"I said it." She roars under the table again. The children shriek.

"It's not true, Mom. Or maybe it's true for everyone else. It's not true for me. My intestines are a wreck. That's not beautiful. I was not good at being married."

"Oh, well I guess I was never much good at that either," she says. "Well you know that. I was a slob and I didn't have you looking nearly as cute as you should have."

"It's okay. I'm not blaming you for that."

"I guess I should keep a list of which things you're blaming me for and which you aren't." She gives another roar to the orphans.

I say, "You're a good lady, Mom."

My feet are getting tickled. I acknowledge that fact with a quick peek.

"You're a good lady too, Digs. A peach of a kid." She punches my shoulder.

"Do you think she'll live through this?" I motion to the door.

"I pray."

"Do you?"

"Oh yes, Digs. And I have had some very good feelings."

"Revelation?"

"Oh, I'm not into revelation much; I'll leave that to Johnny. I've just felt good about Luisa."

"Did you have 'good feelings' about my marriage? Did you think I could make it work?"

She hesitates. "No," she admits uncomfortably. "But I thought if you were going to try, you'd better believe in the chance. I'm sorry."

"I hope the colitis doesn't kill me."

"It won't," she says, and roars again.

Then I start crying. I tell her, beg her, to go back to Belen. To take Dad and go back. This place, I say, is the ship, and you and Dad are Jonah. Go back now, today, so that the fighting will stop. More fighting, I tell her, will kill me.

She is certain my period will start tomorrow.

"But will you go?" I say.

"I'll talk to your father."

Two days later, they left. Dad was disgruntled and Mom half-frantic as they got into the van.

"We'll be back," she shouted. "We'll be here for the birth, Cookie! Guaranteed!" The fifth time she had made that promise since breakfast. "I love you guys!" she yelled to her orphans, who were jumping up and down, flinging themselves up to see their reflections in Doodle Dan's windows.

Luisa and I stood with our arms around each other, watching my parents set off for Belen. Johnny stood in front of us, a witness to their certain departure.

"My strength is going," said Luisa. "My strength is going." Each word was softer than the one before. When Doodle Dan was out of sight, Luisa collapsed. Johnny carried her back to bed, folded her up in his arms, kissing her hair and eyes. "Rest, *mi amor*," he said. Stroking her eyebrows. "*Duermate*. Obey me."

She closed her eyes.

Eighteen

Alberto returned a week later. I went to milk the cows in the morning, and he was there as if he had never gone away. He said, "You are Ophelia."

I said, "This comes as a shock. Welcome home."

"Do you like the name?"

"Ophelia went loony and drowned herself, if I recall."

"Just the name, not the history. Do you like it?"

I said it was okay.

"I will call you that now. I like Shakespeare's names."

I rolled my eyes and told him I had become free since our last meeting; the divorce was final. He said he was aware of that. "I would not have given you a new name," he said, "if you belonged to someone else."

"I'm free," I repeated. He took the hint, kissed my forehead and mouth. He said, "Congratulations."

"You've been to Izalco."

"Yes, Ophelia. Is there a nickname we could use? It doesn't lend itself well, does it. 'Ophy' sounds monstrous. Like an oaf."

"I think I'll just keep my old name," I said.

"No, you will be Ophelia now. To answer your question: Yes, I went to Izalco. Cordelia sends her greetings. She wanted to know—I promised to deliver the message—she wanted to know if you have heard from the cast of that melodrama."

I had sent Cordelia's letter to the cast of "Dynasty" a couple of weeks ago. I told Alberto I didn't know if TV stars really answer their mail. "We'll just have to wait and see," I said.

"As with everything. But you have news for me, yes? You went to San Salvador."

I told him about my visit. I spent two minutes denigrating the fat man and his mansion. I said Luisa insisted Piggott was a good guy, but that Luisa was too sick to think now, and that I was more worried about her than about our tape.

"I am worried about her too," he said. "She raised me, you know. My natural mother gave me up—"

"Yes, I've heard," I said. "You were an orphan."

"No, not an orphan," he said. "My mother is still alive, you know."

I didn't know that. The story we had gotten from Johnny— unless my memory was wretched—was that Alberto's mother had died shortly after begging him to raise her newborn son.

"Of course you know that," he said. "Marta Otsoy is my mother."

Marta. The lady who knelt for Johnny like he was an icon. The one who had clapped behind the van for a couple of miles after the concert of rededication. Marta the "great convert."

"It's news to me," I said. "Why wouldn't Johnny tell us that?"

"There were reasons. We don't need to discuss them. Suffice it to say, Luisa has raised me. It was she who gave me Shakespeare. Yes. I used to be her focus and joy."

"Used to be?"

"You know so little, Ophelia. Your eyes and ears are virgin. You're like Eve before her eyes were opened."

Alberto's eyes weren't fully opened themselves. They were distant, dreamy, a little insane.

"You're losing me," I said. "What about Luisa?"

"Luisa. I was saying that I used to be her joy. Manuelito was as well. We were her sons. She called us her twins, though we were actually a year apart. She lived for us. She hates me now."

"Luisa doesn't hate anyone."

"Ophelia. Virgin. You have used the olive oil on your face, no? Your cheeks are smooth. Like velvet your skin."

"No, I didn't ever get the oil. Oil gives me zits."

"But your face is very good now."

"Is it? I'm not nervous, that's all."

"A beautiful face."

I waited for the kiss. It didn't come.

"It is a lone and dreary world, *mi amor*," he said, stroking my jawbone. "Full of outrageous fortune. A sea of troubles."

"You're mixing metaphors," I said.

"Do you think you love me?" His voice was soft, low, sexy, macho. I had to resist it consciously.

"I think it's early for that," I said. "I'm barely divorced, Alberto. It might take some time for me to believe in love again."

It was a lie. I had never stopped believing in love. I was infatuated with the whole concept. Love was an ineffable truth, something floral and undying that fertile couples came upon during long walks. I thought I smelled it with Alberto, but it would come and go uncontrollably and unpredictably. I wanted to love him. I imagined I did, sometimes, but it wasn't permanent.

"You will love me," he said. "John said you will."

"Oh did he?"

"His prophecies come true. I have seen them come true. He is a man of God."

"He said I'd fall in love with you?"

"You were not informed?"

"Informed?"

"You have a mission here, John said. He has not told you?"

"That much he said."

"I like your eyes. Are they blue?" We were standing in front of the cow. It moved its nose between us and gave a soft snort. Alberto patted it and then took my hands, drew his face very close to mine, looking deep into my eyes, as though he were myopic.

"Hazel," I said. "They look blue when I wear blue."

"I enjoy blue. Why don't you wear blue?"

"I wear it sometimes."

He brushed my nose with his and drew himself back.

There were two buckets of milk. Alberto took one and gave me the other. We started our walk. I headed towards the cabin; he told me we would take the milk to the processing hut today. The workers who normally did this chore were busy with some government jobs. So we walked over a couple of hills, through a grove of avocado trees, and past two cornfields.

Alberto said, "I have two mothers and two fathers. And one of my fathers is a ghost." He laughed. I thought he was going to sing. I thought this was the preamble to a folksong. But there was no forthcoming melody.

"Alberto?" I said.

"I am trying to tell you things," he said. "Listen."

"I'm listening."

"Yes, Luisa is sick. She will die."

Again, it was like a song. "She'll be comin' 'round the mountain" or "Go tell Aunt Rhodie . . ." But no chorus.

"Luisa?" I said.

"Yes, she will die. Then there will be another ghost to haunt me." He chuckled grimly. "Does the sky make your eyes blue?"

"I've never checked," I said.

"Let me see. Yes. Yes, it does. Your eyes, with the sky behind them, they are like John's eyes."

"Are they?"

"His are the most beautiful eyes in El Salvador. Old women tease him. They say, 'Give me your eyes.' He teases them back."

"What does he say?"

"Never mind. Are you afraid of ghosts?"

"Alberto—"

"Are you?" It amazed me how he could speak and move with such energy, and yet not spill the milk.

"You have me confused," I said.

He smiled his sweet, disarming, mischievous smile, still moving gracefully forward. He was feline, like a jaguar, the god of the ruins. "Sometimes I am a child, Ophelia, and I don't want to become a man. I have had to take sides; I had no choice in that. I obeyed the one I loved best. I couldn't see how far the choice would extend."

I braked my steps, came to a full stop, sloshed milk everywhere. "Alberto. Whoa. You know, Piggott thinks you're involved in some political stuff—thinks maybe you're a *guerrillero*. That isn't—you're not, are you?"

He was seven steps in front of me. He stopped, but didn't turn. He said into the air, "No."

"Did you have anything to do with what happened to Manuelito?"

"What would I have to do with that?" he said, turning just his head.

"Am I in danger?"

"No. I think I can love you. Especially when the sky is in your eyes."

"Have you talked to Johnny?"

He laughed. "John knows everything. John knows. Come on, Ophelia. There is more to do than talk."

"Has he given you advice?"

"Constantly."

"Do what he tells you."

"Come. Feet in motion. Is the milk too heavy?"

"It's fine," I said.

He waited until I had caught up with him. "You know, I think you love John," he said. "I think you love him almost as much as I do."

My answer was that Luisa should have her baby in a hospital.

"Do you know what they call the hospitals here? 'Angel factories.' If Luisa were to go to the hospital, John would lose them both—the child and her. Things are as they are. Luisa should prepare herself to cross the veil. It is that simple."

The processing hut was a cinderblock box. Inside was an eye-biting fire under an aluminum vat. A rectangle of bright pink cloth hung like a flag between this main room and the rest of the house. Children were jabbering somewhere behind the flag; a baby was crying.

A short woman in a big black dress came from behind the curtain, smiling. She had a horse's mouth, oversized gums and oversized teeth. She took the milk and poured it into the vat. It would be boiled there and sent off to the next hut, to be packaged. Alberto talked to the horse-mouthed woman for a moment, saying Luisa's name four times in the conversation. He wouldn't translate for me after we left.

All the things I saw and heard in this place—only about a half mile from Zarahemla, but still strange and distant—were new to me. They were the sights and sounds of survival. The milk being poured into aluminum; the squawking of a chicken somewhere nearby, and the blunt pop of an axe in its neck; the screech of a rabbit being flayed (this I saw—a man stood on his porch across the path from us and stripped the fur from the creature); the grunts of a hog on death row eating corncobs. This was a hot and bloody day. It was lunchtime, and there was nothing pristine about the way butchers did their work. Cows were undone with a bullet in the brain, Alberto told me, and chickens got their necks wrung or split open as their purchase price was handed over. All of this was part of the day-to-day world without refrigerators or supermarkets. You didn't buy meat in saran wrap here.

I hadn't eaten in hours, and the smell of animal blood was pungent. I must have paled a little before I stumbled. I landed on my knees in soft, putrid mud.

"Ophelia," Alberto said, offering his hand.

I said, "You're such a sweetheart sometimes and sometimes such a jerk. Maybe it's just you're a man."

"I am sullied flesh," he said.

I looked at myself. Sullied flesh. I was wearing white bermuda shorts which now had black hems. My knees were dripping mud. I did not want to touch them. I knelt again in some long grass and scooted around in a circle until the mud was replaced by green. "By the way," I said, standing, "I'm not giving up on Luisa. I love her too much to give up."

"And you think I don't love her?"

"I don't know what you feel about anything."

"Luisa nursed me," he said, as we started back to the cabin. "Yes. Actually nursed me. She had delivered a child—dead—a few days before I was given to her. She fed me that child's milk from her breast. She was the one I looked to when I was troubled or bored. She was my teacher and my best friend. Until two years ago, she was my greatest provider."

"What happened two years ago?"

He shrugged. "That was when we had to choose. All of us. Manuelito, Luisa, and I. Manuelito went with her. I did not. She thinks I am responsible. You hit one domino and they all fall. But I love her, Ophelia, more than you can guess. I know her. I know the anguish. She has suffered. More than a woman should suffer. And so quietly. If you only knew."

We walked. He took my hand. He said, "What is my duty?" Smiling at me again. That big, ingenuous, secretive smile. "Tell me, Ophelia, what is my duty? Which father do I obey?"

"These abstractions are really hard to follow," I told him.

He turned me to him, gripped both my shoulders in his hands. I felt like I was in a Clint Eastwood movie, about to be raped or shaken. "Then listen," he said. "And tell me honestly. Do you believe in Johnny?"

"Yes," I said.

"He is like God," Alberto said. "Is he like God for you?"

"A little."

"Would you for the world destroy him?" he said.

"No."

"You would never do anything to destroy him or undo his followers?"

"No." I was more aware of his parsley breath and his closeness than I was of his words.

"Even if it might save Luisa?"

I felt his fingernails.

"Save Luisa," I repeated.

"I can save her. I can save her if I do one thing."

"What? What do you mean—one thing? What are you talking about?"

"I can save her."

"How?"

"The how is not your concern. Not your choice, but mine."

"If you can save her, then do it," I said, removing his hands from my shoulders. "And quit talking like you're stoned."

"I'm sorry. I have hurt you."

"You're difficult, Alberto," I said. "Very difficult. Just do what you ought to," I said. "To thine own self—"

"Polonius," he interrupted, "was a buffoon and a wicked man."

"It's still good counsel."

"Can the wicked speak good and the good speak evil?"

"Oh sure they can, Alberto," I said. "There wouldn't be any hope otherwise."

He put his arms around me, and I did not resist. "I would lose you," he said.

I didn't answer. I thought he was being presumptuous. But I returned his kiss.

Nineteen

Rainy season was at its most furious at that time, but waned a few weeks later. Storms came sporadically then. The sky turned merely moody. I had been in El Salvador nearly six months.

One afternoon when I was writing letters by the lake, Johnny announced to me that my "time had come."

The kind of line Indian maidens heard before they were tossed to the gods.

"I am about to let you in on the biggest secret you will ever hear or see, kiddo. You've earned it. Now swear to me. Are you ready to keep it on pain of death?"

I said I'd do my dangdest to keep his secret.

"Follow me," he said.

We walked around the plantation—in circles, it felt like, for nearly an hour. Eventually we went through the jungle behind the cabin. The branches were blunt cut, like a machete had hacked through them yesterday. Johnny walked ahead of me, waving his arms every few seconds "to keep snakes away," he said. He'd glance back where I was following. The grey hairs in his beard would shimmer.

It was dusk when he stopped. We were in a clearing like a baseball field gone to seed, surrounded by little mountains.

"Swear to me you'll keep it," Johnny said.

"I'll keep it, Johnny."

"Say 'by God I'll keep it.'"

I said it.

"It's serious crap, kiddo. Men have died over what I'm about to show you. But God, he's whispered in that still small voice of his, told me you're ready for your next step." Johnny went forward, then turned back like an afterthought. He said, "You're staying in Zarahemla, you know. You won't be going back with your folks."

I didn't answer for a moment. Then I said, "Yeah, I know that."

"You feel all right about it?"

"I think I will."

"Oh kiddo, you'll feel better than all right. This place will burn inside you. This place will brand itself into your soul. You'll feel you belong here like you've never felt anything in your life. That's a promise."

I said that sounded encouraging.

"Take my word. Now, kiddo, why do you think I named this place 'Zarahemla'?"

"You've asked me that before. I still don't know."

"Guess."

"It's a good name. I don't know. It has scriptural meaning. It's sort of the Promised Land in the Book of Mormon."

"Sure. But why not name it 'Bountiful' or 'Cumorah'?"

"I don't know, Johnny. Why not?"

"Do you want to know, kiddo? I mean do you really want to?"

I nodded.

"I called it Zarahemla because that's what it is. Now you look." He pointed to one of the mountains directly before us. I understood. We were on the site of a ruin. These were mounds. Ancient buildings—maybe pre-classic, if Johnny was right—that the centuries had buried and the jungle had claimed. Humps of dirt and untamed, leafy shadows. There were maybe thirty of them.

"What makes you think it was Zarahemla?"

"The Holy Ghost. I'm not fooling. Just stand here, kiddo, and listen. The Holy Ghost rides the wind around here. I figure this place is some sort of playground for kids who died before they were old enough to be baptized. For them and a few well-behaved angels. Just you be still now for a second, and feel God coming around you. I walk here and sometimes I feel like Jesus is right behind me, standing on a gold plate in the air, and I can't look because it's holy ground I'm walking on, and here I am wearing shoes, so I just bow my head and I say his name: 'Jesus. Jesus.'"

I did feel we were being watched, either by God or by some big cats. The wind made a low moan.

Johnny said, "You can imagine King Benjamin on top of whatever's under that hill over there. You can picture Alma and Mosiah and Moroni traipsing over the grounds, praying around, dedicating the place and just waiting for us to figure things out and pay them a visit. Do you feel it?"

I did. There was a holy hush on everything. The breezes were sweet and careful, like they were guided by God, like they were the breath of the ages, the gentle cyclone of the eternal round, keeping things moving and alive, preserving the sanctity of the past.

"I feel it," I said.

Johnny bowed his head. "Can you imagine what might have happened if it was some gold-hungry jerkster or a big shot grave digger discovered the place? Zarahemla would be turned into a— a museum, for hellsake. With motels and a little airport and maybe a whorehouse—all the ruins have whorehouses. Zarahemla—where Jesus came. It would be blasphemy. Sheer, horn-rimmed blasphemy. I tell you by the priesthood, God was guiding me all along—thank you, Father. You know how that works, kiddo? You feel like you're on a Wild Mouse ride and you're headed into a jungle that nobody's ever escaped from and your life is out of control and then—poof—the ride's over and you're exactly where you were supposed to be. It's been God at the helm all along. Makes a person want to shout hosanna and kneel down."

He didn't kneel, but looked at me significantly. "When things got bad, back in seventy-nine, this is where we hid. We brought corn and beans, dug a well—that's it over there, if you look hard—and we lived here for a couple of months or more."

I said, "How many people know about this place?"

"One or two of us have started digging. Found a bunch of precious things. If you want to know the whole story, and I guess you have a right to, Manuelito took some of the gold. For that he died. Not that I had anything to do with it. I couldn't take a man's life unless God told me to."

"I know you couldn't, Johnny."

"Mani had good intentions. He wanted to pay for—you know—guns and bullets for the underground. But the gold isn't for that. This gold isn't. This is God's gold. You see, kiddo, Zarahemla is for better things than politics. You know that like I do, isn't that right. That's why God had to take the boy. Oh, and he was a good boy, too. Don't know when I've grieved more. Even when you know something has to be, you grieve. If you didn't grieve, it would be because you didn't care. The more spirit a person has, the more he cares. You think God didn't care when Jesus was killed? You think he just turned his back? Oh, he cared. When Jesus said, 'My God, my God, why hast thou forsaken me?' it wasn't that God was in some other corner of the universe. I'm telling you by the power of the priesthood, God was right there watching and aching in every bodily part of his. Do you believe that?"

"Yes."

"It's true. You should believe it. You should believe everything that's true and nothing that isn't. So what do you think of the place?"

"It looks like an important center."

"Only a very few people have seen it. God considers you worthy. Now that's a huge compliment from the Almighty. He has a great work for you to do here, if you'll follow his counsel. And you'll do that, won't you."

"You know the answer to that," I said.

"You bet I do. Come on. Let me show you around."

I followed. Johnny took me to each hill, telling me just what he was sure had happened there anciently. I half-listened. I was thinking of Manuelito.

As far as I had been taught in Sunday School, God didn't string people up on trees. He sent an occasional she-bear after insolent kids who called a prophet "Baldy," but the God I had been taught about said things like "Blessed are the meek" and "Love one another."

Johnny was expounding on King Benjamin's speech. I said, "Wasn't it *Orden*, then, that killed Manuelito?"

"What?"

"Didn't *Orden* do it?"

"Oh. Yes. Probably. I told you Mani was political. Everybody knew that. I don't guess we'll ever know for sure who tied the rope. It doesn't matter now anyway."

"You think God inspired whoever it was?"

"Aw, you bet He did. God is jealous of this place, let me tell you. I know that beyond the shadow of a doubt. This place is sacred. You can tell that, can't you."

"Yes, I can tell that," I murmured.

Johnny recited the history of the site, as he imagined it. I touched some gold coins he showed me. I told him, yes, they probably were pre-classic (not that I knew; but I had my degree and sounded authoritative). I looked at him, saw his beaming cheeks and full grin above his beard. I thought, one thing about Johnny: he doesn't let death ruin his plans. That was healthy. If Jason had been able to take his father's death in stride, things might have been different for us. If Jason had already faced up to death, kissed a corpse or read Edgar Allan Poe, he wouldn't have been so angry or so protective. He could have loved me for a longer time, accepted my love, felt some grace.

I thought about Jason as we walked back through the hacked off branches. I thought of the time we visited the crash site. There was scrap metal still interspersed with pebbles and boulders, and Jason found a strip of rubber. He held it up. It was dirty, half-melted, dried. I thought at first it was some decomposed flesh or a small, dehydrated snake. Jason said, "Look." I stood there holding his hand, gazing at the thing he dangled. "Look." He undid my grasp and held the rubber with both hands, cradled it like it was something alive. "It's part of my dad's shoe," he said.

I said, "He must have been so scared when he realized."

"He didn't think he'd die," Jason said, certainly, defiantly. "He was trying to get control. He didn't see the telephone pole. Do you think he wanted to die without leaving insurance?"

"It was instant, wasn't it?"

"No," he said. "He burned."

I held him.

He put the rubber in his shirt pocket. We straddled his motorcycle. As I put my arms around his waist he held them there. He turned to me, his face profiled against the two-toned telephone pole, and said, "I love you."

"I love you too."

He kicked the gas pedal. Dust sprayed out from the rear wheel. Jason's hair blew back from his head. I watched it, wheat-colored and wild. I could tell he was smiling though I couldn't see his face. "I love you," he yelled into the moving air.

"I love you," I answered as close to his ear as I could get. We were riding the wind. I felt my hair behind me like a whipped flag.

He told me later of his recurring dream. In the dream, Jason is waiting for the crash, standing at the site with a firehose. When it happens—and he sees the crash in his dream, vivid and terrible, the plane monstrous, twice as huge as it really was, malevolent—he puts the fire out. The telephone pole—also gigantic—cracks; the plane ignites into a bud of flame, and Jason aims the hose and douses not just the fire but the whole Cesna. The water is a geyser. He has to hold it with all his might or it will escape. Then his dad comes out, drenched, and grabs him, holds him tight, says, "You saved my life, son." The hose goes wild, baptizing everything, and Jason wakes up.

"They lived the Law of Consecration," Johnny was saying. "Jesus set it up himself. All things in common. We're not worthy to live it now. We're rich sons'a bitches."

"I guess that's true," I said.

"And plural marriage, that's been taken back too. Now you think of plural marriage, kiddo. Think about it. You know how I love Luisa, you sense that, don't you?"

I nodded.

"With every wife, that love is multiplied—or would be if we were worthy to live it. It's like having children. Every baby brings more love, don't you think? I know with every orphan that's been given to us, our love has bloomed like a summer rose. It was supposed to be the same with plural marriage. Plural marriage is eternal. New and everlasting covenant. You know what I'm talking about, don't you."

"Sure."

"But people were too selfish to live the law, so God took it away, though he might reveal it now and again to his elect, who knows?"

We were in the middle of the jungle. I looked back at the ruins. What I saw were black leaves and blunted twigs. I wondered if the builders' ghosts could see their undone buildings. I wondered what they would think if they could. Maybe it wouldn't matter to them that everything was rotting away, that nature was digesting their remains, that time had eroded their stairs and bedrooms. Maybe it wouldn't matter that their promised land, their mid-jungle miracle, had turned out to be as ephemeral as the rest of mortality. Maybe it wouldn't matter that even though Jesus had walked there, redemption hadn't lasted.

I looked, squinted to find the mounds through the wild growth. Johnny was talking about the Law of Consecration. I was groping with my eyes, thinking, "Where is the meaning?" and "What will become of me?"

In the distance, a jaguar or some other exotic feline roared. I had never heard a sound so piercing and bold and untamed. It seemed to vibrate under our feet. The leaves and branches shuddered as though the cat were underground and the roar had tunneled up their roots.

"It's okay," Johnny said—to me or to the cat, I was not sure. "Don't be afraid."

I wasn't. I was never afraid with Johnny.

Twenty

"You've seen it, haven't you?" I spoke to Alberto between purple udders the next morning.

He nodded solemnly. "John took you there, yes?"

"Yes."

Neither of us made any brash statements or confessions. We communicated by inference. The ruin of Zarahemla was a secret we had to keep or be damned.

"So what do you think?" he said.

"I don't know."

We filled two buckets and then brushed the cows' hides with the same kinds of burrs Primitivo used on his blankets. The burrs ("teasels," Alberto called them) were attached to five popsicle sticks and spread out like a leaf rake. The cows closed their eyes as we brushed. We talked to them, not to each other, until the job was done. As we cleaned out the burr-combs, Alberto asked me, "How much did he tell you?"

"A lot."

"For example?"

"I know about Manuelito," I said.

"No," he said, frowning. "Everything?"

"Everything, I guess. Do you believe it?"

"Believe?"

"Do you believe God inspired whoever killed him?"

"God inspired Nephi to kill Laban," he said.

This seemed to be a standard scriptural citation around here.

I noticed that I had managed to remove a tick from the cow's hide. It was trying to escape the burr spines. I pricked my fingers when I took the tick between them. A tick, I had been told, is unsmashable. You have to set a match to it if you want to snuff it out. Still, I tried smashing. I even dug my fingernails into its crust. But my fingernails were stubs now. So I just held it there tightly, like my pressure could cut off its blood supply. I watched it and felt it was watching me.

"When I was a kid," I said, "I had God all figured out. He was that bearded man with a bunch of kids around him, one on his lap, one holding his hand—have you seen the picture?"

"Yes."

"My Primary teacher put it up every week. Every week we'd sing, 'I Wonder When He Comes Again' and look at the picture. I got it ingrained."

"Is there some difficulty with that? You don't want God ingrained anymore?"

"God changes."

"That is not true, of course. I don't need to tell you that. If God changed, He would not be God."

"Do you have a match?" I said. "I understand these things have to be lit up to die."

He pulled a butane lighter from his shirt pocket. I put the tick down, and Alberto set it aflame. It ran around for a couple of seconds and then burned. I stepped on what was left of it, smothered the flame, covered the thing with a kick of straw.

"I'm not into killing," I said. "Even ticks." I brushed my fingers through the cow's hide once more, a final inspection. I found only bone and muscle. The cow mooed.

"Ticks fill the measure of their creation," Alberto said.

"They're ugly little snots though. Hard to imagine that unchanging God inventing them. Must have done it on an off day."

"They serve a purpose."

"Do they?" I said.

"Yes. And your eyes are very blue at this moment. Cornflower eyes. Cornflower angel. Don't worry about the tick, *mi amor.* Remember, there can be nothing beautiful without ugliness first." He stroked my cheek. He said, "Adam and Eve had to go through the wilderness before they could return to heaven; Jesus had to die before he could be resurrected. Even you, Johnny has told me, you had to go through an ugly marriage—a wrong marriage—before you could come here. Before you were ready for Zarahemla. One gains no self-knowledge in innocence, Ophelia."

"Please don't," I said.

"What have I done?"

"I'm not Ophelia. I don't want to be. Do you mind?"

"I mind, yes. I want you as Ophelia. Your other name means nothing to me. Your other name is someone else's wife. Can you understand?"

"It bugs me," I said.

"Read the play again."

"I'm sick to death of the play." The complaint burst out of me before I had even thought about it.

"Ophelia." He put the burrs down and stroked my hand. "You are confused."

"Aren't you?"

"I have been. I talked to Johnny yesterday—before he took you to the sacred place. He told me things. About myself, my identity, my mission. He is right. He is a great man. God gave me to him for a purpose." Alberto's voice was soft and utterly devoted. He was giving the kind of testimony you hear sometimes in Fast Meeting, when the testifier has been on the brink of death for three weeks, hasn't held his food down in a month, and is finding it a chore to get oxygen under his words.

"Let's take the milk," I said. I could feel myself distancing from him. I was going the wrong direction. I always went the wrong direction when I was supposed to love a guy.

Halfway to the processing hut I asked him, "You believe God's behind what's happening to Luisa?"

"Yes." He was certain about everything today.

"Then what good do all those prayers do?"

"They help the ones who pray," he said. "Is the bucket too heavy for you? I have a free hand."

"Oh I've got farmer's muscles by now. Haven't you noticed? Why do you always ask me that?"

"I am here to help you."

"I know," I said. I was on the verge of tears. I had no idea what was causing this rush of emotion. Hormones, I suspected, but the tears had something to do with my being mad at God, too. I was furious with God for moving around after Primary. For letting people die. For hoarding his miracles.

"You must abandon your fears," Alberto said. "Abandon fears and awake your faith. That's from *The Winter's Tale*. Have you read *The Winter's Tale*?"

"No."

"A good play. Full of faith. Perhaps it should be the next one we undertake. Shakespeare knew about faith. What good can come with no faith? We are on the verge of a great miracle, Ophelia. If we can have the faith . . ."

"Was it true what you told me?" I said. "You said you could save Luisa. Was that true?"

"Her life. But only God can save her soul."

"Do you know what you sound like?" I said. "You sound like a Great Lama. You sound like some freak who lives at the top of a mountain eating locusts and honey and growing hair and spouting cliches. Were you always like this? I don't remember you being like this." I had an urge to push him. I wanted to see the bucket go flying from his hands, the milk become two white wings above his vulnerable head. I wanted him to get angry, furious at me, to grab my fists and threaten to brain me. I wanted him real and out of control. His righteousness was exhausting.

"Don't be upset. Please, Ophelia."

"Ophelia," I said, exaggerating the sounds. "Ophelia. Don't I have any say in my name? Sometimes," I said, "you're a real bastard." My voice was ugly and familiar. I was talking to myself, though my words were loud and perfectly aimed—as though of their own volition—at Alberto.

When he turned to me, I thought my wish for violence would be granted. His eyes gleamed. I thought he would slap me, and braced my jaw.

"That is an ugly word," he said in a low, over-controlled voice.

"You're a bastard," I repeated, more softly this time, looking straight at him. There were other words in my mind—shocking words about total incompetence—that I didn't speak.

Alberto took a long breath. He stood there glaring and mute. "Would you call Jesus that?" he said. "His father was not the man his mother married, but would you use that word to describe him? The connotations are enormous. Richard III was a bastard. Edmund was a bastard. Caliban was a bastard. It is a hateful word."

"Yes it is," I said. My eyes were tearing. I didn't want to blink.

"Did John tell you I am a bastard?"

"Johnny adores you."

"What did he say?"

"I didn't memorize what he said."

"Of course you didn't. I wonder, sometimes, how prepared you are. I wonder how prepared John thinks you are. I wonder how much he will reveal to you, and how soon. Do you know who you are, Ophelia?"

"Yes, damn it, I know who I am. I'm not Ophelia."

"You are fury's slave, that's who you are. Your blood is fiery, isn't it."

"Sometimes," I said.

He set his milk bucket down and took mine. I asked him what he was doing.

"I am going to kiss you." He put my bucket beside his. "It is awkward doing that with milk in my hands. I am loving you at this instant, Ophelia."

He held out his arms. It was a simple and utterly seductive gesture. I hesitated, thinking what a fatal ruse sex is, then gave in to my hormones and the passion of the place.

We were at the top of the tallest hill, like bait for lightning, and we kissed as we had during the thunderstorm.

I opened my eyes as his lips moved down my neck. Zarahemla was spread out before me. The place of my spiritual fantasies and folklore, the mysterious, numinous Kolob where Johnny dwelt. Ten acres: little huts where anonymous Indians and Latins lived and worked; barns, chicken coops, spinach, mangos, gardenias; the lake with its schools of carp; and the cabin at the center of things, like a pulsing heart. Zarahemla was lush. Erotic.

Alberto's hands moved over my face, down my shoulders and hips. He knelt, clung to me around my thighs. I put my hands on his head, my fingers through his thick hair. "I love you," I said. "I do. I love you. Forgive me for everything."

The earth quivered, as though it were Alberto accepting my submission.

"Earthquake?" I whispered.

"No," he breathed. "Just the earth. Speaking approval."

He kissed me again, and twice more before I said, "Enough."

Twenty-one

My farm duties were now secondary to my nursing duties. Johnny told me I would be directly fulfilling a Book of Mormon prophecy when I cared for Luisa. "The Book of Mormon," he said, "talks about the gentiles being nursing fathers and mothers to the Lamanites. You want to know something, kiddo? Moroni, when he gave that prophecy, he saw you. And I mean you specifically. He saw this very day, the very struggles we have here, and you watching over Luisa like she was your baby. You haven't known that, have you. You've read that scripture maybe hundreds of times and not seen what Moroni saw. You. Aw yes, kiddo, it's right that you do this. God loves Luisa. God's heart is breaking too, you know. He's cried real tears, if you want the truth. God has cried real tears for her."

Every day she grew weaker, paler. I finally wrote Mom and begged her to come back. It was getting scary, I said in my letter. I don't know what to do. My jokes don't work on her like yours do. Luisa, I said, is dying.

Johnny promised to mail the letter, and thanked me.

*   *   *

Often, she just wanted me to hold her hand while she slept. When she was awake, I bathed her, took care of her personal needs, brushed her hair, massaged her womb. There were usually a couple of hours a day when she felt well enough to talk, though she rarely said much. She asked me about my life, about Jason, about divorce, about love.

"Do you love him still?" she asked me once.

"Jason?" I answered. "No, I don't love him. It hurt too much to love him. When someone's clawing into your heart every other day, it's hard to keep the good feelings rolling."

"Yes, it is hard," she said. "I imagine it is very hard."

"But I feel bad for what happened. I feel like if I had loved him enough, maybe he would have come back to the Church and we could have been happy. Do you understand me?"

"But he was killing you, no?"

"Or I was killing myself. I don't know. There was a lot of pressure in that marriage. Sometimes I thought maybe I should let myself die, just to get out—or to be redeemed maybe. I was crazy. Once I imagined myself dead, and I thought I'd save him that way. I'd make him feel so guilty that he'd dump all his sins and all his anger into a vase of flowers over my grave, and I'd just sort of drink them in and sprout dandelions."

"He was the first man you loved?"

"Yes. Or the first who loved me. I never imagined myself with anyone else."

"Are you aching still?"

"I'm all right," I said. I looked at her etchings. She had once been, she told me, a very good artist. The talent was still there. The etching of Johnny with soft eyes reminded me that my mother had had another love before Dad.

"This Daniel Castillo guy," I said, "how serious was that?"

She looked at me strangely. "What do you mean?"

"Do you think Mom would have married him if he hadn't come back here?"

"No. They would not have married."

"No? Why not?"

"Because Daniel did not love her."

"She thought he did."

"Daniel," she said, "was following ME."

I felt that I had tresspassed on intimate territory. I put the etchings back in their place at once, and helped Luisa turn on her side to sleep.

Outside, Alberto was singing. Luisa's window was open, her yellow curtains blowing softly. We could hear his voice on the wind.

Al decir adios,
vida mia,
Te digo eso:
Te quiero
Y te estoy agradecido.
Te veré, amor,
En los cielos.
Te miré, amor,
En mi jardin.

"He has," murmured Luisa sleepily, "a beautiful voice. He always had a beautiful voice. He used to sing for me. No more."

"He thinks you're mad at him."

"No," she moaned.

"He told me something. He said—never mind. I don't understand half of what he says."

"He is ashamed," she answered, her words slurring. "He knows too much."

Alberto began "A Poor Wayfaring Man of Grief." I hummed it with him.

> A poor wayfaring man of grief
> Hath often crossed me on my way,
> Who sued so humbly for relief
> That I could never answer nay.
> I had not power to ask his name,
> Whereto he went or whence he came.
> But there was something in his eye
> That won my love, I know not why.

"Why don't you sing with him?" Luisa whispered.
I did, very softly.

> Once, when my scanty meal was spread,
> He entered, not a word he spake,
> Just perishing for want of bread.
> I gave him all, he blessed it, brake
> And ate, but gave me part again.
> Mine was an angel's portion then;
> For while I fed with eager haste,
> The crust was manna to my taste.

"Yes," she said—her last words before she slept—"you harmonize well. Oh Julie—help him. Help him be good!"

We sang:

> I spied him where a fountain burst
> Clear from the rock; his strength was gone.
> The heedless water mocked his thirst;
> He heard it, saw it hurrying on.
> I ran and raised the suff'rer up;
> Thrice from the stream he drained my cup,
> Dipped and returned it running o'er;
> I drank and never thirsted more.

"Keep singing," I told Alberto, though he couldn't hear. "It's so pretty. You make everything soft."

> 'Twas night; the floods were out; it blew
> A winter hurricane aloof.
> I heard his voice abroad and flew
> To bid him welcome to my roof.
> I warmed and clothed and cheered my guest
> And laid him on my couch to rest;
> Then made the earth my bed, and seemed
> In Eden's garden while I dreamed.

Twenty-two

I tried to find the ruins the next morning. I had not realized how full the jungle was. It was a labyrinth of leaves. I would never find the real Zarahemla without a guide. I gave up on it, went back and picked corn, which was to be dried until the kernels were hard as pebbles, then shucked for future tortillas.

The cornstalks were taller than I was now. Everything was growing and blossoming. Popsicle sticks would sprout here. Even weeds put out magnificent purple flowers—like morning glories— and dared you to unearth them.

Alberto and I sang again that night, and I made him promise to take me "there" in the morning, after milking.

As it turned out, Mom and Dad arrived just after breakfast. I saw Doodle Dan snaking down the nearest mountain as I was heading towards the barn. I yelped, and Alberto, frowning, told me to wait for them; he would milk the cows himself. My father made him nervous, I knew that.

Johnny was with Luisa, reading scriptures to her. When I told him I had seen the van, he frowned too. "I don't know," he muttered, "that God's going to be real pleased with this. God feels strongly about Belen. He doesn't like his workers taking off like that."

"But I asked them to come," I reminded him. "You mailed the letter yourself."

"Oh the letter. Yes, that's right, I did mail it. Well maybe I shouldn't have."

"Mom's here," I cooed to Luisa, stroking her forehead.

She did not open her eyes. "Thank you," she said, like a prayer.

I ran outside and jogged up the road to meet them. My burdens were falling off. The Good Humor lady was coming.

Mom opened Doodle Dan's door as I approached. The van was still in motion. Dad hated it when Mom did that before he had come to a full stop. He shook his head as he braked.

"No pain no gain!" Mom yelled at me.

I hopped in, closed the door, and Dad continued to the cabin.

"You got my letter," I sighed, out of breath.

"What letter?" Mom said.

"Damn these Salvadoran mails," I muttered. "But anyway—you're here!"

"Your father had a spiritual impression, Digs. Felt we should come. How about that, huh? I may have to get down his halo polish from the cupboard after all."

Dad shook his head again.

"How's Luisa?" Mom asked, and I told her. The pregnancy had sapped her strength and made her helpless. "She needs you," I said.

Was it her orange scarf, her smile, or just her presence that calmed me? I was suddenly unworried, even joyful, in the van with my parents. Zarahemla looked small, pretty, not so full of shadows.

Luisa was sitting up in her bed when we entered. She reached her arms for mother and the two of them embraced. "My hay-ell," said Mom, still holding her, "you look like death twice warmed over, Cookie. I'd better buy you some strawberries to rub on your face, huh?" She loosened her hug and kissed one of those pale cheeks. "Oh look—the baby!" She cupped her hand over Luisa's womb (the canteloupe had grown watermelonish) and whispered into Luisa's navel: "Hello in there! Howzit goin'?"

Luisa's face—how can I describe it: Everything half-alive, half open. Grief, pain, sorrow. She had brushed her hair after I told her that Mom was here. It glistened, but made the rest of her seem so pale, the grey-blue shadows under her eyes so stark. This is what her ghost would be: white robes and black hair blowing; arms raised, beckoning, blessing; a face that embodied grief; half-blind, pleading eyes.

"My first stop," said Mom, "is the marketplace. I'm buying you boysenberries, Cookie. And chicken soup."

"No," moaned Luisa. "Stay. Please stay with me." This request was directed exclusively to Mom. Luisa seemed to be telling the rest of us to leave.

Mom laid her back down and promised to stay. Dad and Johnny and I went outside, though Johnny didn't stay with us long. He said he had business elsewhere and made a quick split. I saw him on the appaloosa a minute later, galloping across the rim of Zarahemla's biggest hill.

Dad put his hands in his rear pockets and silently surveyed the plantation. He seemed so tall to me then, so much taller than Johnny, and powerful. What was there about my father that frightened my uncle and unnerved Alberto? Why had God not wanted him here? I imagined myself in a Vietnamese barn, staring across a hay bale at this huge white warrior. I felt suddenly sick. It had been wrong of me to write that letter to them, wrong of me to pray them here. Dad brought his apostasy with him. He and Mom turned this holy place common, made jokes where God walked.

"You didn't get my letter?" I said, wanting to be sure.

"No." He didn't look at me. I knew his stony face: he was boiling inside. This is how he would have looked at a National

Guard summer camp. ("Here, men, is the jugular vein. It must be severed in this fashion . . .") Yes, my father was capable of terror.

"Dad—"

He turned to me. If Luisa was grief's ghost, Dad was the spirit of rage. I stepped back.

"What, Julie?" he said.

"How's Belen?" My voice was thin, flat.

"Full of crap, same as here. You have anything you want to tell me?"

"No."

"How's Alberto?" His eyes bored into me.

"He's fine."

"You haven't eloped or anything."

I tried to laugh. "No. Still single, Dad. Single me."

"You ready to head home?"

That was his knife, quick and to the heart. "Home?" I repeated. "Stateside, you mean?"

"Home."

"No. No, I'm not ready."

"Why not ready, Jewel?"

"It's not time, Dad! Timing's off."

"We've been here over six months."

"There's more. Come on! Come on! There's Luisa. There's —there are things for me to do here. I don't—Johnny's told me that there are things—"

"And you believe him."

"Sure I do."

Dad laughed, once. "You see that avocado tree, Jewel?"

Of course I did; it was as tall as a two-story building.

"What say we race there?"

"I don't know, Dad. Luisa might need me."

"When did you race me last?"

I shrugged.

"Try to remember."

The memory was there, ready to be snatched from its file. I am seven years old. It is autumn. Dad and I are running through yellow leaves that rustle around our feet. He lets me win the race and picks me up, swings me around in a circle, holds me. It is chilly, on the Other Side. Home. And that man—that sweet and playful Daddy—and the one who killed a Vietnamese kid in a barn are one and the same.

"It's been a long time," I said.

"Who won?" Dad said.

"I don't remember."

He was trying so hard to be light, it was pathetic. His laugh was forced, adolescent. "Sounds like a challenge," he said. "Come on, Jewel, take me up on it. Race me to the avocado tree." I knew what he wanted was to be where no one would hear us, and maybe, too, there was energy in him that needed to burn.

I glanced at him, then took off. I heard him behind me and imagined that this was another jungle, that there were tigers and panthers watching us, and there were mines and snake pits waiting to be tripped up. His feet were heavy behind me. I thought of Manuelito. Had he run from his murderers? Had it been like this for him? And the kid in the barn—had he run from my father? Had he heard those very steps I was hearing now, and were those the last sounds he heard?

He passed me just as I came to the trunk. "Good job," he said, and, exhausted, I started to cry.

He watched me. He paced back and forth, cooling down. "I'm sorry," he kept saying. "I'm sorry. Sorry we ever came."

"That's not it. I want to be here, Dad! I want to stay!"

"Stay?" He stretched his arms behind his back. "Stay here—you mean here—in El Salvador? For how long, Jewel?"

I wiped my eyes. "Forever," I whispered.

"Uh huh." He looked at me, then quickly away. "You mean you might stay even after Mom and I leave, is that it?"

"Yes." I wiped my eyes again and looked east, where dark clouds were moving in. I thought, I'm becoming just like this place. These quick bursts of moisture with no warning. Zarahemla, the powerful, had taken me into its heart.

"Has Johnny told you to stay? Has he told you that, honey?"

"Dad," I said, "you know, there are things of the Spirit I don't expect you to understand."

"Oh good night, Jewel! Who do you think I am? Attila the Hun? This is your father speaking." He took a sharp breath, then spoke more softly. "Listen, honey, I won't try to control your life, but please listen. All I want to say is—is be careful. Jewel, I'm not sure I believe in Johnny. Let me phrase that more clearly. I know about sin, understand me? Hey, this is Mr. Apostate speaking, right? Put it this way: I won't be surprised if Johnny has been wearing my shoes for a long time. There are times I can smell them on him, Jewel. Times I can smell the stink."

"Not Johnny," I said.

"I'm just saying I won't be surprised." Dad's forehead and cheeks were beaded with sweat. He lifted his T-shirt and wiped his face with it. "I don't think you should decide to stay here unless you're absolutely sure about things," he said.

"I'm sure."

"You Mormons!" He was trying to tease me, to lighten things up, but his eyes still brimmed with deadly accusation. "Come on—race me back," he said. "Race me back to the cabin."

I didn't want to think about Dad's words—I tried not to—but all afternoon they were echoing off walls, radiating around my recent memories.

"I can smell the stink."

"I won't be surprised if Johnny's wearing my shoes."

"Are you sure?"

"Are you sure?"

"Are you sure?"

I thought about Johnny, and about Manuelito. When I prepared a chicken on the kitchen counter after lunch, Mani was there. I heard him as clearly as I had the first time. "*Hola. Me llamo Manuel.*"

Yes, I know that, I answered in my mind.

"What do you know?" (His English accented.)

The chicken's neck had been wrung and plucked. My fingers went to it, stroked the cold, porous skin. I imagined Manuel before me, black bruises across his throat, his posture unnaturally straight, stretched, his head tilted, cocked like a curious kid, his eyes accusing—like Dad's.

"*Hola. Me llamo Manuel.*"

The chicken guts came apart in my hands. The smell was putrid, excremental, overwhelming, mingled with Manuel's.

Are you an apostate? (To whom, this question?)

"*Hola—*"

That night—did you know you would die?

"*Me llamo—*"

Did they chase you first? For how long did you struggle with them? With the tree?"

"*Manuel . . .*"

Did Johnny know? Did Johnny know?

Are you an apostate?

Are you sure? Sure? Sure?

I was dizzy, faint, sick. I left the chicken guts on the counter and went in to Luisa. Mom was with her too. I washed my hands and we rubbed her down. Mom sang her kiddie songs like "Little Bunny Fu Fu" and "Five Little Monkeys Jumpin' On the Bed." Luisa smiled weakly. My questions pounded in me with each heartbeat. Questions about fate, death, Johnny, Manuelito. "You're not going to die, are you?" I wanted to say. I wanted to bless her, that's what I wanted. In pioneer times, Mormon women blessed each other before childbirth. They (the authorities) don't let us do that now. Women give blessings in the temple, but otherwise, it's just men who act as God's official conduits. I have resented this at times; I resented it then. My hands wanted to cup Luisa's head. I wanted power to pray her well. But my hands were so unworthy anyway, so divorced—why should God come through them? And if Johnny was right and it was God who wanted her dead—as he had wanted Mani dead—why should he let me undo the curse? I stroked her forehead after Mom finished "Little Bunny Fu Fu" the second time. "You all right?" I asked.

"Sure," Luisa said. And in the way she said it—her softness, her weakness, her other-worldliness—I knew she would die. Johnny was a prophet.

One month, and Luisa would be due.

Twenty-three

I still wanted to see the ruins again, but Johnny and Alberto made themselves scarce after my folks arrived. Johnny blamed me, I felt, for their coming, for all the confusion they had brought.

When I milked the cows in the morning, Alberto joined me. I asked him to take me to the ruins when we finished. He agreed. But as it turned out, Mom had other plans for me: a visit to the marketplace to buy those berries for Luisa. Mom's orphans came with us. We took the van.

A Salvadoran marketplace is pungent. The natives—mostly Latins here, not Indians—wear clothes that look like the thrift store castoffs of 1955. They sell fruit, vegetables, freshly-slaughtered meat (pig, beef, chicken), blood from the slaughter, fabric, wall hangings, dried and salted fish, tamales, flowers, you-name-it. The displays are set apart by tent-like arrangements of cloth, held up by bamboo. The friendly haggling can be heard a block away—high-pitched, insistent, full of laughter and savvy.

The orphans went immediately to the mango man, who served them strips of unripe mangoes dipped in lime juice and brown sugar. Next they wanted a rice drink (*atole*), and finally insisted on some clothespin dolls. Mom gave in to everything. Mom was a marshmallow. She had been for me too, when I was a kid. If I could draw out my "pleeeeease" for three seconds, she'd get me anything. The orphans didn't even have to say "please." They just had to look at something and gasp.

Mom carried a basket and filled it with all sorts of junk we didn't need. She couldn't resist the sweet, desperate eyes of the merchants either. She even bought a dozen eggs, though she knew the chickens of Zarahemla were over-productive as it was.

I said, "Well, you're quite the comparison shopper, aren't you."

"I do get off on it," she said. "This is what the tourists love to photograph, you know? A typical marketplace. I saw a couple of tourists last week. One of them was wearing bermuda shorts with little pink hearts on them."

"A man tourist or a lady?"

"Man. Gringos are silly, Digs. We may as well face that."

"You're right. Best to face facts as soon as possible in this life."

The orphans were everywhere. Little old ladies would beckon to them and when Mom went to pick them up, the little old ladies would hold up their wares. Mom would pass out money, laughing, loving, filling her basket, talking Spanglish ("*Que pretito!* I am so *impressionada.* Give me *dos.*") Eventually, she had to buy another basket too, and filled it within fifteen minutes. Both baskets were packed by the end of our spree.

Mom stood at the edge of the plaza and waved at everyone when she had to agree we had bought all we needed (and a whole lot we didn't). At least twenty people waved back and adored her.

I told her she was the most popular lady around. She said, "Oh no, not me. These are just loving people is all. You give them a little love and they smother you with what they give back. Beautiful people."

"Hard to imagine a war here," I said.

"Hard to imagine a war anywhere. Of all the ridiculous inventions of men." She gave me a basket. It must have weighed twenty-five pounds.

"How was it to be in jail, Mom?" I said, grunting, heading for Doodle Dan Van.

"I beg your pardon?"

"When you were arrested for protesting Viet Nam—I haven't forgotten that."

"Well don't remind me. My hay-ell. I can't believe some of the stuff I did back then."

"But how was it? Really."

"Really? Not too bad. A lot of streetwalkers. One cop thought I was one too. I called him a very bad word and told him my crime had been a legal one. He laughed like I was an idiot. That was humiliating. Otherwise, it wasn't so bad."

The orphans were following us, but were easily distracted by streetside vendors. Mom had to keep calling them back—without going to get them herself, or we would have had to buy another basket. "Now stay here," she told them—as though they could understand English. Then to me: "In the sixties, spending a night in jail was sort of a rite of passage. Honorable. Most of the protesters had done it. A few liked to brag about it. There was one guy who was trying to spend a night in jail in every state in the Union. Utah was number thirty-two for him. He probably accomplished the goal. Some goals you really can meet."

"Would you do it again?" I said.

"What? Go to jail?"

"Yes. Protest a war and go to jail for it."

"Probably. I'm still a hippie at heart."

"Do you think war is ever justified?"

"War is stupid, Digs. It's an invention of men. The only way it's justified is when men have done other even stupider things that make it necessary. Men like Hitler, spit spit."

"Do you think God would ever inspire one man to kill another one?"

"Good gravy, Digs, where are these questions coming from?"

"I don't know. I'm curious to know what you think, though. Would God inspire one guy to kill another guy?"

"Well, there's Nephi—"

"That's what everyone says. Forget Nephi. Is God in the habit of telling someone to commit murder?"

"Well no, not if you put it that way. Of course, everyone wants to think God is behind their side in a war. Everyone wants to think God wants their enemy dead. But everyone doesn't know a lot about God or they wouldn't be having a war in the first place." To the twins: "Now you stay here!" (Giggling is the answer.)

"If someone told you that God had inspired somebody's murder," I said, "would you believe him?"

"Well, I'd have to know the situation. Most likely, I'd be skeptical."

"If the guy who said that was a Mormon, would you think he had apostatized?"

"I might. My hay-ell, you're full of questions, Digs."

"Full."

"Your dad might give you different answers from mine, of course."

"I don't know, Mom," I said. "He might not."

We loaded our groceries and miscellany into Doodle Dan, buckled the orphans in, headed back to the cabin. It was lunchtime before we got back. Alberto and I didn't get started on our trip to the ruins until nearly noon. I knew better than to announce to everyone where we would be going. I told Mom we had "errands."

Alberto broke through the first vines of the jungle like they were annoying threads, nothing more. Three steps and the path was clear, machete-hacked. He instructed me to never tell my father or mother about the ruins. My father was too political, he said, to be trusted. And Mom was too much a child. She wasn't ready for something so serious and so sacred.

I said I hadn't told anyone. I had promised Johnny not to.

"This is a sacred place," he reminded me again.

The path was serpentine. It would seem to stop abruptly, come to a dead end of foliage. Alberto would simply pull a few vines and point me to the uncovered continuum.

"A person could get lost in here and die with no one knowing," I said.

"It's happened."

"If I didn't trust you, this would be worse than a spook alley."

"You trust me, yes?"

"Of course I trust you."

He kissed my cheek. "I could ravish you right here and no one would know," he said, then kissed my mouth, long, hard. This was an intense, full-hormoned boy. The jungle gave him passion.

"I don't think Johnny would approve," I answered when the kiss ended and he was coming at me for another, his hands moving down my ribs.

"Oh you don't?" He kissed me again, and held my waist—just as my busdriver had. His eyes were full of bright, powerful lust. His hands hurt me, and he kissed me until I could hardly breathe. "Don't—" I said when he let me catch my breath, but he kissed me again and again until I was melting inside. "You love me," he said. It was an announcement or a command, I'm not sure which. "You love me." Then there was sudden movement, cracking sticks close by which made me push him off me and tighten. I pictured first a jaguar, then a terrorist with crazy eyes. I took Alberto's arm.

"*Tranquilate*, Ophelia," he said, smiling, relieved himself to have identified the noise. "They are only monkeys. Spider monkeys. The jungle is brimming with them." He was amused, his eyes no longer dangerous. He brushed my eyebrows with his lips. "I'm sorry," he said. "John warned me, you know. He said I would feel this, that I would love you strongly. But there must be some control, yes?"

"Yes," I murmured. I looked up and saw a monkey staring right at me, then making some monkeyish accusation and swinging itself away.

Spider monkeys have always been troublemakers to the Maya, as well as great comedians. In the *Popol Vuh* the twin heroes, Hunahpu and Xbalanque, turn their half-brothers into monkeys, who can only be saved if their grandmother restrains her laughter when she sees them. It's a bold, useless condition, though, because the monkeys are monkeys—funny by nature. They pull their lips out at their grandmother and scratch themselves, dancing around her, one playing a flute, the other making ridiculous contortions with his mouth, like a four-year-old kid who's just learned the Bronx cheer. Finally the old lady roars laughter, and the monkeys are banished forever to the forest.

It's no wonder the Maya conjured folklore like that; the critters look so much like little men, observing us interlopers with their wise, hilarious monkey eyes.

"Are we close?" I asked as we walked. Alberto held me to him, moving his hand up and down my hip bone.

"Look."

I could see the mounds between leaves. Alberto moved two more branches. We were there.

It was much more spectacular now, at noon, than it had been at dusk. There were more mounds than I had remembered; the trees on the towers were bigger and greener; the blossomed weeds were bright and ubiquitous. There were orchids. One mound was covered with little pink orchids. There were olive trees with branches spread wide as jets.

"Jesus walked here," Alberto said.

"That's what Johnny believes."

"It's true. After his resurrection, Jesus had other sheep, not of the Jerusalem fold. They were here, in Zarahemla. They were my ancestors. He held their babies and blessed them. He gave them commandments. He broke bread and sanctified it for them to eat. You have, of course, read the book."

"I have, of course."

"'Behold, I am Jesus Christ, whom the prophets testified shall come into the world. I am the light and the life of the world. Arise and come forth unto me, that ye may thrust your hands into my side.'"

"Have you got it memorized?"

"The words I love stay with me."

"I've noticed that."

"They will stay with you as well, and with our children. 'I am the God of Israel and the God of the whole earth, and have been slain for the sins of the world.' This is holy ground, Ophelia."

"Ophelia," I murmured, rolling my eyes.

"Listen to me. This ground has been preserved. It has known no ugliness since the visit of Jesus. It was burned with fire before He came, and all its inhabitants were burned too, and then it was made holy and never desecrated afterwards. God would not allow it. It has been preserved for this day. I will give you proof. I will show you the writings. The temple. Come."

We passed the orchid mound and a small bush of white, lacy flowers whose perfume was so rich and sweet it seemed narcotic. Alberto plucked three blossoms.

"Ophelia." He presented me the little bouquet. "I would I had some flowers of the spring that might become your time of day."

"Thank you," I said.

"From *The Winter's Tale*. Beautiful, no? Come this way." He took my hand, kissed it (there was reverence now in all his actions) and led me past the orchid tower and an olive tree. There was a stairway leading underground. It looked to me like it might go to a sauna where ancient priests would have heated stones and sweated themselves clean.

"You won't be afraid of the dark, will you?" he said.

"Are there bats?"

"A few," he laughed. "Not many. They won't disturb us."

The stairs led to a tunnel. Alberto took a flashlight from his pants' pocket. "So shines a good deed in a naughty world," he said.

I followed the beam. He pointed it to a wall carving—a *bas relief* with familiar pictures.

"The tree of life, in the shape of a cross," Alberto announced.

"Is that what Johnny says it is?"

"See for yourself."

I rubbed the dirt under the leafy cross. The form was already quite visible: a sacrificial victim with the tree sprouting from his heartless chest.

"It's a heart sacrifice," I said. "And this god here, this is Chac, the rain god." I pointed to the grizzly, full-lipped face beside the cross.

"It is Lehi's dream of the tree of life," said Alberto. "Look at it. Look."

"No it's not," I countered authoritatively. "I'm sorry. It's a common picture. This guy's soul is going to climb up the tree-cross to get to heaven. He's going all the way to the thirteenth heaven, because he's just been sacrificed to this ugly little monster over here. Chac."

"No. That is not true. In fact, it's a lie."

"Archaeologists aren't all idiots," I said.

"Look here, then." He pointed to another wall carving. "Nephites and Lamanites dancing together, living the Law of Consecration after the visit of the Lord."

I was familiar with these images too: a circle made up of white-faced and black-faced men holding hands.

"A ritual dance," I said. "They painted their faces like that for Chac."

"I don't believe you."

"I didn't say you had to believe me. Believe what you want. Just don't write any books about it or you'll be laughed out of the library."

"This is Zarahemla."

"I'm not arguing with that. Maybe after Jesus left, the people became wicked—they're not exactly saints when the Book of Mormon ends."

"The people wicked? No! After Jesus came, this place was undefiled. It will always be undefiled!" He was rubbing the dirt under the tree-cross, tracing the form of the prostrate victim, holding his finger where the guy's heart should have been.

"Come on, Alberto, they were feeding the women their husbands' flesh in the last chapters of Moroni."

"Not here."

"All right. Here they were just planting trees in people's chests. Impaling their hearts on olive branches."

"This was a temple!"

"God doesn't let bloodthirsty men build temples, dear."

"You don't know!" he said. "Who do you think you are to say such things? Incompetent! Incompetent!"

Jason's definition of me. Berto was quoting my ex like a war tract.

I stiffened, rage building, simmering in my gut. For using that word, I wanted to kill him. And if volume could murder, he would have been dead at my feet the next second.

I drew myself close to his face. "I KNOW!" I yelled, roared, my intestines clenched against all those forces that had ever wanted to destroy me. With every cell, every screaming atom, I was defending my past, my intellectual honor, my integrity, my whole self as though this were the devil's court and Berto my ex-husband's scheming lawyer. "I know! Who do you think YOU are?" I shot the words at him like nasty tasting nails. "Just who the hell are you?"

I felt even taller than he, until he pointed the flashlight like a gun at my chest and poised his other hand above my cheek, ready to strike. "You would use such tones here?" he hissed low. "Such words?"

"Hey, hit me if it will make you feel better." (Yes, I had said this before. This whole conversation was sickeningly familiar.)

"No." He lowered both his arms. The flashlight made a white circle on the floor. I could barely make out Alberto's profile in the dark. When I did, I saw that it was Johnny's profile too.

"Tell me about your father," I murmured, my rage abruptly over, replaced by the horror of what was before me. Numbness was spreading through my body like a rush of cancer, starting in my stomach, branching out to my arms and legs. How had I missed it? How had I missed seeing what was here?

"My father?" said Alberto.

"Who is he?"

"Don't you know?"

I knew. I knew. "It's Johnny."

"Yes. Of course yes."

I was suddenly cold, shivering inside, as though my cells had been flash-frozen. "Johnny," I repeated. "Johnny. Oh no." It was dark, dark where we were. "Berto, raise the flashlight," I whispered.

He did, focusing on the sacrifice.

We did not speak for a long moment.

"Do you feel the ghost?" he said at last.

"The Zarahemlites?" My voice barely sounded.

"The ghost. Is he in you? Speaking through your mouth? Are these his questions? His fury?"

"Whose questions?"

"My other father. My mother's husband."

"I'm alone with you."

"He wants revenge. Oh, he is wicked!"

My body tingled. I was floating through space. No foundation. No weight. Nothing to hold me. "So," I said, unsure my voice could get past the cold black of my throat. "So you really are a bastard."

"Don't. Please. You asked who I am. I will tell you. I am a bastard, yes, but a holy one. Do you understand me? I am not like Edmund or Caliban. I am like Jesus Christ. I have a mission to perform—and you with me."

"Let's get out of here," I said, starting for the outside. The air seemed thicker than my body. I felt I would have to swim to escape.

Alberto pulled me back. "You must awake your faith!" he said.

I pointed to the picture on the wall. "That's what they told that guy there." My voice echoed back to me strange and distant. "Thank God my grandma's dead. She worshipped Johnny. Thank God she was spared this."

"You must believe in John. There is purpose to everything he has done."

"Are you his only child?" I was remembering the sandy-haired kid Marta had presented to him when we first went to Izalco.

"No."

"Does he have other wives?"

"Does it concern you?"

"Hell yes."

"There are others. He was commanded by God to take them."

"Do you believe that?" I asked.

"I believe."

"He could get exed for it. He should get exed."

"Only Piggott would excommunicate him. And he is too afraid of John to act. He knows John is a man of God."

"You really believe it." The numbness had ceased. Now I was merely sick.

"John is fulfilling the prophecy. Can't you understand that? Feel it in your heart? Listen. Remember: The Lamanites will become a white and delightsome people—or pure and delightsome, if you prefer. Do you think that metamorphosis, that evolution, will happen without biology? God works within his laws. You and I, Ophelia, are destined to begin the change." He shined the light on my breasts.

I sat down on the cold rock floor, suddenly crying. I said, "It's a lie. Johnny's off the wall. He's an apostate. A damned sinner. Dad knew it. Before any of us saints, Dad knew it. And this—I promise you—is a room for pagan priests. This is no Zarahemla. It's a pre-classic ritual center for cannibals."

"John is a man of God," Alberto repeated, unemotionally, out of habit.

I didn't answer. I was crying and damning Johnny to Hell.

"Pray for peace," Alberto said, putting his arms around me. I was shaking, getting hideous-looking in his embrace. I thought he might start kissing me again, and pushed him away.

"The night before I married Jason," I said, "I felt like there were clouds in my brain cells, lead in my corpuscles. Stupor of thought, call it that. Everything shadowed, oppressive. I thought—what an ass I was—I thought it was Satan tempting me away from my mission, away from this pathetic guy I was going to save. What an ass! Crap!" I sobbed again till my nose was dripping into my hands. I wiped it on my sleeve. "I was almost as confused as you are," I cried.

"What are you saying?"

"Maybe your ghost is your conscience or some good angel trying to rescue you from John. And I'm saying Luisa can't die! You told me you could save her. Well you do it! You do what you have to do. Don't you let her die!"

"The will of God—"

"Do what you have to do, you bastard!"

"God will do what he has to do."

"It's all wrong. It's all wrong. Oh God! What has happened here? Alberto, is this all—all—holy crap! Holy, holy crap!" I cried hard and long. Alberto kept his arms around me and, after a long while, cried too.

This moment was my apotheosis—or anti-apotheosis, as it happened. I was in a fragrant abeyance with no foundation whatever, crying with my cousin, letting my illusions dissipate. I hadn't realized it until then, but it had always been Johnny's sunlit face surrounded by the little children in the Primary picture. It had been Johnny at Gethsemane and on the cross. Johnny had been the luminous angel, the haloed messenger from heaven. Now someone had pulled the plug on him—zapped his light. Johnny was a dead star. And the rest of us, we were just hanging around, receding from the big bang, grappling with gravity and meteorites, floating away to our separate distances. We were aimless, and I the most aimless of everyone because I knew I was. All my doubts—the precious secrets and wonderings I had pushed to the fringes of my faith—were orbiting me as I drifted. They popped, like the snaps of a cap gun, reminding me they had been there forever but no longer mattered. Others of my illusions—my diary brides, my Primary pictures—didn't even have the strength to pop. They were just gone as Johnny was gone. I understood that they had been trying for a long time to disintegrate. They had started to melt once or twice, like chocolate under my tongue, and I had spit them out and grabbed them. But I couldn't stop them now. They were gone. They had beamed away. I was completely divorced. I had nothing but this half-Latin boy and my diseased body. Even my parents were irrelevant shivers of an unremembered conflagration. There was no God. There was no rule, no morality, no Law of Consecration. There were two impotent mortals holding each other, making each other into symbolless statues, comforting each other with meaningless grace.

"Let's go outside," I repeated.

He let me go this time, and followed me to an eroded stone—an altar of some kind, probably to another bloody god—where we sat. I asked him questions; he gave me answers. Sometimes he would repeat that there was purpose to everything Johnny had done, but it was too late for testimony. Alberto would not admit his confusion or ambivalence, but it was around him like a stink. Neither of us believed.

"How long has he had other women?"

"Years."

"Luisa has known?"

"She has suffered. I told you that. But it is good to suffer. It is better to pass through sorrow, that we may know—"

"Did he tell her she would die?"

"He told her God would take her if she did not support him and the other wives. It was a prophecy. In a blessing, he told her she would die. It was an act of mercy. It gives her time to prepare. Foreknowledge."

"And she hasn't told anyone."

"She loves him. He is a man of God."

"Did he kill Manuelito?"

"No."

"Did he kill him, Alberto?"

"No. I said no!"

"Did he have anything to do with it?"

"It was for his soul. Mani's soul. Mani's blood had to be shed—for atonement."

"So Johnny had the hanging done."

"He did not like the hanging. John was sick about the hanging."

"Luisa knew he had part in it?"

"Maybe she knew. I don't know."

"How much did Johnny pay to have him killed?"

"How much? The worth of a soul—"

"How damn much?"

"I don't know the amount. The amount doesn't matter. He did it—believe me—for the sake of Mani's soul."

"Did you see him hanged?"

"I was spared that."

"But you knew it would happen."

"Not that he would hang. He was to have been shot."

"You knew he would be murdered."

"I knew, yes. But understand, it was the only way for Mani to go to God. He had sinned. Blood must be shed for a man's sins. He should have been shot. He was to have been shot."

"By *Orden*."

"Yes."

"Blood atonement."

"Yes."

"God."

"Yes."

I inhaled deep and long. "Are you communists here?"

"We are no more political than Jesus was. We believe in the poor." He was shrugging and blinking a lot, like someone psychotic. His eyes would moisten and clear, moisten and clear. His voice would be sometimes thunderous and sometimes a whisper. I felt pity such as I had not known since I married Jason. I wanted to hold Alberto and cry. I wanted to be his vessel of empathy, to merge all his existential angst with mine.

"And you have had Cordelia?" I said.

He watched his feet. "John gave her to me. Two years ago he called me to be his disciple. He called Mani too. Luisa rose against him then. Mani and I had to choose between them. We had to take sides."

"And you were to have me too?"

"Yes." He laughed grimly, blinking, shrugging.

I could see the vision: my children by Alberto would have fairer skin than he, and our grandchildren, after some intermarriage, would be fully white. Johnny was taking control of the prophecy. Johnny was making things happen the way he knew they should. He was taking control in a land where control was rare. Being the leader people could depend on. Mom and I were like him in that: we loved righteous power, the glory of saviorhood. We wanted to be there when the plane crashed, to put out the flame with a baptism of water and spirit.

I asked Alberto, "Did Johnny have Piggott's wife?"

"He dreamed that Sarah had covenanted with him in the pre-existence. She left her husband. She couldn't consummate the alliance with John."

"It's not that Johnny's evil," I said.

Alberto repeated that John was a man of God. It was vain repetition. It came from him like a hiccough, habitual and involuntary, the noisy gas of the shrunken, dead star he had swallowed like an Alka Seltzer.

"He's not an evil man," I said.

In my mind were the angry, lusting eyes of my bus driver. I had seen them again in Alberto. Adultery was not hard. I knew that better than I knew anything else at the moment.

I pictured Cordelia in all her magnificence, her brown shoulders gleaming, the waterfall behind her, the sulphur mists rising between her breasts, eyes luminous, face unblemished, everything about her young and nubile. I knew that Marta must have looked like that some twenty years before. Adultery was not hard.

"Is there anything else I should know?" I said.

"Is there?"

"Will you call me Julie now?"

"You are sure that's what you want?"

"Yes."

"Too late for other things?"

"Too late, yes. I want to go back to the cabin," I said.

He nodded absently. "How can one be so certain one moment and so confused the next?" He was asking the orchids. "There was a night I awakened," he said, "feeling there was a devil in my room, breathing on my shoulders. I could feel his breath. Cold. Icy. I said, 'Who are you?' Do you know what it said in reply?"

"What?"

"It said, 'Murder most foul.' Familiar, no?"

"That's all it said?"

"Yes. Those words and no more. It came again the next night. I felt like Joseph Smith did just before his vision—without power to speak or move, trapped by that spirit of night. Five times it came, quoting speeches from the ghost of Hamlet's father, calling me the name you used."

"Bastard."

"Yes."

"You were dreaming."

"I wish I had been only dreaming."

"It sounds like a dream."

"It was no dream. And now, you are telling me the ghost with icy lungs was from God?"

"I don't know where it came from. Sounds like it came from Shakespeare."

He stood, looking around himself, glancing over one shoulder then over the other. It was a scene from *The Exorcist.* He shouted, "Are you there? Are you there?" He spoke Spanish into the air, and then dialect until he was screaming like a mad man: "*Tata-ahhhh k'o chicaaaaah!*"

"Alberto." I went to him, embraced him, kissed his cheeks until he quit the noise. But after his mouth was closed there came a sound from the jungle almost like the one he had been making—a tormented, hellish roar: an answer. It was the jaguar, I knew that. Jaguars are gods to the Maya.

"My father," moaned Alberto. His face was dripping sweat. He fell into my arms—nearly knocked me down—and clung to me. I stroked his wet hair, kissed him, put my cheek against his.

"Do you love me?" he said.

"You're my cousin."

"Even so. Do you love me?"

"Sure I do, Alberto."

"Do you know who I love?"

"Tell me."

He sobbed. "Her!"

"Cordelia?"

He shook his head.

"Luisa," I said.

"Yes, Luisa. You think I don't love her? She nursed me with her own breasts! Held me—like you are doing now, but with so much more feeling, so much more. You cannot imagine her goodness, her purity. She was the one I went to when I was troubled. All the words I love were the ones she read to me. I love her better than anything in this earth. Do you know that?"

"Sure, Alberto."

"But it's too late for her."

"Why too late?"

"She hates me now."

"She loves you."

"I can't undo it."

"You told me you could save her. Is that true?"

He moved his head to my breasts, clung to me like a baby wanting to be suckled. He cried, "How do I know where to turn?"

I gave him the only answer I had to anything: "I have no idea."

Our faces were both streaked and dirty when we went back through the jungle. We said very little to each other. It was nearly dark when we returned. We milked the cows without speaking.

"I will take the buckets," said Alberto.

I said that would be fine, and stayed there alone for a long time—hours—stroking the cow's hide.

When I went to the cabin, I ate a tortilla, gave a few words of groundless comfort to Luisa, then walked around, watching how the jeweled night came. I didn't want to sleep, and went to the lake instead. It was a mirror of the sky. I took off my clothes and flung myself deep into the mirage, erased the stars, made a dent in the pretense of heaven. I stayed buried a long time and looked up. The lake was my lens to the black-branched world, the carp my companions. I swam like a lazy frog, and then flutter-kicked myself in circles around and around and around. "Piranha Lake," my Mom had called it. Amazing I had believed her.

When I got out, Mom was waiting for me.

"Are you all right?" she said.

I was naked. She handed me Luisa's white bathrobe.

"I can walk," I said. "I guess I'm all right."

"Then say your prayers. Your aunt's in labor."

Twenty-four

Luisa was cadaverous. All of her life seemed centered in that great fruit. Her eyes were sunken, her face bloodless. I thought she was unconscious when I entered the bedroom.

Johnny had gone for the midwife. Dad was who-knows-where. It was just the women in the room now, and the premature event.

"You're doing fine," Mom whispered to Luisa's inert arms.

Luisa's eyes fluttered open. One side of her mouth turned up as if caught on a fishhook. She made a sound like a hoarse cat—a long, painful sound, as limp as the rest of her.

"Over in a second," Mom said. "I know, Cookie. It hurts. Babies hurt."

Luisa drew out her groan until it was a long, thin mew. She went flaccid. Instinctively I put my hand over her heart. She covered my palm with hers. She said something I couldn't hear, and I put my ear to her mouth. Her hand came around my head, cold and limp as death. "My gardenias," she said.

"They're fine," I whispered. "Guzzling mango juice. Doing great. I fed them today."

She lifted her lip into that lopsided grimace, her eyes still closed.

Mom told me the pains were about fifteen minutes apart. Hard labor was a long way off, she said, but things had started. Luisa's water had broken; there was no going back now.

I could not imagine that this wilted body on the bed could really accomplish delivery. Luisa would die and the baby would be pulled from her like entrails from a chicken. Dead.

I thought an unaimed prayer: "Come on. Come on. Be."

Mom told me to moisten a washrag with cool water and put it across Luisa's forehead. "You've never seen sweat till you've seen a delivery," Mom said. "Five weeks early. That's not so bad. Lots of babies are five weeks early, right?"

Luisa mewed.

"You're tired, aren't you, Cookie," Mom said to her. "Rest. You'll need your strength for pushing. Sleep if you can."

There were tears at the corners of Luisa's eyes, glittering under her lashes. I dabbed them with the washrag, then folded and smoothed it over her forehead. She made a quivery noise, a rattling in her throat, like something from an ancient ritual.

"You're fine, Cookie," Mom repeated. "There is nothing on earth lovelier or harder than labor. Oh I know that. Scares the crap out of you when it's you delivering, but brings you closer to the veil than the grittiest prayer you'll ever make."

Luisa murmured, "Yes."

Mom stroked the washrag over Luisa's brow. She said, "Some people say there's a light in the room when a baby comes, like the angels are doing escort service. I want to see about that. I want the lights out so I can see if there's some trail of glory from Heaven. Doesn't that sound tremendous? A glacier of light for the kid's spirit to slide down. Angels holding his hands. Gotta see it."

Luisa moved her head.

"Oh yeah. It'll be wonderful," said Mom. "Old Boinky here, he's probably saying 'bye bye' to all his friends right now. He's probably watching us this very minute. I imagine he's a little uneasy about getting born, too. A little scared of how he's going to get that body of his out." She made her voice childlike. "You nervous, Boinky? A teeny bit frightened? Now don't you worry. Everything's set up just like it should be. Your Aunt Em and cousin Digs are right here to meet you. Things are fine. Just fine." Back to normal: "Now Cookie, do you feel like you can sleep?"

"You might need to stop talking before she'll sleep, Mom," I said. I was the one sweating.

"Am I bothering you, Cookie?"

"No." Almost inaudible.

"I'll shut up and let you sleep," Mom said. "Sleep between the pains if you can. That's it."

Mom seemed half-oblivious to the possibility of tragedy. Not that I would have expected otherwise. But I knew she wasn't an idiot. Somewhere in that orange optimism of hers there had to be fears. She couldn't be blind to Luisa's diminishment.

Luisa tensed and let out an exhausted whine of pain. Her head moved from side to side on her pillow. The washrag slipped off her forehead. I took it and wiped her cheeks and neck. Mom held Luisa's feet, as if that would sturdy her. "Breathe through your nose, Cookie," Mom said. "Like your tummy is a balloon and you're going to blow it up. Come on, now, Cookie, breathe with me." Mom inhaled deep. Her mouth was a pucker, her eyebrows lifted high. "Again. Breathe with me, Honey." Luisa opened terrified eyes. She obeyed. Her mouth was shaking as she copied the pucker. It shook through all her breaths. Her knees shook too. Mom pressed harder on her feet. Luisa went limp again, closed her eyes, moaned, "Over."

Mom patted Luisa's ankles. "Good job. Damn, you're good. Oh, what am I saying? There are probably a hundred angels around us here, and off I go using my mouth. God should really strike me mute sometimes. I mean that. He really should. Oh, but you were perfect, Cookie! You see how it works? Just like blowing up a balloon. Oh yeah. You're going to do great." She looked at her watch and glanced at the bedroom door. "How far is that *aldea* where the midwife lives?" she said. Trying to act casual.

"Not far," Luisa managed.

"Well those rascals," Mom said. "They've probably stopped for a soda pop or a taco. Did they think we were kidding about this labor stuff? Those rascallions!" She laughed, but shot me a quick, desperate look.

"I'll check if I can see them coming," I said.

The curtains were drawn and the kitchen lights dangling brilliantly. I had no clue to what was waiting outside until I opened the front door. There was a slide of lights out there. I gasped and thought "fire" and then "angels" until I realized what it was: the Zarahemlites and their neighbors were holding a candlelight vigil for Luisa. A group of women—women Mom and I had romped with in the stream as they washed; the processing woman; the egg-sorter woman; anonymous women I had seen at the marketplace—about a dozen of them—were kneeling reverently a little distance from the cabin. Others—hundreds of others—were coming to join the prayers, two by two, holding long, white candles. They were coming in utter silence, though a few of the kneeling ones were counting beads. Their rows of candles shone like an ascending runway. All around them, hardly distinguishable, were fireflies; above them stars. This was a light show.

The nearest ones saw me. A couple of the women I had worked with gave me knowing smiles, though none broke the stillness.

I watched the trail of candles zigzag around trees and chicken coops. Two by two, the faces above the candles appeared. Each light moved slowly downward as its holder knelt. Within five minutes there was a magnificent throng of candles and brown faces. Mostly women, but one or two men.

I held up both my hands in a gesture of thanks. They were watching me expectantly. With my hands up like that, it seemed I was ready to give a message. I did not want to talk, their reverence was so moving, but they were waiting for my news.

I said, "*Nada.*" I meant that nothing had happened yet. It sounded, I know, like a statement of nihilism, full of pessimism. But it was the best I could do with my Spanish. "*Nada. Gracias.*"

Their faces were devoted. I wondered if Johnny had any idea how much they loved their Luisa. I suspected he did.

I repeated "*Gracias*" several times, until the jeep lights appeared at the rim of the hill.

Johnny had to have seen the candles. He flashed his headlights on and off several times, like the Woodward Avenue bus driver had done to tell me hello from his distance.

The crowd turned its collective face to the lights. Johnny revved the engine. The jeep could be loud with some prodding from the gas pedal. It made the kind of VARROOM little kids imitate with toy race cars. A good, long, high-speed noise that seemed to echo off the hills to signal an earthquake or heavenly visitation; a noise like rushing waters or a crackling wind. The people watched the roaring lights come over the hill and through the same zigzag they had just negotiated. Johnny honked, flashed his brights, pulled up next to them. The midwife had arrived.

The candles made her face quite visible as she got out of the jeep. It was the most wrinkled face I had ever seen. More wrinkled, even, than Primitivo's. It was a study in oval: the face shape itself was oval, as were the wrinkles extending from forehead to chin, and those around her baggy eyes and around her flaccid cheeks. She had a set of the most incredible jowls I had ever seen on man, woman, or dog.

She grinned. She had no teeth that I could see. As I had done, she held up both her hands. But where my message had been impotent, hers full of power: it was herself, her merciful arrival, her ancient, victorious presence. She was wearing several black shawls with long fringes. As she lifted her arms she looked magical and bird-like—something you'd expect on Halloween. She cackled too, like a happy, benevolent witch. Thrilled to be on hand for the Gringos.

The people smiled gratefully, watched as she went inside—limping and hunchbacked but energetic still—with Uncle Johnny. Then they returned to their prayers.

Inside the cabin, Johnny was boiling water and noisily sorting out medical instruments; Mom was going in and out of the bedroom, doing miscellaneous tasks like unfolding blankets and fluffing pillows; the midwife was happily—laughingly at times—barking out instructions in a mix of Spanish and her shrill dialect.

I asked Mom how I could help. She told me to wet the washcloth again. I took it from Luisa's forehead, telling her as I did about the women outside. She gave a vague nod. "Our way," she said.

"So how far apart are the pains?" I asked Mom.

"Ten minutes. She's doing great."

Mom hadn't reapplied her lipstick in hours. It was flaky and creased in her pucker lines. I noticed, too, that she had some silver hairs. I had forgotten she dyed her hair.

The midwife was taking Luisa's clothes off. Luisa was a rag doll, willing but lifeless. When at last she was naked, the disproportion between her thin arms and legs and that full, stretched stomach was grotesque.

The midwife put her ear on Luisa's navel, then cupped her hands around the solid lump of her middle. She seemed to be measuring the child. Luisa groaned. Again the midwife measured, and again, as though she were not satisfied. Then she stood and proudly announced, "*Hay dos.*"

"Twins," Mom gasped. "Oh hell." For the first time, her composure was gone. She turned her face so Luisa wouldn't see, and pressed her eyes. Of course, when she turned back a few seconds later, she was beaming like a bride. "Two for the price of one," she gushed.

"Price," moaned Luisa.

"Twins! How about that, Cookie? Hey, did you hear how I understood that Spanish? You're a good teacher. The best."

The midwife was silly with mirth. I could not understand a word she said, but she seemed to be teasing Luisa. She talked incessantly, laughing, gesturing, smiling patronizingly through all her instructions as though she were addressing the babies, not their mother.

I would have thought her senile if I hadn't watched her hands working over Luisa's crotch. Those wrinkled hands were expert and agile. They massaged Luisa's thighs and perineal muscles, then made a circle that indicated how big Luisa would have to get before the birth could proceed. Through all of this, she chattered gleefully on and on. Sometimes, between pains, she demanded that Luisa respond to her teasing. She displayed her pink gums and repeated insistently, "Eh? Eh? Eh?" until Luisa gave an answer, however weak. During the pains themselves, Mom breathed with Luisa. The midwife observed this enthusiastically, opening her eyes wide, clapping her hands, exclaiming, "*Buenissimo!*" and "*Que mujer!*"

Johnny came in and laughed right along with the old lady. They were affectionately mocking the delivery, joking about the thinness of the cervix and the veil.

But this birthing didn't stay pleasant. Sometime late into the labor, the midwife measured Luisa's opening and made a futile gesture with her hands. The night was half over, the pains almost continuous, and dilation had stopped. The midwife changed her expression from glee to anger so abruptly it was melodramatic, manic-depressive. She scolded Luisa for her smallness, shook her finger and spoke sharply.

Luisa's eyes rolled back in her head. She said, "*Padre Nuestro que estas en los Cielos, santificado sea tu nombre.*"

The Lord's Prayer. She was reciting it like a catechism.

"*Hagase tu voluntad como en el cielo asi tambien en la tierra.*"

Her fingers were moving on her chest, counting invisible rosary beads. She was reverting to a Catholic right there in the childbed. She cried as she recited.

"*El pan nuestro de cada dia, da nos lo hoy, y perdonanos nuestras deudas como tambien nosotros perdonamos a nuestros deudores.*"

Barely audible. A whimper. A plea. Johnny's expression changed too, from amusement to a sublime tenderness only he could manufacture. None of this was bothering him. He could watch her decompose, I thought, and get loving inspiration from her bones. I hated him.

"*Y no nos metes en tentacion, mas libranos del mal, porque tuyo es el reino y el poder y la gloria por todos los siglos, amen.*"

Her eyes shut tighter. Her naked stomach moved, tightened.

"*Ay Dios!*" she said. "*Madre Maria, ayudame.*" She whimpered, gave two little sobs, calling again and again on the Virgin.

The midwife was making vigorous circles where the babies would emerge. Her face was grave. There was no teasing now.

Mom took Luisa's left hand (Johnny was holding her right one) and said, "We're here, Cookie. You've got to get your strength up. Come on, now. You're going to do just fine. We're all with you."

Like the whole lot of us would stand guard. No angel of death would wrap her up with us beside her.

"It'll be over soon," said Mom. "Oh I know this hurts. Cookie, I've been there. I know."

"Luisa," said Johnny, "Luisa, sweetheart, I've loved you—loved you with all my heart. It's been worth it."

Luisa panted, sighed, and let her head fall sideways on the pillow. Her eyes were glazed and half-open.

Mom patted her hand. "Come on," she shouted, trying, as it were, to scream into the next world. "Come on, Cookie! Almost done! Everything's fine!"

Luisa did not respond.

I watched the scene as if from a great distance, as if I were under water. Everyone seemed frozen, bending over the still, pregnant body. All the faces but Luisa's were full of pity and anguish. Luisa's had no expression. I thought, now they'll cut into her and take the babies out. They'll use one of the knives Johnny boiled. Luisa is dead, I thought, and Mom is a compulsive liar.

Unconsciously I was moving toward the bedroom door. I heard the knocking outside like thunder. I went to it numbly, half expecting to find a faceless, black-robed figure pointing his scythe at the bedroom. The invited guest.

It wasn't Death, it was Dad. Beside him were Alberto, Piggott, and a Latin guy with soft, gentle eyes who I somehow knew was Daniel Castillo.

I said, "You're too late."

Piggott moved me out of his way and strode into the bedroom. Daniel Castillo went behind him. I watched from the kitchen as Daniel anointed Luisa's head with oil. Piggott gave a long, inaudible blessing. His hands seemed much larger than Luisa's head. Someone who didn't know the Mormon ways might think he was slowly crushing her skull.

"No good," I said. "Too late."

"Julie," said Alberto. (How long since he had called me that?) "Julie, remember: you must awake your faith."

Luisa's hand moved.

"You see," said Alberto, "the statue comes to life."

"Alive," I murmured.

Dad whispered, "She was just asleep. Women sleep before the last stage."

"I wouldn't be too certain, sir," said Alberto.

"Well, son," whispered Dad, "as you might have heard, uncertainty is one of my pastimes."

We watched Luisa through the bedroom door. Her face went tight. Dad said, "Here it comes."

She cried out "*Jesus!*" pronouncing it "Hey Zeus"—like she was calling to Mount Olympus. Her mouth stretched into a grimace. She growled.

"*Hombres afuera,*" said the midwife, shooing Piggott, Johnny, and Daniel Castillo into the kitchen. Then to Luisa, "*EMPUJA!*"

The bedroom door shut behind them. There were two separate worlds now.

"Do you want to go in?" Dad said to me.

"Pretty gory, isn't it?" I said.

"Go on in," he said. "They might need you."

I did. Luisa was sitting on the bed. Mom was bracing her, hoisting her up from her armpits. Together they were breathing sharply. The midwife grabbed my arm and put me on the side of the bed. It was my job to bring Luisa's knees to her chest when the midwife said, "*Ahora.*"

"*Ahora!*" I pushed the knees into the chest and Mom pushed in on the shoulders. Luisa screamed and bore down.

"*No!*" shouted the midwife. Luisa, she said, was making too much noise. The midwife mimicked her. "*No como una cochina,*" she insisted, making pig noises as though she could humiliate Luisa into proper labor. "*Asi. Asi.*" The old lady modelled the way to push a baby out. She clenched her fists and held her breath. Even her incredible wrinkles seemed to tighten. Luisa went purple with her soundless imitation. The midwife nodded, rewarding her with a satisfied smile. Luisa tried to smile back; her teeth were chattering uncontrollably.

"*Ahora!*" said the midwife.

I think I will never hear the word again without hearing earthy, bestial, strangled breaths of a woman in labor.

"*Ahora!*" It went on for nearly an hour, the midwife mimicking, shouting, scolding, mocking, teasing, laughing, shrieking. "*Ahora!*" Then Luisa gave us a look of terror, a wide-mouthed, wide-eyed look like the mask of tragedy. She panted a high-pitched "*Ya, ya, ya.*" The first baby's head, guided by the midwife, was born. It came out bloody and compressed and seemed to blossom in the midwife's hands. Two more pushes and the rest of the body emerged. A boy—tiny, unnaturally wrinkled and red, but very much alive. He gave a lusty wail and peed on the midwife's chest.

Luisa fell back into Mom's arms. Mom lowered her to the pillow and let her rest until the next set of pushes began, about fifteen minutes later. The second baby was a boy as well. He peed on his mother as the midwife held him up.

Mom shouted to the closed door, "John, you're the father of twin boys!"

John yelled the news to the crowd outside. We heard him, and his echo: "*Gemelos! Varoncitos!*" We heard the applause of the Zarahemlites too, like a rainstorm.

Luisa lifted her arms. She was still shaking. Mom held one boy and I held the other against her breasts. Luisa sobbed and brushed her finger across her babies' cheeks.

"Oh damn!" Mom said then. "I can't believe what an idiot I am. I left the lights on, can you believe it? Why there could have been angels tap dancing on the bed. There could have been a whole aurora borealis on the ceiling, and I had to go and leave the damn lights on! Can you believe it? I may not see angels again till I die. Damn!"

The midwife was working with the afterbirth. The tissue sloshed into a bucket she held under Luisa's legs. When she had it she grinned her toothless victory and rattled off some instructions to me. I told her I didn't "*entiendo*." She repeated her words more loudly.

"*No entiendo*," I said, matching her volume.

This time she spoke slowly and loudly, giving me the same patronizing smile she had given Luisa. She finally took me by the elbow, holding the bucket in her other hand, and led me to Johnny in the kitchen.

"You've got the old lady climbing the walls, kiddo," he laughed.

"I don't speak Spanish."

"What she wants you to do is bury the placenta and plant a tree over it. It's a custom in these parts."

"Oh." I accepted the bucket as the midwife nodded and showed me her gums. I started outside, but before I got through the door, Mom was screaming, "Blood!" the way teenagers do in spook alleys. I set the bucket down and ran back to the bedroom.

Yes, there was blood. A pool of it under Luisa's legs. The midwife stood watching it flow out of her, shaking her head.

Daniel Castillo entered, carrying a black valise, which he quickly unpacked. He told me to get ice. "Some *tienda* will have ice. Knock loudly. Wake the owners up. Have your Daddy take you—or the *Presidente*. Quickly. Bring me ice. Pull the curtains from the windows and fill them with ice. Be fast."

Dad took me. He knew of a little *tienda* equipped with a generator, that sold soda pop and *hielo*. We drove the jeep there. When we returned, Daniel was working over Luisa, massaging her abdomen. His hands were in high motion, but his face almost calm.

He took the icy curtains (Luisa's former wedding dress) and pressed them around her bleeding. "Get more," he said. "Please." He smiled like he was asking for a newspaper or a donation. He said to the midwife, "*Soy medico.*" She congratulated him with her gummy grin.

I don't know how long the hemorrhaging lasted. It was the kind of crisis that shuts down time. I remember it sometimes as hours, sometimes as minutes. I know Dad and I had gone to three *tiendas* for Luisa's ice before Mr. *Medico* said to Johnny, "*No se vaya morir.*—She's not going to die." Daniel Castillo had no accent. He sounded fluent and articulate—like he could have been Piggott's scribe and surrogate (as Alberto was for Johnny?). "Today is not for dying," he said to my uncle.

"Well let's thank God for that," Johnny answered.

"Yes," said Daniel. "Let's." Those gentle eyes turned hard for Johnny, hard and stern. Daniel gave Luisa an injection of iron. She winced and closed her eyes.

"Let her rest," said Mom.

"I will stay with her," Daniel said, taking Luisa's hand in his, feeling for her pulse. He sighed deeply.

"She's okay?" I said.

"Fine. She's fine. Thank you."

Luisa was still naked. Daniel took a sheet that lay crumpled on the floor and covered her with it. "She wouldn't like to be seen like that," he said. "She was always modest." He tucked it under her chin. "Always modest, always chaste." His voice was as tender and full of love as his eyes were. He sat on a chair beside her bed and took her arm into his lap. He kept his fingers on her wrist.

Mom puttered around, cleaning up droplets of blood, checking on the babies. She told Daniel Castillo he had hardly changed and, oh my gosh, it was so good to see him again.

He acknowledged her with a friendly, tolerant smile. "Good to see you too," he said. But you could almost see him counting the beats of Luisa's pulse as he spoke.

I asked Dad to come with me to the mango tree, where I had chosen to bury the placenta. I took John's spade from his tool box. Dad took a flashlight which, as it turned out, we did not need. When we passed the flock of worshippers, they followed us. It was an old ritual with a Shakespearean feel to it. Alberto should have come. I could imagine a procession such as ours in *Julius Caesar* or some other history play I haven't read and never will. It was a ritual that must have been re-enacted for centuries.

We led them to the place I had in mind. They made a circle around the tree, like they were cherubim set to guard it. Dad and I dug the hole. I started to tip the bucket, but Dad stopped me. "I think we're supposed to pray over it. If I remember correctly," he said.

The Indians began the recitation at once. It was a Catholic prayer, full of rhythm and emotion. I couldn't understand it. When they finished, Dad said, "Thanks to the Almighty," and poured the placenta into the hole. An old Indian woman dressed all in black took a mango pit from the pile of them on the ground, and dropped it in. I had no doubt but that a good, full mango tree would grow there, survive us all, bear fruit when we were dust.

Alberto was standing just outside the cabin when we returned. He gave me a salute, blew me a kiss, and disappeared into the night. It was the last I saw of him.

The midwife was washing her hands in the kitchen sink. When we entered she put her palm to my stomach, pointed to herself, pointed to me, back to herself, and cackled. I got the gist of the message: "I'll catch your baby whenever you're ready to pop it." Clearly, she thought I was staying.

The babies were both crying.

"They're going to be a handful," Dad said.

Johnny was trying to quiet one of them; Mom was holding the other, sticking her pinkie into its mouth, saying, "Suck, you little Boinky. What do you think this is—a lobster? Let me tell you, this kid is a boob-a-wack."

Luisa was asleep, still quivering, Daniel still holding her wrist.

"Digs," said Mom between the babies' wails, "why don't you stay in here with your Aunt Luisa while Johnny and I calm these boinkies outside. Cookie needs her rest."

Within twenty minutes both the babies were asleep in a little cradle next to the bed. The midwife was asleep on the floor beside the cradle. Mom was driving around in the van somewhere, checking out *tiendas* for disposable diapers. Johnny and Piggott were eating in the kitchen. Daniel Castillo was in exactly the same position he had been in for an hour, connected to Luisa by her pulse.

Dad came in to spell me off.

"Have they gone home?" I asked.

"The candle people? Yes."

"Quite a night."

"You saw more of it than I did, Jewel. So, was it beautiful?"

"Beautiful?" I had to think about that one. "Yes," I said at last. "And scary."

"I'm glad you got to see it." He glanced at Daniel. "I don't believe I've introduced you to Daniel Castillo, Jewel."

"I figured that's who he was," I said.

Daniel looked at me curiously. I just smiled and said "hi," then to Dad, "How did you know to bring him?"

"It was Alberto's idea," Dad said. "I just played taxi."

"Your playing taxi maybe saved her life," I said.

"Well, Jewel, I guess we'll never know."

Luisa stirred in her bed, opened her eyes. Daniel came part way to standing. "*No te muevas*," he said. She gasped and said his name. His eyes moistened. He did not speak.

"*Un sueno?*" she said. "Did I dream it? Am I dreaming?"

I came to her. "You have twin sons, Luisa," I whispered, very close to her ear.

"*Todo esta bien?*" she said. "Yes? Like the hymn: all is well. Yes?"

"You betcha," I said.

Daniel wiped her forehead. The tears flowed down his cheeks now.

"Did *Presidente* come with you, Danny?" she said, holding out both her hands to him. "Or maybe that I dreamed."

I answered for him. "*Presidente* came, Luisa. He's in the kitchen."

"Get him for me, Julie. Please. I want to talk to him."

I did. She kept one hand in Daniel's, and held the other out to President Piggott. He took it. She said, "You both are my answer."

Piggott actually blushed. "Now *Hermana*," he said, "it was Daniel done most of anything worthwhile. You and me both know I'm nothing much by myself. Why, I'm a fat old man. I'm a bump on a log."

"No, *Presidente*. God works through you. This I know. *Presidente*, I prayed you here. I did not think my prayer would be answered. I did not think I would be worthy. But you came. God brought you here. And Danny—" (She turned to him, weeping) "God let you come to me, Danny. Perhaps—do you think?—perhaps this is why we have loved so—this day is the reason. So that when your hands touched my head, I would be renewed, kept here. *En la tierra*. This is how our love was to be spent: to open a way for God to pour light to my soul. God let you bless me, Danny. God is merciful. *Dios es misericordioso*."

"Well now," Piggott said, "that's true for sure. God is more merciful than we'll ever know or imagine. He's just up and give you and John a couple of beautiful kids there. Perfect bodies from what I can tell."

"Yes."

"Now you better take and get some sleep, *Hermana*. You've been through a mighty big ordeal here."

"I will sleep," she said.

"You do that."

"*Presidente?*"

"*Si, Hermana?*"

"What shall I do?"

He stood looking at her for a long time. His eyes teared too. They were all three of them crying. "Well now, you just get rest," Piggott said. "Right now, you just sleep some." He turned off the light. Dawn was a pink line beneath the lacy yellow curtains.

"*Si, Hermano,*" she said.

Piggott and Dad went into the kitchen. Johnny was already there at the table. I stayed in the bedroom with Daniel and Luisa, closed the door, listened.

Twenty-five

I heard only their voices. Had I not known them, I could have imagined three missionaries at early-morning scripture study. But I didn't want to hear any scriptures from them, or pious scripts. This was the moment of confrontation. There needed to be one hell of a head-on collision.

By contrast, the bedroom brimmed with peace and unearthly warmth. There were heavenly lights there, around Daniel and Luisa, around the babies. Not lights you could see, but feel only. I believe, I truly believe, there were angels with us—hovering around their wards, enjoying some respite from the battles and sins outside, lounging around in a sweet, ephemeral comfort zone. There was this little world of beginnings and faith and love and all those beautiful Edenic words we want so desperately to possess, and then there was the world of the next room, ready to explode.

I was between. I wanted to enjoy the angels' intermission, to stay in the glow, to ignore anything but the bloom of heaven here; yet I wanted justice done in that dreary, sin-flecked kitchen. If Dad and Piggott didn't know what Johnny was, I would tell them. I imagined myself courageous, though I had never been that before, imagined myself leaving the glorious bedroom, saying, "Don't you see? Don't you? See!"

As it happened, they knew what they were dealing with. Johnny's laundry time had come.

This, as best I can reproduce it, is what I heard:

Dad: So, John, what do you say: truth or dare? For old times' sake.

Johnny: What the hey. Don't tell me—you want to know if I ever kissed *Hermana* Grille. Well, I did. On the cheek, her last day here. To give her a thrill. She wrote me love letters for two years afterwards.

Dad: The girls always went for you, didn't they. And you were one *coqueton*. But to be honest, whether or not you kissed Sister Grille hasn't preoccupied me much. Not like some other questions. You ready to give answers?

Johnny: Sure. Just like you used to give me answers back then when we were missionaries.

Dad: Back then. Back then this place was Eden, wasn't it. I went around with you two, naming every creature—I even named you gentlemen, didn't I?

Johnny: Yeah. You did. I was *Ojos*.

Dad: That's because your eyes were so pretty and blue-green. You'd drive the ladies crazy. Sister Grille. Yeah. I'll bet you still drive women up the wall, don't you.

Johnny: I never ask.

Dad: Oh don't you now? Don't you really? What about you, Dave? Didn't I give you some special, some sacred name?

Piggott: *Mago.*

Dad: *Mago.* That's right. I remember now. You were the *Mago.* One of the three wise guys.

Piggott: It was short for *estomago.*

Dad: Was it? How rude. I was a rude S.O.B. back then, wasn't I. But at least I had the courtesy to keep my doubts to myself. Who knows? Maybe I was a spiritual giant. Maybe we all were. When I think of us, I see awfully pretty pictures. Maybe there was something holy about us. Or something holy about the place. It was Eden.

Johnny: Still is.

Dad: Could be. But only for the ones who haven't taken the fruit, John. That doesn't include any of us. Maybe it includes those new sons of yours, but it doesn't include you.

Johnny: And what do you mean by that?

Dad: As much as you want me to mean by it, I guess, John. So, hey, let's get down to the game.

Johnny: What do you mean, doesn't include me? Out of all of us, I'm the only one who kept the dream.

Dad: Did you, John?

Johnny: Look around you, this ain't Detroit. God walks this place, fella. Why there are things here I can't even mention, they're so sacred. God told me to keep them in my breast like a pearl.

Dad: I see. And not to cast them before swine or Piggotts, is that right?

Johnny: I haven't lost the dream.

Dad: It was some dream, wasn't it. The three of us, governing Zion. One in three and three in one. The righteous trinity. Some dream. So. John, truth or dare?

Johnny: You're serious about this entertainment stuff, arncha.

Dad: Truth or dare?

Johnny: Truth . . . . I said Truth.

Dad: Have you apostatized?

Johnny: Have I what? Apostatized? You're asking me?

Dad: I guess I am.

Johnny: Seems a little strange to have you be the asker.

Dad: Maybe the question would work better if it came from Dave.

Piggott: John, you may as well know. Alberto's told us everything. There's nothing we don't know.

Johnny: I see. Uh huh. And is that supposed to make me pee my pants or something? You guys! You dope-faced guys! Don't you know about Alberto? That boy's been telling stories since he learned to talk. He's a drama-maker, that's what he is. Reads Shakespeare like it was his only nourishment. Believes it too. You tell that boy that Romeo and Juliet were made up and he'll bop you one on the nose. Gullible as the high school airhead who thinks manual labor is the president of Mexico. And a born liar. You ask that kid a question and he doesn't know a good answer right off, he'll just up and invent one. I wouldn't trust him far as I could toss him. I don't care what he told you.

Dad: Truth or dare?

Johnny: I told you the truth.

Dad: How many children do you have?

Johnny: Now you listen to me, you two. Every kid who's hungry, every kid who cries on my doorstep, every kid who's hurting, that kid is mine. I felt that the first time I saw one of them, when we were missionaries. I saw a little kid with dirty snot all over her face, and she came to me holding her arms up like this, and I lifted her up not caring how dirty she got me, and I knew she was mine. My responsibility. She was a little Jesus, one of the least of these, and she was mine same as Jesus was. Now I don't know how Alberto construed that up, but that's the truth. Out of my actual loins I have two sons, and they're lying asleep right there in that room. Out of my spirit, I have hundreds of kids, given to me by God.

Piggott: Well now, what Alberto said was that you had relations with his mother and then arranged for her husband to be killed. What Alberto said is you're his actual and true father. From your own loins.

Johnny: That's a lie. Why that's a story he pulled out of the

Bible. And he pulled it over on you. Where—may I ask—is your spirit of discernment?

Dad: Mine's in San Francisco, I think. I haven't used it in a while. But my logic is pretty keen. And I could see Alberto's face all the time he was talking. I've noticed it before, John, he looks an awful lot like you. Too much like you. Now you're pretty dark-skinned, but you're not as dark as the Latins. And neither is Alberto. Truth is, you can't hide from your genes. I think maybe you can't hide from God either.

Johnny: I'll assume you're talking to yourself.

Dad: I'm talking, by God, to you. From my own life. My own soul! I'm saying to you, John Barley Ashworth, I'm saying repent, for the kingdom of heaven is at hand. I'm saying to you straight from Perdition itself that there is nothing worse than losing everything. Whatever you're doing, however you're covering up and justifying your sins, the price is too great.

Johnny: My hell, Chuck, you sound like you've been memorizing scriptures again.

Dad: Oh, they're still in me somewhere.

Johnny: You make me remember you like you used to be.

Dad: Do I? Well you know, John, I believe what I'm telling you.

Johnny: You believe Alberto's story.

Dad: I do.

Johnny: How about you, President. Or do I even have to ask.

Piggott: I believe the boy.

Johnny: I'm not exactly shocked. All right, then, I think maybe it's your turn to play now, Dave. Isn't it? Truth or dare?

Piggott: Truth—

Johnny: No, man, take a dare. Take this dare, Pres-ee-dent-ee. You listening? I want you to listen and I want you to hear what I'm saying. The dare is this: Ex me. Go on, I mean it, ex me. See what happens to the community around here. See what happens to the Church. You want to be my judge? I dare you. Ex me. You believe what Alberto told you. You believe his words over mine. Sure you do. You believe him because you hate me. You couldn't control Sarah when she started loving me and you've been hunting down revenge ever since. You've built this whole thing up. You're the one who made Alberto's story. You're the one in charge of this whole thing, isn't that right. You have money, don't you. You've found out how powerful money is. Why, you can buy anything in this world with money. How much did you offer the kid to lie? What was the price of my head, Dave?

Piggott: John—

Johnny: Why you could probably just provide him with a couple of your maids and he'd go away humming. The guy's a sex fiend, I tell you. He's laid every half-boob female this side of Izalco. Give him a couple of grand, a woman or two, and you've got any story you want. Why, he could even print it up for you in the underground press, did you know that? You should have gotten him to write you a nice long article. With his abilities, he could even sell it to some big-time Stateside rag. Now the story might look a lot like *Macbeth*, but it'd be a good story. So if you're going to do it, Piggott, why not go all the way? I dare you. Go the limit.

Piggott: There was a time I would have.

Johnny: No kidding?

Piggott: There was a time I could have bit you to death, John. You'll never know the hours I took and spent on my knees. I begged God like I never begged him before. I pled with him. I told him, I said wash out this dirty heart of mine. I begged him. For a year or more, every night on my knees, I took and prayed like that. Every night. Prayed like Enos did, to love my enemies. I asked God to pour his love into my bloodveins. And He done it, John. I don't want to kill you or hurt you in any way. Sarah's gone. I know that. I could damn my soul if I dwelt on it. John, there's some kind of grace or something swimming in me right this moment. I don't want it to freeze up.

Johnny: You want to know something amazing? Something that might just blow your mind? I believe you, Dave. How about that? I give you the trust you won't give me. All right, maybe you don't hate me. Maybe you're just too gullible to know when someone's lying to you. I tell you now in the name of God: I've kept the faith.

Piggott: John, no. I'm speaking to you as your priesthood leader. Please, John. Anchor your soul. Unburden yourself. That's why I'm here.

Johnny: Aw no, Dave. You're here because Alberto told you some fairy tales.

Piggott: I come to bless your wife.

Johnny: And she needed that. I thank you. She had no faith. God was going to take her from me because of her unbelief. He revealed that to me sure as I'm standing here. I begged him not to. I prayed like you must have prayed in your own confusion. To lose a wife is a terrible thing. Believe me, I understand that. I didn't know if I could go on without Luisa. Well, God heard my prayer. He couldn't go back on his word—He is God, after all—but He chose to be merciful. Chose to find someone to help her faith. Someone with money, because she believes more in money than she does in other things. God chose you, Dave, to bolster Luisa. He answered my prayer through you—even through your money. God can work like that. Mysterious.

Piggott: From what I hear tell, you give Luisa a blessing or two yourself. You told her she'd die when she delivered. You told her that every day for a while, from what I hear tell. Seems like to me if you take and tell a woman she has cancer, and you repeat that every so often, seems like to me her body might just take to dying so good you wouldn't have to worry about no other poison.

Johnny: Part of that's true, Dave. I did tell her what God had revealed to me. But I told her out of love. I wanted her to go pure to Jesus, not fearful. I wanted her to repent is all. To be ready. Out of love.

Piggott: You know, she told me I was the answer to her prayer. Daniel and I was.

Johnny: Well you were, in a way. You see, Luisa was raised rich. An Alfaro. She can't believe in a god born in a manger. It has to be another god. Catholic god. There has to be a 14 kt. gold halo around his head. There have to be candles and money around his feet. And that's your function to her. That's your function to all your people. To your maids and to your little Americans in that subdivision of yours. You see, Dave, you can give them money. You can turn stone to bread, right? You fill their guts with yummy morsels. Aw, they worship you. They have faith in you like they could never have in the real Christ. All of them. And Luisa does too. The only way she could believe in God was to see you again. Feel your hands on her head. Do you know how she was praying when you "answered her prayer"? She was *recir*-ing. Saying her *Padre Nuestro*. Giving Catholic verses, Dave. And then you and Darling Daniel barge on in and put your hands on her head like she was your own woman. I could have stopped you, you know. I could have reminded you that I was the head of my household. But I wanted her faith up. I said my own prayer. I prayed that if somehow—even through you—if she could start believing again, I prayed to God to let me keep her.

Piggott: That's not true.

Johnny: Quite a job you have, Dave. It's a good thing you're such a big guy. Whether you're saying grace or "Fee Fie Foe Fum" the people are going to fall on their knees to you. It's power you've got, Dave.

Piggott: Power? Not of my own, John. Only what the Lord's give me is all I have.

Johnny: Aw, you know better than that. Don't you know better? Your strength is in your belly and in your pocketbook. You think for one minute if you were a skinny old guy with calloused feet—well like these here; look at my feet—you think if this was you the people would pay one iota of attention?

Piggott: If God was with me, they'd listen. Sure they would. I know these people.

Johnny: You know them, do you. Hell, you've fallen for every temptation the devil ever gave Jesus. Especially that first one. Turning stone to bread. You're rich, Dave! My God said it'd be harder for a camel to get through a needle than a rich man to get into heaven. That's what my God said. What about yours? Which God is it you're serving anyhow?

Piggott: God's give me money to help the people.

Johnny: God never intended for you to live in a palace, Dave.

Dad: And God never intended you to be his hatchet man, John.

Johnny: What the hell does that mean?

Dad: It means Manuelito and Marta's husband and whoever else you've had done in.

Johnny: I had nothing to do with any of that.

Dad: You only financed the executions, right? You didn't actually pull the trigger or tie the rope. At least Piggott spends his money on pretty furniture. At least his money doesn't bleed.

Johnny: I had nothing to do with any of that. And even if I did, I think it's mighty ironic to have you tell me about murder. How many have you killed with your own hands? Aw Chuck, if Piggott fell for the first temptation, you've gone flat on your nose for the second one: the power. Oh, you have power, from what I understand. You've raised up popes and priests, armies and navies. You're reigning with blood and horror on this earth, arncha. My connections tell me you've been asking some pretty interesting questions.

Dad: My connections tell me you have some pretty interesting answers.

Johnny: Maybe I do. But I haven't—and I won't—shed blood for them.

Dad: Is that right, John? You and your miracle machines. You and your angels. You and your bread, and your "connections." Why you're twice as powerful as Dave and I are—and probably twice as bloody—and you know it. You have more money and more power than anyone around here, and you complain about Dave's mansion like it was his tragic flaw.

Johnny: Isn't it?

Dad: Hell, I don't know. Maybe it is. Maybe we've all sold our souls for different sets of coins. But it seems to me we've strayed some from the issue at hand. The issue isn't whether Elder Piggott—Dave—is rich or whether or not he should be. The issue here is—come on, Dave, this is your place, not mine. You do it. I'm an apostate myself.

Piggott: John. John, maybe we can't prove anything about those—those deaths, and maybe you didn't pay for them—I'm willing to believe you there. I know you was awful sad about losing Manuel. I know you cried over him, Alberto said you did. But there's something else maybe you won't deny. Now John, you've covenanted to have no sexual intercourse with any woman except the one—the only one—to whom you're legally and lawfully married. Have you kept that covenant?

Johnny: You're enjoying this, aren't you Dave. You've wanted to be in the judge's chamber for a long time now. Wanted to nail me to your wallpaper. Well I'm sorry to disappoint you, big guy, but the answer to your question is yes. I've kept that covenant.

Dad: The hell you have!

Johnny: If you don't believe the truth then take my dare, you bastards. Ex me! I'm the plug to the whole Church organization down here. Take me out and everything we've worked for since we were missionaries—everything!—gets sucked down the drain. Believe me or ex me. Truth or dare.

Piggott: Well then, John, if that's how you want it, I guess we have no choice but to convene a Church court.

Johnny: I mean that much to you. You've waited years to say those words, haven't you, Dave. You've probably dreamed them. You've dreamed of me with whipped cream glopped on my head, ready for you to devour. I know you. You'd sacrifice all our work just to get me out of your way. You little prick.

Piggott: If I had my way, you'd just plain confess your sins. You'd be forthright and honest—

Johnny: I have been forthright and honest. You have your own damned agenda here. Now you listen to me, Piggott. I am going to prophesy, and you listen good. It'll be to your reward or to your condemnation, whichever you choose. Now God has called me to this mission and ordained a sacred place for me to live—a place so sacred I can't tell you. There are prophecies to be fulfilled, and I'm the one He's called to fulfill them. If you boot me out of the Church, I tell you by the power of my priesthood, you'll be booting God out too. You'll be left with your money and your mansion, but God's Spirit will abide with me. His Church will flourish in the wilderness and His children will not be deceived by dollar signs. Any distance you put between yourself and me, Piggott, you put between yourself and God Almighty. This is God's word to you, worlds without end. And to you, Chuck: God sent you to me for a purpose, and part of you will remain with me. You've let God down, and he's mighty upset about that, but He will redeem you through your daughter. When you were supposed to be building up Zion in this region, you were off smashing gooks in Viet Nam. Your only hope of redemption is in Julie. I tell you that by way of prophecy. She is to stay here. She's got a mission to fulfill. She will be your Savior here on Mount Zion, and your only hope. That is a prophecy in the name of the Lord, and some of it's verbatim from His mouth. Amen.

Dad: God said "gooks"?

Johnny: I said some of it was verbatim, not all. Don't push me.

Dad: You're truly amazing, John. I almost believe you believe this crap.

Johnny: Don't trifle with things sacred, Chuck.

Dad: Oh John, come off your cloud. Come on back to earth.

Johnny: You're speaking to me? You who chose of your own free will and choice to leave the Army of God and serve in the Army of Mammon?

Dad: Well, I'm a pretty poor voice, I'll admit that. But at least I'm close enough to the ground that my fall won't hurt me much. But yours, John—yours! You're up there in that Tower of Babel on the top floor. Every bone is going to shatter when you finally land.

Piggott: He's right.

Johnny: And this is the fat man talking.

Piggott: John, it's not just me—

Johnny: My words will be fulfilled, every whit.

Dad: Holy hell, he's turning into Charlton Heston.

Johnny: The Lord is my God, Piggott. Go ahead and ex me. If that's God's will, if that's the price He wants me to pay, I'll do it. I'll risk whatever I have to. Even excommunication. But you have been warned of the consequences.

The front door opened then and Mom yelled, "Well good morning Sunshines. If it isn't the three musketeers! Hope I'm not barging in on a mission reunion here. How's Luisa?" She peeked into the bedroom, then entered, holding four packs of disposable diapers. She had re-applied her lipstick and was ebullient. "How's the little mother?" she whispered, approaching the bed.

Luisa moved her head. A shaft of light beaming through a gap in the curtains illumined half her forehead and the white pillow under her. Her hair was obsidian around her cheeks. She was wearing a soft, dreamy half-smile. She was Mona Lisa, and this was that miracle moment of unsought beauty that could stun a common artist to an act of genius.

On the nightstand next to Luisa, Mom set down two gardenias which she had somehow kept undamaged beneath the diapers. Luisa opened her eyes and smelled the flowers. She said, "My sons?"

"Asleep," Mom whispered. Even she sensed that it wasn't right to speak in normal tones here.

"They're fine," I added.

Mom sat on the bed. Daniel let her take Luisa's hands. "Gosh, you're amazing, Cookie," Mom said. "I was scared there for a moment, I'll tell you that now. Thank God for doctors, right, Daniel? Oh look at you, Cookie! The color's coming back into those rosy cheeks of yours. You're looking like your same old spunky little self. Do you hurt anywhere?"

"No. I think perhaps my breasts are leaking."

"Oh you just wait until your milk comes in. Your breasts will turn to petrified cottage cheese. Will she show you how to nurse the little men?" Mom gestured towards the midwife, who was asleep on the floor.

"Yes."

The conversation reminded me that I hadn't milked the cows. The morning was fully under way now. I excused myself and started for the barn. Mom called after me—still using quiet tones—that I had had a rough night and would need a long nap after my chores.

As it turned out, I took the nap without milking the cows. When I opened the front door I found two buckets of warm, frothy milk. Elves or angels—I would have believed in either at the moment.

Twenty-six

The next couple of days were filled with exits. Daniel and President Piggott left first. There was no climactic moment, no final confrontation between Johnny and the Pres; no love scene between Luisa and Daniel. One morning, Piggott came into where Luisa was lying, shook her hand, said, "Take care, *Hermana.* Have a good rest now." Daniel, who had left Luisa's side only to use the outhouse, rose and went with the President, looking back at Luisa, saying nothing. I believe he had not slept since coming. He walked with a slight swagger and a limp, not speaking until he saw Johnny. Then he said to him, "You take care of her." His voice was underscored with such threatening power that it made me shiver. Piggott said to all of us, "Sure good to see you folks. You all have a good day."

Almost the same exit line I had used with Jason. The last words I said to him were "Have a nice day, dear." At the door as he left for work after his lunchbreak. My gut throbbing. My suitcase hidden, packed, under the bed. "Have a nice day." An exit line to rival the one I used on Fag Cummins after a half hour of his insults: "Good to have met you." I was a wimp in my exit lines. I had that in common with Piggott. It was the second pathetic characteristic I shared with him, the first being divorce. We were both stupid, I surmised. We had made big mistakes in marriage; we were klutzes in goodbyes.

I watched Piggott leave with Daniel. Piggott took big steps, like he was striding mud puddles. Daniel was dainty and careful. They got into a blue sedan and drove off. I watched until the glint of the blue Chevrolet was a butterfly in the pines.

After Luisa's milk came in, the midwife hovered around her, teasing all the time, as the twins nursed. Luisa's nipples bled. The old lady scolded the twins for biting, though they had no teeth. She said a few words of Spanish to Luisa, gave a great cackle of joy, lifted both her fringed arms in a triumphant goodbye, and went out to the jeep, where Johnny was waiting for her.

Dad helped me milk the cows. He told me our exit would be the next one. I had felt it coming.

"When?" I said.

"Maybe day after tomorrow."

"Will Luisa be all right?"

"Sure she will. She's fine."

When I told him I had heard much of his conversation with Johnny and Piggott, he arched one eyebrow. "So what do you think?" he said. "Do you know what the truth is?"

This was not a characteristic question for Dad. Dad thought truth was subjective. You couldn't know something was true any more than you could know what the weather would be tomorrow. Knowledge, he's pointed out in countless arguments, is a strange thing to Mormons. Mormons pass knowledge around in testimony meeting with Wonder Bread and the microphone. In the Mormon Church, the questions of the ages are tossed around like ping pong balls. Catchwords that have stumped philosophers are accessible and easy in a Mormon chapel. Even if you've been doubting life itself ten minutes before, the microphone brings your testimony with it. You pick it up and hear your amplified, emotional voice declaring itself and what it knows. Truth and knowledge, Dad has said, are commodities in the Mormon supply store.

But here he was, asking the question. Did I know what the truth was?

"No," I told him.

"No?"

"No."

"Then how about the lie? Do you know about the lie?"

"That I know, Dad. The lie I know."

"So. You finally got down and smelled Johnny's feet, did you, Jewel?"

"How's Mom taking it?" I said.

"Taking what?"

"You've told her, haven't you? About Johnny?"

"What would I say?"

"I don't know."

"He'd deny it. Anyway—no—I'm not ready to do that to your mother. Not yet."

"She'll have to find out someday."

"Sure she will. But maybe by then she'll have a replacement. Jesus or me or somebody else. I don't know."

I turned to the cows and spoke gently to them. They gave me their milk with affectionate moos. The cows had their exit lines down pat.

"Can you be ready to go by the day after tomorrow?" Dad said. "To the other side?"

I shrugged. I didn't want this world to become a picture on the TV screen. I didn't want my concerns broadened, flattened, made into pretty cliches and coordinated wallpaper. I felt heavy just thinking about shopping centers and fashion catalogues, school, movies, dates, visiting teaching, long talks about profound and challenging subjects using very big words and rhetorical jargon.

The world of El Salvador was smelly, bloody, putrid, and stratified. Nonetheless I had found it full of unencumbered wonder and private joy, beauty itself in all its dimensions. When I thought

of skyscrapers and fashion shows, the images were flat and distant
—pictures on a TV screen. They were the ghosts behind static snow
in the pharmacy.

We had been in El Salvador for over six months. I had been
concerned with gardenias, cows, unborn children, love, manure,
memory, sulphur pits, waterfalls, fireflies, blankets, fleas, spinach,
murder, orchids, jaguars. I did not ache anymore. I hadn't had
diarrhea in months. Some wound inside me had healed, and there
were new longings where the pain had been.

I longed to hold Luisa's babies and show them the Southern
Cross. I longed to watch the mango tree grow, and tell the twins
how it had started. I longed to be utterly fertile and married and
full of awe for the mysteries of the abiding, irrepressible, expanding
jungle that eventually took over all monuments to time and
civilization, covered up each people's deceptions and heroics,
buried their secrets and their discoveries, sprouted from their
sacred books and from their bones. I wanted to love under the
stars, to continue on, to build a house, and make an effort to tame
the leaves and branches. Plant something edible. Live next to the
jungle with no fear of being buried or of finding death hanging
from a tree—but knowing it could happen. I wanted to make
prayers where there were no walls to contain them. I wanted to be
in touch with all things bright and beautiful. Oh no, I was not
ready to go to the Other Side: the skyscrapers, the asphalt, the
parking lots for shoppers, the desert of desire with perfunctory
commercial breaks. I wasn't ready to pass on to that.

So I lied. I said, why sure, I could be ready by the day after
tomorrow.

He said, "I'm not looking forward to the trip."

Ten days. I remembered. Soda pop and green butterflies. This
time we would go from the green to the brown. From the garden
to the desert. It would be near winter when we got to Orem, Utah.

The cow I was milking turned to look at me as I released her
udder. I stroked her brown head and called her the sweet names

Alberto had used. *Querida, Mi virgen, Mi amor.* Dad took one bucket. I took the other.

When Johnny returned from the midwife's *aldea*, he found me sitting by the lake. He said, "Picked up a letter for you at the post office. From Hollywood, California."

I opened it, though it was actually addressed to Cordelia, in my care. An autographed picture of Linda Evans, Joan Collins, and John Forsythe was inside. It said "Best Wishes to Cordelia." I put it back in the envelope and said I would take it to her on the way home.

Johnny's eyes went into shock. "Home?" he said.

"Yeah. Home."

"Hey, now, you're not going anywhere."

I looked at him and felt ambivalent.

"Come on, kiddo. Come on! You can't go. I tell you that in the name of Christ," he said. "You know good as I do that God has a mission here for you. You leave it and you'll be taking damnation into your soul. Every turn of the wheel and you're closer to Hell, Julie. That's a prophecy and it'll happen. Your mission is here. Feel those words, Julie. Feel them!" He grabbed my elbow. "They're God's truth."

I took a deep breath and extricated my arm from his hold. I gave him the exit line I should have given Jason: "I'm sorry."

He lurched back like my words were a baseball coming for his nose. "Aw no," he said. "Julie, no, you can't. What have they told you, anyway?"

"Who?"

"Hell, I don't know. Piggott? Your Dad? Alberto?"

"They didn't have to tell me anything, John. I knew already."

"Knew what?"

"John," I said, "I think you're right about one thing: God never intended Piggott to live in a mansion. That's true I think. But I also think God never intended you to do what you've done. God never intended you to fork over money for somebody's head. And God never ordained you to be His sacred stud." I stood and went inside.

We loaded Doodle Dan the next day. Luisa got up and dressed, and made us spinach sandwiches. Her big concern now was what to name her children. I suggested *Hunahpu* and *Xbalanque*, which I thought would be symbolic and inspirational names. Mom reminded us of the time Joseph Smith had been invited to name a baby. He took the kid in his arms and named him Mahonri Moriancumr, after the brother of Jared in the Book of Mormon. "Can you imagine the faces on the kid's parents when they heard that?" Mom said.

In the end Luisa settled for a couple of generic names: David and Jonathan.

Luisa stood by Johnny when we left, surprisingly healthy and radiant. Mom looked at the orphans with madonna tears in her eyes, then she sobbed. She hugged them, kissed them, called them Benjer Bom Boop-ups and Munchy Crunchy Cha Cha Cha. She promised she'd mail them Snickers bars. "Esneekers," she said, like a native.

The orphans dried their eyes with their fists and waved when Luisa told them to. Mom got into the van, her orange mouth held in a tense, shaky frown, her cheeks wet. She waved and puckered her chin against more crying. Luisa and Johnny waved back, happily, and Dad and I waved, as if this had been a pleasant little vacation for us all. But Johnny squeezed me a curse through his eyes as Dad put Doodle Dan in gear.

Twenty-seven

We went first to Belen, where Mom gathered grapefruit (most of which we would leave at a Texas border station) and hugged and kissed her adorers goodbye.

The next stop was Izalco. The road was familiar to me now. I directed Dad to Primitivo's place with no trouble. The old man was at his loom. There were three black pots of boiling herbs in front of the kitchen hut. Cordelia was dyeing the wool in them, and keeping their fires burning. When she saw me she held out her arms as though we were long lost sisters. We hugged. She chattered excited sounds and I answered *Si, si* when it seemed appropriate. I gave her the envelope. She let out a shriek of joy as she opened it, and embraced me again, crying. "*Que dice?*" she said.

Dad translated the words for her.

"*En Ingles,*" she said.

I told her. "Best Wishes to Cordelia."

"*Base weeches,*" she mimicked, repeating it over and over. "*Base Weeches.*" I knew she would stick the photo on the adobe wall, maybe next to the picture of the temple. Maybe she wouldn't know the difference between the meaning of the two.

But Primitivo would know. Primitivo was a holy man. I believed that with a fervor. I believed he had seen messengers from heaven. He was the kind of guy they'd visit: a third-world, uncombed Einstein.

He grinned at me from his loom and said a greeting in a mix of the dialect and Spanish.

I complimented him on the blanket. "*Muy bonito,*" I said.

"*Es matrimonial,*" he said. A marriage blanket. There were two quetzal birds facing each other in the center, and blue deer and red crosses around the borders. "*Ya voy a terminar.*" His loom was like an inverted piano—the strings vertical, the wild artist's face beaming behind them. He worked the pedal. The loom made its primitive bang of progress. Five more trips of the skein and the job was done. He knotted the wool at the blanket's end, made fringes an inch apart, carefully removed his creation. It was rough and dirty. He grinned at me as he hung it over a clothesline. I helped him comb it with the popsicle stick teasels. The next step would be the final washing—*batanando* at Salto Blanco.

"*Voy con usted?*" I said.

He stepped back. "*Adonde?*"

"*Salto Blanco,*" I said.

He laughed hard, relieved, I suppose, that I wasn't propositioning him. "*Si,*" he said, nodding buoyantly. "*Si, si, si.*"

Cordelia was beside me then, offering a glass of warm Orange Crush. ("*Croosh,*" they called it.) I had been so involved in helping Primitivo finish the blanket that I hadn't noticed she had gone for the pop.

Mom and Dad were already drinking theirs. I told them we would visit the most beautiful place on earth that day, with Primitivo.

We went late in the afternoon. One last time around the curves and ravines. One last time to the sulphur and the falls.

Primitivo wore the blanket on his shoulders. He led the way, reviewing with Mom and Dad the whole story of Christ's visit. Dad translated.

We heard the roar of Salto Blanco, and then it was before us.

I knew I wouldn't see it again. I smelled the musk of the green orchids, the watercress under the foam, the salty, rocky, yellow sulphur mists. The Indians were sitting in the earth holes, scrubbing each other's backs with pumice, laughing, glowing.

Primitivo put his blanket down in a puddle of sulphur water and began slowly dancing on it, talking all the time about Jesus. Dad said he was quoting Isaiah. "The guy's a walking Bible," he said.

"Living Scriptures," said Mom.

We changed to our *camisones* and sat in a lava pit by where Primitivo was *batanando*. Cordelia poured cold water into the hole.

The old man was telling how Jesus had blessed the little children. I couldn't understand his words, but I knew what he was saying. He mimed a baby in its mother's arms, and showed how Jesus placed his hands on the baby's head, embraced the little body, kissed the little cheeks. He did the whole scene for us, his feet moving all the time. "Suffer the little children to come unto me, for of such is the kingdom . . ." No one needed to translate. Primitivo didn't need words. If he had said that he had been one of those children who sat on Jesus' lap, I would have believed without understanding.

I watched his dancing legs. His white pants were rolled up again around his knees. I noticed that his shins were hairless. Indian men were smooth-skinned. No whiskers, no fuzz in the armpits, for all I knew. Indians admired hair. Jesus was always bearded and tall and white in the passion parades. Sometimes he was an outright Gringo.

The warm waters came around me like a prenatal dream. I could have closed my eyes and slept. Primitivo talked and danced, repeated the name of Jesus and the name of his angel—yes, the angel had a name, though I don't recall it now; it was a dialect name, not English—made the rhythmic sounds of his language as though he were singing a hymn, lifted his arms as the midwife had done, declaring himself to be who he was, bearing his testimony with neither microphone nor Wonder Bread.

Mom's cheeks were crimson. Sulphur brought out color in a person's cheeks. I thought that God must not have understood Mom's color charts. Her cheeks clashed with her lipstick.

"What a gorgeous place this is," she said. "If this place were in California, someone would make a mint off it."

Dad stroked her temples as gently as Alberto had once stroked mine. "You're hot," he said. "Should we go?"

She brought her knees out of the sulphur water. They were young knees, brown and shiny. "I guess so," she said. "This is a jacuzzi, you know. A natural jacuzzi."

"I know," I said.

"I hate to leave the luxury." She stood.

They were all standing before I was. Primitivo was wringing out his blanket. I knew that when I stood, we would leave. I would not come here again. I wanted another story, another song, a few more minutes in the roar of Salto Blanco. Mom and Dad were looking down at me, waiting. I leaned back in the water, let my hair drag through it, then slowly, slowly stood.

It was already dark. We changed to our regular clothes, lit our candles, and went up the winding road, around the green canyons, away from the smell of the sulphur and the noise of the falls, back to the hut. Primitivo hung his blanket up to dry. Cordelia served us tortillas and black beans. I would crave this food for years, I knew that.

I woke up early, before dawn, and went outside. I had one last date with the Southern Cross. It would appear just before dawn and vanish at daybreak.

The air was moist and warm, the sky perfectly black, ornately jeweled. The Southern Cross was just above the horizon. The Big Dipper was upside down, rising with the crux. Some of the constellations I would have known on the Other Side were so filled with strange stars that I could hardly recognize them. Even Orion was concealed in a glittering curtain. I could imagine all the familiar constellations caught behind a storm of star-drops. So vast, so eternal, so foreign. The stars had different names on this side of the world. I didn't know what they were.

I held my knees. My nightgown shone in the moonlight, though the moon was only half full. I thought the words of that ancient prayer—the one we Mormons avoid sometimes because it has become memorized and Catholic. Luisa's prayer: "Our Father which art in Heaven, Hallowed be Thy name. Thy kingdom come, Thy will be done, on earth as it is in Heaven."

Heaven was full of contradictions, yet ordered and obedient. Magnificent, incomprehensible, awful. There were stars that had shrunk into black gravity and hung around as holes devouring asteroids and meteors. There were poisonous gasses; planets colder than any place on earth; planets hotter; suns and moons and stars and empty space, expanding. Yet there was life and the means to sustain it.

"Give us this day our daily bread, and forgive us our debts as we forgive our debtors."

In Mormon scripture, the jewels of heaven are "filling the measure of their creation," along with seeds in all their varieties, and animals and fishes. Things go on as planned.

"And lead us not into temptation, but deliver us from Evil. For thine is the kingdom, and the power and the glory, forever and ever and ever and ever and ever and ever."

"God," I said—still with no face in mind for Him, still with my faith shaking in dusty aftershocks, "God, there's no end at all."

Leaves rustled, stars sparkled, filling the measure of their creation. Dawn made overtures. Black became indigo, then turquoise. A line of light appeared at some unidentifiable horizon —as if the sky were a circus tent in a peach-colored world, and God were slowly lifting it.

Mom came out of the hut. "The early bird catches the worm," she said. "Maybe that's why we call you Digs. Couldn't you sleep?"

"Didn't try. I've just been thinking."

"Penny for your thoughts."

"A penny is nothing, Mom."

"A nickel then."

"I'm thinking," I said, "that I don't notice the fleas anymore. It must be that we get used to them after a while. Indians don't scratch their fleabites; they must just get immune."

"Maybe so."

"But I still hate mosquitos," I said.

"So do I. I always figured the devil made mosquitos. When I make my worlds, there won't be any bugs that bite."

"Mom," I said, and looked at her.

How innocent was she really? How much of her mirth was an act? When she raised us kids, she consciously put on cheer some mornings—so she wouldn't throw us out the window, and all our toys behind us. And she had known, despite her dramatic smile, that Luisa had been ready to die that night. What could I tell my mother, and what difference would it make? Had she been fooled by anything here? Maybe she had known about Johnny for years. Maybe we came because she wanted to use her glee on Luisa. Maybe an angel had appeared to her, saying "Hie thee hence to El Salvador, for thy brother is behaving himself like a schmuck, and thou must save his wife." Maybe Mom was the best savior of us all, and her pretense of blindness a girlhood habit. Maybe in the future Johnny's name would come up in our conversation and we would exchange furtive glances and change the subject, both of us knowing what we knew; both of us keeping things pleasant.

"Mom."

"What, Digs?" There was apprehension in her voice. I couldn't say what I had planned to say.

"Mom, the thing about sunlight," I said instead, looking towards dawn, "is that it covers up the stars."

"Ironic, huh?" said Mom. "Reveals and covers up. It's the way things work, though. I suspect our poor eyes couldn't bear to see everything. It would blow us away."

As though she had read my mind.

"Your color," I said, motioning to the sky. "Dad hates it, though."

She laughed. "No he doesn't."

"He does. He only puts up with it because you like it so well."

She laughed more. "Digs," she said, "you are a monkey."

"You owe me a nickel," I said.

From the hut, Primitivo called "*Buenos dias!*" We answered the same. His blanket was dry now. He was combing it one last time. He held his burrs in both hands and straddled the blanket where it hung, then combed both sides at once. The wool had become smooth and soft.

"I wonder who's getting married," I said.

"Who knows?" Mom said. "Maybe the old man is. Remember that joke I used to tell about the guy who goes into the doctor's office, and the doctor says, 'You're in great shape for a man fifty years old,' and the guy says, 'Who says I'm fifty? I'm seventy.' So the doctor says, 'My hay-ell, man, you're in fantastic shape. Was your father this healthy before he died?' and the guy says, 'Who said my father died? My father's ninety-three and he got married last week!' So the doctor says, 'Who'd want to get married at ninety-three?' and the guy says, 'Who said he *wanted* to get married?'"

"Yes," I said.

"What?"

"Yes, I remember that joke. It's a good one, Mom. You are a funny lady."

"That's true, but looks aren't everything." She grinned. That happy, oblivious smile. Revealing and covering up.

Primitivo was taking the blanket off the rope. He brought it to us and held it out.

"*Muy bonito,*" I said.

Mom said, "Wow," which was a word that worked either in Spanish or English. Primitivo grinned and pushed the blanket into my arms.

"*Muy bonito,*" I repeated.

"*Un recuerdo,*" he said. "*Para usted.*"

"*Como?*" I said.

"*Se lo regalo.*"

"He's giving it to you," Mom translated, as though I couldn't understand.

"What?" I said, "I can't accept this—this is—"

"*Un recuerdo.*" He was giving me his canine grin.

"Thank him, Digs, for goshsake," Mom said. "The word is—"

"I know the word," I said. "*Hermano—hermano, gracias.*"

He waved his hand as though the gift were nothing. He arranged it around my shoulders. "*Hace frio en el otro lado,*" he said.

"He says it's cold on the other side," Mom translated.

"I know what he said," I answered. "*Hermano.*" He was already starting for the kitchen hut. Smoke was coming from the roof. There was no chimney. None of the adobe huts had chimneys. The houses always looked like they were on fire when tortillas were cooking.

Dad was the last one to join us. He had been checking out Doodle Dan's fan belt and oil. His hands were black. He wiped them on his jeans.

"Everything's set?" Mom said.

"All set."

"Well then, you ready to head back to the butterflies?"

"Absolutely," said Dad. "You ready, Jewel?"

"Sure," I said.

I took a last bite of tortilla, then performed the ritual of thanks. In Indian houses, everyone thanks everyone else after a meal, and everyone answers, "*Buen provecho.*" In dialect, it is "*Tiosh-ooh-oh.*" We gave Indian embraces to our hosts, placing one of our hands on one of their shoulders and patting, while they did the same to us. Cordelia walked with me to the van. "Base Weeches," she said.

"Best wishes." I put my blanket around my shoulders, and stepped up into the American Flag.

"*Buen viaje,*" called Primitivo, standing straight and proud, waving with both hands. "*Que les vaya bien!*" Waving, waving, all of us waving.

Dad turned the key, sent a plume of smoke out the exhaust that left Cordelia and Primitivo coughing, moved the gearshift, started away from Izalco.

There were three naked Indian boys playing with a dirty bicycle tire in the road. They squealed and hopped around like rabbits when Dad honked them out of our way. There were maybe twenty Indian girls off to the side of the road, carrying bright pots on their heads, going for their water. There were avocado trees, mango trees, gardenias all around us. The stuff of dreams, the stuff of dreams, getting smaller and smaller. We rounded a bend, and Izalco was replaced by pines. Near the bottom of a hill I looked up and saw the flamingo fountain, small enough to fit inside a television screen. I wanted to memorize this picture. And I wanted Alberto to appear in it, one last time.

What would I have told him? What would I have asked?

Where are you going, Alberto? ("To the mountains," he says. "Up there." I am inventing his speech—just as he invented me, and Cordelia, and John.)

What will you do? ("Be or not be. Seek answers. Same as you.")

He calls me Ophelia again, tells me I know what I know, and that readiness is all.

He will die, I am afraid, a violent death, and then haunt me. Some misty evening in Orem, Utah, I will be on my way to 7-11. I will switch on the car radio and hear him sing:

Al decir adios,
Vida mia . . .

And there he will be, standing where my headlights shine. He will put a bloody hand on my car and tell me to remember him.

I will be married. I will have children of my own. (Yes, I will risk my guts again: risk them for a less mystical and more enduring love; risk them for babies who will give their first cries in a more antiseptic but no less threatening world.) We will be living a normal Gringo life, my family and I: attending church, watching the nightly news, reading the Newbery winners, seeing war portrayed by an all-star cast, giving monthly charity to the movie stars' causes, clinging to our comforts and our cliches. On Sundays we will sing of crucifixion and resurrection—grateful that God sees all, more grateful that we don't. We will have clocks, calendars, schedules, conferences. We will eat cake at weddings; send roses to funerals. We will read great questions and learn the jargon of answer. And in rare moments we will feel close to understanding what is essential about our lives, ourselves, the ties that bind us. We will doubt and wonder and hope and pray—sometimes pray very hard.

Alberto will know these things about my life, and I will know nothing of his, though I will suspect courage.

"And in your own," he will say, "has there been courage in yours?"

"Well," I will answer, "I've told the tale."

He will kiss me through the dashboard window, give me a knowing look, and *desaparecer.* As he does now. As he does now. As all of it does now.

We are headed home.